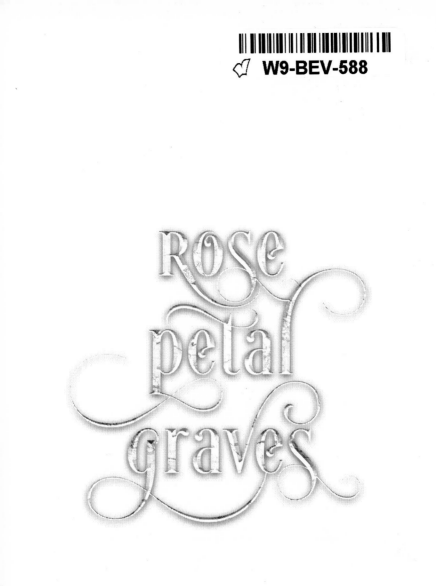

rose
petal
graves

DISCLAIMER

The Gottwas are a fictional tribe inspired by the Ojibwe People. I did not want to cause offense to Native Americans by writing about customs and traditions that aren't mine.

GOTTWA GLOSSARY

aabiti: mate
adsookin: legend
baseetogan: fae world; Neverra; Isle of Woods
bazash: half-fae, half-human
chatwa: darkness
gajeekwe: the king's advisor, like a minister
gatizogin: I'm sorry
Gejaiwe: the Great Spirit
gassen: faerie dust
gingawi: part hunter, part fae
golwinim: Woods's guards, fireflies
gwe: woman
ishtu: sweetness
kwenim: memory
ley: light
ma kwenim: my memory
maahin: come forth
Makudewa Geezhi: Dark Day
manazi: book
mashka: tough

mawa: mine
meegwe: give me
meekwa: blood
naagangwe: stop her
tokwa: favor

FAELI GLOSSARY

gajoï: favor
lucionaga: faerie guards
mallow: an edible plant, faerie weed; doesn't affect humans the same way it affects faeries, and hunters are immune
calidum: lesser faes; bazash
Neverra: baseetogan; Isle of Woods
vade: go
valo: bye
ventor: hunter
wariff: equal to a *gajeekwe*

CHARACTERS

Adette: Taeewa's mate; the *bazash's* daughter
Ace Wood: Linus's son; Maximus's grandson
Aylen: Nova's sister; Cat's aunt
Astra Sakar: half-fae; owns Astra's Bakery
Bee: Beatrice; owns Bee's Place; Blake's grandmother
Blake: Bee's grandson; Cat's friend
Cass: Cat's best friend in Rowan; Etta's daughter
Catori Price: main character
Chatwa: Iya's mother; twin sister to Holly's mother, Ley; hunter
Cometta: known as Etta; part fae; daughter of Astra; sister to Stella
Cruz: fae; faux medical examiner; friends with the Woods family; Lily's fiancé; Lyoh & Jacobiah's son
Derek Price: Cat's father; Nova's husband
Elika: Negongwa's mate; Gwenelda's mother
Faith Sakar: Stella's daughter; bad blood between her and Cat
Gregor: current fae wariff; soulless narcissist
Gwenelda: huntress; first to awaken; absorbed Nova's soul
Holly: Ley's daughter; fae; Iya's cousin; Cat's great-great-aunt
Ishtu: Kajika's mate; looked like Cat
Iya: Chatwa's daughter; Cat's great-grandmother

Jacobiah Vega: fae; former wariff; Cruz's father; killed by Lyoh Vega

Jimmy: Cass's brother; Etta's son

Kajika: Ishtu's ex-mate; Gwenelda's brother-in-law

Ley: Chatwa's twin sister; fae

Lily Wood: fae; mute; Ace's sister; Linus's daughter; Cruz's fiancée

Linus Wood: Lily & Ace's father; fae; wealthy

Lyoh Vega: Jacobiah's wife; Cruz's mother; killed her husband; killed Ishtu

Maximus Wood: Linus's father; ruthless, lawless, bloodthirsty leader

Menawa: Gwenelda's mate; Kajika's brother

Negongwa: revered leader of Gottwa Indians

Nova Price: Catori's mother; Derek's beloved wife

Satyana: Aylen's daughter; Shiloh's twin sister

Shiloh: Aylen's daughter; Cat's young cousin; Satyana's twin sister; has the sight

Stella Sakar: part fae; daughter of Astra; sister to Cometta (Etta)

Taeewa: Gwenelda's youngest brother; the 13th hunter

Tony: Aylen's husband

Woni: Iya's daughter; Nova's mother; Cat's grandmother

*TO MY CHILDREN AND HUSBAND
FOR THE FAIRYTALE LIFE THEY'VE GIVEN ME.*

PART I
FAE

THE NEWCOMER

*T*he silence was compassionate, but it came off as oppressive. I wished people had kept talking when I arrived. I wished they hadn't stared, but their curiosity didn't surprise me; it simply irked me. Like drivers slowing to absorb each detail of a car wreck, they were attempting to decipher how many sad little pieces I'd been broken into.

Unwrapping the thick scarf from around my neck, I walked with my head held as high as my aching neck could carry it toward my father. Gently, I shook his shoulders and whispered, "Dad, I'm here." He was slumped against the varnished bar Bee kept in pristine condition since she'd inherited the restaurant from her father. "How much did he drink?"

"Two tumblers of whiskey, but he was a bit woozy when he came in," Bee said, drying a glass and setting it neatly on the wooden shelf behind her. Her real name was Beatrice, but everyone called her Bee. "I took his car keys away. Exchanged them against the drinks. Here." She slid them over to me.

"Dad," I tried again. Still no reaction. I stroked his back, hoping that in his numbness, he sensed I was there—that I was back.

"How was the flight, sweetie?" she asked.

"Bumpy. I hate flying."

"Never been on a plane," she said.

"That's because you never leave," said Cass, one of my high school friends turned waitress at Bee's. "Hey, Cat." She gave me a small, sad smile that mirrored the one Bee wore. "I'm so sorry." She placed a platter of empty drinks on the counter and they rattled. Then she came to hug me. "It's so horrible."

"What did I tell you about learning some delicateness?" Bee asked her, probably to lighten the atmosphere.

Cass pulled away, rolled her eyes, and blew on her long bangs. "Why did I ever sign up for this job?"

"Because you get to eat my grandson's cooking for free, that's why. And he's the best darn cook in all of Michigan."

"Hear that, Blake?" Cass exclaimed.

Blake stuck his head out of the kitchen hole. "Catori!" He abandoned his pots and pans and came out into the main room, making a beeline straight for me. He crushed me against him.

When he released me, I asked, "Can you help me get Dad home? If it's all right with you, Bee."

"I'm offended you're even asking," Bee said, planting her wrinkled hands on the shiny counter. "Get Derek home. And stay as long as Cat needs you." She raised her voice. "For those of you waiting on your food, the next round of drinks is on the house."

"And for those of us who got our food?" old Mr. Hamilton asked. He used to be a famous actor back in the day. At least, that's what he claimed. We'd never seen him in any of the movies he bragged about.

"Everyone gets a free round," Bee said.

Cass nodded. "On it."

As she went around the room, Blake ducked under Dad's arm and hoisted him up. I was offered condolences and patted so many times on my way out that when I stepped onto pavement, it felt like freedom. I took a deep breath of frosty air. Snow was coming. I could taste it.

"It's a wonder Dad made it here in one piece," I told Blake when I spotted the hearse. It was parked across the street, with three of its wheels propped on the sidewalk.

I swung the passenger side door wide, and Blake deposited Dad in the seat and fastened the seatbelt across his chest. After he shut the door, his good eye roamed over my face. I almost didn't notice his glass eye anymore, just like I almost didn't notice his flattened nose, his missing right ear, and the scar tissue covering most of his face. "I'll follow you in my car," he said, jogging toward the back of Bee's Place.

I settled into the hearse and turned the key in the ignition. Since I'd been in no state to drive sixteen hours cross-country, I'd left my car back in Boston. Now I was stuck driving this gleaming monstrosity that reminded me of Mom. She'd taught me how to drive in this car. How I hadn't destroyed it was a mystery. Once, she suggested we go on the highway, but halfway through our driving lesson, she remembered she'd forgotten to sew Mrs. Matty's mouth shut and if she didn't do it before the wake, bad smells would leak out. Even though I was sort of bummed a corpse took precedence over me, I made a U-turn in the middle of the highway. I thought it was very fast and furious of me; Mom thought it was very fast and stupid.

The lump, which had been building in my throat since Dad phoned me with the news a few hours before, grew so big I could barely breathe. A tear dripped off my chin and plopped onto my jeans. And then another. They blurred everything around me, from the shop awnings to the mailboxes planted next to every white picket fence on Morgan Street.

I slapped the steering wheel. "Shit, shit, shit!"

Dad stirred beside me, but didn't wake.

Blake slid his blue Jeep around the hearse. Blotting my eyes with my hoodie sleeves, I pulled away from the curb and followed him past the peninsula covered in ancient sand dunes that dipped into Lake Michigan, past the vast bean fields and Holly's plantation of naked sour cherry trees that blossomed white in the spring, down a gravel path that snaked through tall pines and ended in the cemetery. *Home sweet home.* The land had belonged to my mother's family for several generations.

We lived on top of the graveyard in a two-story house that my grandparents had built to replace the one falling to ruins. We'd all resided together, my grandparents downstairs, and me, my parents, and my aunt upstairs. Aunt Aylen had left first. She'd gone to college in Arizona with no intention of coming back, except for the holidays and a few weeks in the summer. Then my grandpa passed away. Five years later, my grandma joined my grandfather.

As I gunned the hearse through our property's broken, rusted gates, I noticed a car parked in front of the house. Probably another mourner with a casserole. Dad told me he'd been receiving roasts and baked pasta dishes all day, so many that he'd put some away in the cold chambers in the basement. I didn't know how he had the courage to go down there. Even though Mom's body wasn't laid out, she was there, in one of the metal fridges, awaiting the medical examiner to establish cause of death and prep her for her final rest.

A man leaned against the parked car. He didn't look like a mourner; he didn't look like anyone I knew for that matter.

Blake was already parked and out of his car. He closed in on the out-of-towner. "You lost?" he asked.

The man, who must have been a couple years older than I was, pressed away from the hood of his sleek car. His face was smooth and moonlit, and his raven black hair fell in curls over his forehead. "I'm the medical examiner."

"You're not supposed to arrive for another two days," I said, coming around the hood of the hearse to stand next to Blake.

He narrowed his eyes at me. They were startlingly bright considering how dark it was. "I was free early." He stuck out a hand. "Cruz. Cruz Mason. You must be Nova's daughter."

I eyed his hand. It shone white as though illuminated from within. Perhaps it was due to the contrast with the black leather jacket he was wearing, or perhaps it was because he was standing underneath the porch light.

A retching sound broke the silence. Blake lunged toward the hearse, yanked the door open, and pulled Dad out, but he wasn't fast enough. My father was already covered in vomit, and so were the dashboard and leather seat. My stomach flip-flopped at the idea of having to wash it out.

"I'll get my bag," Cruz said, pulling back his hand since I'd made no move to shake it.

"You don't have to get started tonight."

"It wasn't to get started," he said, taking out a black bag from the trunk. "I was told there would be an extra bedroom I could use."

"Oh." I shot my gaze over to Dad who was in no state to confirm this. "I'm sure Blake can accommodate you. Right, Blake? You have some free rooms over the restaurant?"

He nodded.

"I wouldn't know how to get there," Cruz said.

"Your fancy car doesn't have a GPS?" Blake asked. Even his glass eye seemed expressive.

Cruz glared at him.

"Blake's heading back there in a sec. Just follow him."

"Don't you want me to stay?" Blake asked.

"I'll be fine. We'll be fine," I said, looking at my father whose head lolled against Blake's broad shoulder.

"You sure, Cat?" Blake asked.

I nodded.

"Okay. Let me get him to bed," Blake said

"You don't need to carry him upstairs. Just put him on the couch, Blake," I told him as he climbed the porch steps.

The toecaps of Dad's boots scraped against the floorboards and then against the doormat as Blake swung the front door open and stepped in. The wind chime Mom had suspended on the porch ceiling during Christmas tinkled, scattering sound across the otherwise silent expanse.

"You don't lock your door?" Cruz asked, once Blake and Dad were inside.

"Most people come here to visit their dead relatives." I gestured toward the headstones. "They don't come to pay us a visit."

"And I bet you believe that thing you hung over your door will keep people out?" Cruz asked.

I glanced at the cluster of tiny, silver bells. "Mom put it up. She said it was to ward off evil. She was superstitious like that. You should see how many dream catchers I have in my bedroom."

"Are you going to keep it up?"

"What? The wind chime?"

He nodded.

"Why would I take it down?"

"I heard talk of a blizzard."

"It's pretty solidly attached," I countered.

Cruz raised one palm in the air. "That was just me giving unsolicited advice. I do that too often."

I peered up at the large hook Mom had screwed into the porch beam. It looked sturdy, but what if Cruz was right? I didn't want Mom's creation to fly off.

"Is the big guy a friend of yours?" Cruz asked, watching the gaping doorway.

"He is."

"What happened to his face?"

"IED blast. He enlisted after high school." I folded my arms tightly against my chest. "I should get inside."

"You should."

I walked up the porch steps, but stopped midway and turned around, contemplating whether to let the vomit sit until tomorrow. I was afraid the stench would penetrate the fibers of the seat and floor mat. On the other hand, it was dark and I would probably miss spots. I was better off doing it in the morning.

"Forgot something?" Cruz asked.

His face was so bright that I checked my hands to see if my skin also glowed; it didn't.

"Catori?"

"How do you know my name?"

"Your dad told me. Weren't you heading in?"

I nodded. "I was, but I think I should clean the car first."

"I'm sure it can wait until tomorrow." He walked to the trunk of his sleek ride, popped it open, and tossed in his bag. "I'll see you at nine?"

"Sure." I turned around and went inside. Blake had settled Dad on the couch. He'd rid him of his soiled shirt and had pulled a woolen plaid over him. He'd even set out a glass of water on the low table.

"Call me tomorrow if you need anything." He kissed my cheek and left.

I closed the door behind him. And for the first time in my life, I locked it.

BROKEN HEARTS

"Eat?" Dad hollered from the kitchen where he was banging cupboards. "Where's the Tylenol? My head is killing me."

"In the drawer."

"Which one?"

"Same drawer it's always been in," I said with a sigh.

Mom babied Dad, cooking all of his food, fetching him glasses of water before he even asked for them. He got used to it, and now he was going to have to get unused to it, because I would be heading back to college right after the funeral.

I pulled the drawer open, took out the pillbox, and shook out two tablets into his palm. Dad swallowed them without water.

"You should really eat something," I told him. "You want me to make you an omelet? Or reheat some of that bread pudding Bee dropped off?"

"I'm not hungry, honey, but *you* should eat. You're getting too skinny." Said the man whose middle was still concave in his mid-forties. He patted my shoulder as he walked past me. "I'm going to bed."

"The medical examiner arrived last night."

Dad paused on the stairs. "He did? Wasn't he supposed to get in tomorrow?"

"He was, but he's here now. Don't you want to meet him?"

Dad's eyes were bloodshot. "Not really in the mood. Can you show him around? Show him"—a sob caught in his throat—"show him where I...where I put your mother?" he whispered the last part.

My eyes heated up, but I reined in the tears until Dad had climbed the rickety wooden steps. Those stairs had gotten me into so much trouble when I was in my early teens, sneaking out to parties and coming home past curfew. Even though I tiptoed, one would always creak and give me away. And Mom would come out of her bedroom, with her reading glasses on and a paperback dangling from her fingers, and ask if I was all right. I'd thought it was her way of guilt tripping me, but now, I believed she was just worried about me. I pressed the heels of my hands into my closed eyes to squeeze out the tears, and then, when I sort of had myself under control, I headed to the closet where we kept the cleaning supplies.

I grabbed a rag and a bucket that I filled with soapy water and then headed out to the hearse. The fresh air stung my cheeks and blew against the wind chime, making it swing back and forth. The noise was deafening. Dropping the bucket and rag, I dragged one of the wicker chairs toward Mom's last creation and climbed up to unhook it.

The bells were as cold as icicles and prickled my still-warm palm. They hadn't served their purpose; they hadn't kept evil out. Maybe Mom had gotten it wrong. Maybe bells above a doorway were an invitation to malevolent spirits. I tore the chime off the big hook and walked over to the Dumpster. Without hesitating, I flung them inside, and then I just stood there and stared, half expecting our garbage can to burst into flames, or the bells to start careening, but neither happened. Only the wind whistling through the bare branches of the rowan trees disrupted the otherwise blissful silence.

I returned to the porch, pushed the wicker chair back against the wall, and picked up the cleaning supplies. Old snow crunched underneath my boots as I plodded toward the hearse. I placed the bucket on the hardened earth and dragged the passenger door open. The rag I was still holding slid through my fingers and fell into the bucket, settling on the filmy surface.

The car was spotless. Not a splatter of vomit remained. I checked the seams of the leather seat, but found nothing to sop off. I sniffed the air, but even that was clean. I popped my phone out of my pocket to text Blake a thank you when Cruz's car rumbled down our long driveway. He came to a stop inches from me.

"Morning," he said, stepping out. "Beatrice said these were your favorite." He handed me a bakery bag smudged with grease stains.

I slipped my phone back in my pocket and checked the contents. Two corn muffins with real bits of corn were nestled at the bottom, still hot from the oven.

"You took it down," Cruz said.

I followed his gaze to the bare hook. "Yes." I didn't tell him that I'd thrown it away.

"Want me to take this back in for you?" he asked, tipping his clean-shaven chin toward the bucket. "You don't seem to be needing it."

"I don't. Blake washed the car already."

One of Cruz's dark eyebrows arched up. "Did he, now? How kind of him." He sounded sarcastic. I guessed he and Blake hadn't hit it off. I was about to grab the bucket when Cruz bent over and seized it. His skin didn't glow like it had last night. It was normal, perhaps even a little tanned.

He followed me up the porch steps and through the front door. While I hung my coat, I pointed out the kitchen. He walked straight toward it, trekking bits of snow onto the hardwood floors.

"You can just leave the bucket in the sink. When you're ready, I'll show you—" My voice broke. I crumpled the bakery bag in my clenched hand. "I'll show you downstairs."

"You don't have to."

"I do." I tossed the bag on the wooden kitchen island and headed toward the door, which Mom had painted bright yellow. She'd thought that adding cheery paint would help me get over what lurked behind it. Instead, it had increased my distress, as I'd always found myself staring at it. I wrapped my fingers around the knob, but couldn't bring myself to turn it. Several minutes passed. Finally, Cruz put his hand over mine and pressed down to accomplish the task I was unable to. As soon as the latch clicked, I pulled my hand out from under his.

"I got it from here," he said.

I stared straight into his face. Cruz's eyes were green, like the clusters of lanky leaves that sprouted from the rowan trees planted around the oldest section of the cemetery. "I'd like to see her."

"How about I establish cause of death first? And then, when she's dressed and ready—"

"I've seen a lot of dead bodies, Mr. Mason—"

"Cruz. I'm twenty-four, not forty. And yes, I imagine you've seen your fair share of corpses, but this is your mother we're talking about."

I swallowed, but yanked the door open nonetheless and clambered down the stairs. The morgue reeked of roses. Dad had probably stuck some bouquets in one of the cold chambers to keep them fresh for the funeral. On autopilot, I walked over to the back wall—where Dad told me he'd placed Mom—and pulled on the lever of her chamber. Her straight, shiny black hair gusted around her snowy shoulders.

"She always wore it in a braid," I told Cruz.

My gaze roamed over the rest of her face that I knew by heart, over her high cheekbones, over the twin peaks of her upper lip, over the upward slope of her eyes, all remnants of our Native American ancestry.

"You look a lot like her," he said, hanging up his coat next to Mom's mortician robe. It drooped, as lifeless as her body.

I did look like Mom. I had the same black hair, black eyes. I even had the same sloping lips. The only difference between us had been our build. I was an entire head taller than she'd been, and slender like Dad.

Cruz circled around me, hooked his fingers around the shelf's handle, and slid it out...slid Mom out. Her skin, which was always brown, even in the winter, had turned alabaster. Only the unnatural blue tinge of her lips and eyelids shattered her otherwise colorless complexion.

"What does Catori mean?" Cruz asked, his voice slicing through the thick silence like the blade of the scalpel that would soon slash through Mom's sternum.

I took a step back to allow him to slide the drawer out completely. "It means 'spirit' in Hopi."

"Aren't you of Gottwa descent?"

"Yes." I gazed down at her closed eyes, willing them to open again. "But Dad liked the name."

"And Nova?"

"It means, 'chasing butterflies'. When my mother was born, three butterflies landed on her crib. At least, that's what my grandma told me." Her lids didn't flutter. For a second, I saw myself as a child spooked by a nightmare, tiptoeing into my parents' room to find comfort in their bed. I would always come around to my mother's side because she'd lift the covers and let me crawl in, whereas Dad would carry me back to my bedroom, promising the dream catchers would trap my next nightmare.

"Catori?"

"No one calls me that. Just Cat."

"That's too bad. It's a beautiful name." He raked his hand through his wavy black hair. "Look, I'm going to start...*examining* your mother. I think it would be wiser if you left."

"I'm a medical student."

"If you want to keep her memory intact, don't stay for this."

"I'm staying."

"Why?"

"Because"—I gaped at the thin white sheet covering her chest and legs—"her heart didn't just stop. Someone stopped it. And I want to be there when you find out how."

THE BOOK

"What makes you think your mother was murdered?" Cruz asked me, tilting his head.

"She was forty-four, in perfect health. There's no way she had a heart attack."

"People have heart attacks all the time," Cruz said.

"People with poor eating habits, heightened stress, or genetic predispositions. Mom had none of those. I won't interfere with your work, but I'm staying."

"Suit yourself," he said. He flung the sheet off Mom's pallid body, but it seemed to lift in slow motion, caressing her collarbone and her chest, slipping over her navel and thighs, gliding over her calves and feet, finally pooling onto the tiled floor like milk.

I blinked, and the quiet unveiling was replaced by the horror of her naked body sprawled out on the steel bed. I stumbled backward, but caught myself on the metal instrument rack. The shiny, sharp tools rattled in time with my pulse.

My stomach contracted, and the orange juice I drank earlier shot up my throat. I just made it to the metal sink. I gripped the edges as more spasms hardened my insides. I wasn't sure how long

I stayed hunched over the sink, but white and black dots started dancing before my eyes.

Wordlessly, Cruz's hands settled around my elbows. He guided me back up to the kitchen where he sat me down and crouched next to me. "I'll come to get you when I'm done. To tell you if I find anything in her system, all right?"

I nodded. Although I looked at his face, I couldn't see him. All I could see were those damn monochromatic dots, like static on a television screen. As his shoes thudded against the basement stairs, I breathed in and out, waiting for color to flood my eyesight again. When it did, I rose. Walking proved difficult as my legs were still wobbly, but I didn't give my body a choice. I needed to pull through this. Mom would have wanted me to stay strong.

My gaze locked on the yellow door. *Damn door!*

Inflamed by the need to make it disappear, I went outside, braving the wind that swirled snowflakes around the tombstones. I hurried to the shed at the back of the house where my parents used to store a bunch of unnecessary items, like my first bike and extra car tires that didn't fit any of our cars. I shoved things around, aiming my phone's flashlight on the hoarded mess. Finally, I found what I was looking for: a paint can and a roller brush. The dried paint around the lid was white. Not yellow. *Perfect.*

After grabbing both, I locked the wooden doors and returned to the house clutching the swinging bucket and brush. I discarded my jacket and sweater on my way to the kitchen. They landed on the back of the crackled brown suede armchair, but slid onto the rug. I snatched a paring knife from the wooden block and popped the lid off the can. Grabbing yesterday's newspaper, I plastered the floor with the broadsheets, and then I dipped the brush into the can and rolled it over the yellow color until sweat and paint dripped along my bare forearms. It took three coats to get rid of the color. By the time I was finished, even the doorknob was white. I backed up and stared at it, and then I started crying because I'd just gotten rid of something else my mother made.

The doorbell rang. I prayed it wasn't another visitor armed with a casserole and unsatisfying words. Blotting my eyes with my knuckles, I went to open the door.

Matt, the postman, stood before me in his furry, flap-eared hat. "I got a delivery for you, Cat," he said, handing me a heavy box.

"I didn't order anything."

"It's—it was for your mother. You want me to return it? I can just—" He shifted and his rubber boots squeaked on the porch boards.

"I'll take it."

"Um...you got something on your face. Makeup or paint or something."

"Oh, yeah. I was redecorating."

"I did that when my momma passed away. It helped."

It didn't help me.

"Well, you have a good one." He gave me an awkward thumbs-up. "And stay warm," he added, trotting back to the post truck.

Hugging the cardboard box to my chest, I shut the door and raced up the stairs to my bedroom. I kicked the door closed and placed the box on my feather-printed comforter. Using the tip of a pen, I sliced through the packing tape, pulled the tabs open, and combed away the Styrofoam peanuts.

"What the hell?" I murmured, lifting a thick, leather-bound book that smelled musty, as though it had been sitting in someone's basement for half a century.

I ran my fingers over the embossed gold title. *The Wytchen Tree*. Mom tended to the cemetery garden, but a book about a tree was downright eccentric, even for her. I crossed my small bedroom toward the shapeless beanbag next to my window. The purple velvet cover was threadbare in places, but I'd never wanted to reupholster it. That purple fabric had captured my tears of anger when I was a child and my tears of heartache when I was a teenager. Replacing it would mean getting rid of my childhood, like covering an old plush toy with new fur. Hadn't I gotten rid of enough things already?

As I propped the heavy book open, the beanbag molded to my body and supported my elbows. Delicately, I flipped from one page to the next, curious what had been going through my mother's mind these last few days. In the first chapter, I found out that a wytchen tree was just a fancy name for a rowan tree, the very trees in our cemetery. I read about its virtues, about the berries' use in jams and medications. And then I came upon a passage that made me understand why my mother had purchased the book.

In 1812, Negongwa, the revered leader of the Gottwa Indians, espoused the American cause in exchange for a plot of land that spanned from the coast of Lake Michigan to the edge of the Manistee Forest. This land later became known as Rowan.

Negongwa, along with his entire family, lay beneath our property. Negongwa, my great, great, great, great, great, great, great-grandfather. *The Wytchen Tree* spoke about our ancestors. My mother had always been fascinated by our lineage. She hadn't bought this book to learn more about trees; she'd bought it to learn more about her roots.

It was rumored that the Gottwa tribe possessed supernatural powers. Some said they were related to the Pahans or "little people," but others described them as Pahan hunters. When they settled by the Great Lakes, they planted wytchen trees around their land that served as both a natural border and a shield against faeries, witches, and disease.

I snorted. I couldn't help myself. *Faeries?* Seriously. When Mom told me stories of our ancestors, she'd always made them out to be magic-wielding semi-deities. But that was Mom, who'd believed there were more dimensions to our world, dimensions our ancestors could penetrate thanks to magic but which were lost on us rational humans. Most of my friends would lap up Mom's stories and insist we go sit in the circle of rowan trees at twilight, above the graves, and call on the dead. I'd done it—several times—and nothing had happened.

I closed the book and brought it back to the cardboard box, dropping it on the pile of Styrofoam peanuts. Some drifted out like clumpy snowflakes, sticking to my comforter and gray jeans. As I brushed them off, something whacked my window, making me jump. "Just a tree branch," I murmured to myself.

The snow was coming down hard, sheets of white slanting out of the dull sky. The branch struck my window again. This time, I was prepared so I didn't react. I just watched the wild spectacle, mesmerized by the power of nature.

The power of nature.

I glanced at the book again. Perhaps there was power in a tree. I shook my head to dislodge the irrational idea. If a tree could really repel disease, wouldn't it be planted next to every hospital? Wouldn't houses be built only from that material? The future doctor in me couldn't believe there existed a miracle barrier against disease. As soon as the blizzard blew over, I would head to the post office and send the damn book back.

I heard Dad and Cruz talking downstairs, so I shoved the box underneath my bed and went to join them. "You've met Cruz," I said, gathering my hair in a ponytail.

Dad turned toward me. "I was just telling him that he couldn't drive in this weather." He squinted. "What happened to your face?"

"I painted the kitchen door. I hope you don't mind."

"Wouldn't have changed much if I had, would it?" he said gently, but there was a reproach there. He'd always thought I was too headstrong. Mom said it was a wonderful trait for a girl to possess. Dad didn't agree. That wasn't to say he would have wanted me to be submissive, but perhaps more soft-spoken.

"I wouldn't want to impose," Cruz said.

"Impose?"

"I told him he should stay in the guest room."

Super. "What did you find?" I asked Cruz, to avoid dwelling on the fact that a complete stranger would reside under our roof tonight.

Dad furrowed his blond eyebrows, which accentuated the new lines that had appeared on his forehead and around his eyes.

"She suffered a stroke from a blockage in her carotid artery."

"Show me."

Cruz narrowed his eyes. "I already sewed her up."

Dad's hand settled on my arm. "Cat, please, let this go. It's already so hard. Leave your mother in peace now."

"She didn't die because of a clogged artery," I said. "She was healthy, Dad. So healthy."

My father squeezed my arm. "People have strokes all the time."

"But she was forty-four—"

"I know, Cat. I know." My father's voice was gentle but firm. He pulled me into a hug. I banged my fists against his chest, which made him hug me tighter.

"It's not fair," I sobbed. "Not fair."

"You sure you want to be a doctor, honey? Because you're going to see a lot of things that aren't fair." He caressed my hair, running his fingers through it like he used to when I had nightmares. And like when I was a little girl, the gentle stroking soothed me. "How about I dig up something for us to eat while you show Cruz to the guestroom?" he suggested.

I wanted to suggest we reverse roles, but Dad was already on his way to the kitchen. Wrapping my arms around my chest because it was damn cold in the house, I crossed the living room. "It's over here." I almost tripped over the upturned corner of the rug. "I need to nail it to the wood," I muttered, mostly to fill the deafening silence.

"You seem cold. Do you want me to build a fire?" Cruz suggested.

"I can do it."

"I'm certain you are capable of it, Catori, but I'm also certain you have other things to do. Like take a shower." His gaze struck my paint-splattered forearms.

"Fine."

Cruz smiled.

My grandparents' old bedroom contained a queen-sized bed pushed against a wall, a nightstand, and a small dresser. It was modest, but cozy. For years, I'd asked my parents if I could move into it, but they'd refused, suspecting that my incentive to live downstairs was based on my desire to break their rules.

"Bathroom is through here." I pushed through a door that led to a room paved in mosaics with a claw-foot bathtub and chrome and porcelain sinks.

I tucked my hands in the back pocket of my jeans. "Only bathtub in the house."

He rested one of his hands on the curved ceramic edge. I must have imagined his skin glowing the other night because it didn't tonight.

"How long do you think you'll be staying in town?"

"A few days."

"The snow should stop by tomorrow, so you should be fine to leave then." He frowned, probably because he picked up on my not so subtle attempt to get rid of him. "Let me get you a towel and some fresh sheets for the bed."

As I headed back into the bedroom, Cruz's voice rang out, "Did you put a tarp up on that plot you dug up?"

"What plot?"

"The one between the rowan trees."

"What, are you a botanist too?" I asked, pulling out a set of pressed white sheets and fluffy navy towels.

"My dad taught me about the fauna and the flora. He was a nature-lover."

"Was?" I placed the towels on top of the dresser and the sheets on the bed.

"He and my mom died in a car accident when I was a teenager."

"Oh."

He shrugged. "You grieve, and then you forget the pain and you move on."

I didn't think I could ever forget the pain of losing my mother, but it wasn't worth debating with Cruz. For all I knew, he hadn't been that close to his parents.

"So, did you cover that plot?" he asked as I turned to leave. "With all that snow falling—"

"That's not where we're putting Mom," I said.

"Then why did you dig it up?"

"Mom did. The headstone started caving and she was afraid there would be a landslide. She wanted to solidify the foundations."

"So that's where the old casket downstairs came from."

"What old casket?"

"Didn't you see it? It was in the middle of the room."

"No. I…I didn't." All I had seen was Mom.

"Could you open it for me?" he asked.

"There's probably nothing left inside besides bones. "

"Still, I'm curious. Aren't you?"

"Seeing my ancestor's remains isn't at the top of my bucket list."

"Your ancestor? One of the twelve rumored to be powerful?"

I snorted. "You've heard the stories?"

"Stories? You don't believe them?"

"Are you really asking me if I believe in faeries?"

"I am, Catori." His green eyes seemed to glow brighter.

"Sorry to disappoint you, but I don't. And I don't think anyone in their right mind should believe in little people wielding magic sticks."

"Little people?" He chuckled. "Why would you assume they're little?"

"They were called *pahans*, which means 'little people'. Haven't you seen Tinker Bell? She's tiny."

"And she's also a piece of fiction," Cruz said, still smiling.

"Just like all faeries. Anyway, I should get cleaned up. I'll see you at dinner."

4

ROSE PETALS

"*I*t wasn't me," Blake said. I could hear he was at work from the sound of oil sizzling.

"What do you mean it wasn't you?" I asked, putting my cell phone on speaker so I could pull off my jeans.

"Maybe your dad cleaned it up?"

I frowned as I turned on the shower. "Maybe," I said, but considering the state my father was in that morning, I doubted it was him. "Is your grams keeping the place open tonight?"

"Yes and it's packed. Who knew blizzards could be so good for business?"

"People are getting dinner and a show."

Blake laughed. "Did the new medical examiner already leave town?"

"Nope."

There was silence on the other end of the line. "Is he still at your place?"

"Yep."

"Is he staying the night?"

"Yep." I picked up the tweezers from the mug in which I kept my makeup, the one with the quote written in rainbow colors that read, "Don't count the days. Make the days count." Bee had given me that mug for graduation because of the calendar I kept pinned to our fridge on which I would tick off the days until college. She knew how excited I was to leave home. I plucked stray hairs around my eyebrows, then dropped the tweezers back into the mug.

"He knew there'd be a snowstorm," Blake said. "He should've left your place earlier. He did it on purpose."

"Look, I got to go."

"Call me later?"

Steam blurred my reflection in the mirror. "Sure, but don't worry."

"I care about you, Cat. I cannot *not* worry," he said as I dragged my finger through the condensation.

I'd drawn a heart. I wiped it off. "I'll be fine." Blake had feelings for me. He'd had feelings for me since the summer I'd turned thirteen and we'd kissed in his tree house. "I'll call you later," I said, and then disconnected.

I placed my phone on the edge of the sink and stepped into the shower. The dried paint flaked off my skin and glided down the drain along with the warm water. I scrubbed my body with the lavender-scented bar of soap Aylen cooked up in her kitchen. Making soap was her hobby; she was a naturopath by profession. Like Mom, she believed in the power of nature, which had led to heated conversations around the dinner table when I'd announced my desire to be a *real* doctor. Aylen had taken my comment to heart. Although she was quick to forgive me, she was also quick to point out the flaws in modern medicine.

As I dried off, a plate broke in the kitchen. When I heard my dad swearing, I hurried to get dressed, pulling on a fresh pair of jeans and a red sweater. I hurtled down the stairs just as a glass shattered. My father was crouched on the floor, scooping up the pieces of porcelain and glass with his bare hands.

"Let me take care of that, Dad," I said, helping him up. Both his palms were bleeding.

"She's not coming back, Cat. Never coming back," he murmured. His eyes were puffy and bloodshot.

I guided him toward the sink and ran cool water over his hands, then I blotted away the blood and water, sprayed antiseptic on the cuts, and plastered bandages that would probably not hold.

"Am I interrupting?" Cruz asked from the doorway. He was holding a bottle of wine with a peeling, yellowy label.

Dad sniffled. "No, no. Just clumsy, that's all."

"I brought wine," Cruz said.

"That's very kind of you," he said softly.

"The corkscrew's in the top right drawer," I told Cruz, as I walked Dad to the living room and sat him down. I passed him the box of tissues and fluffed a pillow behind his back, then returned to the kitchen to clean up, but Cruz had already swept away the mess, which reminded me... "Did *you* clean the car?"

"I did," he said, twisting the screwpull into the cork.

"Why?"

"Do I need a reason to do something nice?"

I bit my lip. "No." The cork popped out. "Thanks."

"You're welcome. Now where are your wine glasses?"

"Over here," I said, opening one of the cupboards. I took them out and brought them to the living room.

"Should I be serving you alcohol?" Cruz asked as he poured a glass for Dad. "Aren't you a minor?"

"I'm nineteen."

Dad snorted a laugh. "Good luck telling Cat what to do." He took the glass from the table and sipped it. "This is very good. What is it? Pinot?"

"It's a 1973 Bordeaux."

Dad sputtered and some wine dribbled down his chin that was in dire need of a shave. "Nineteen seventy-three? It must be expensive."

"It is, but a good bottle should never be drunk alone."

"Don't you have any friends?" I asked, swiping the second glass from the table.

One side of his mouth perked up.

"Catori," Dad hissed. He only ever used my full name when he was angry. "That's not nice."

"Well, do you?" I asked again.

"Do I strike you as a very unsympathetic person?" he asked.

"Sort of."

"That's enough," Dad said.

"What? I'm allowed my opinion," I said.

Cruz laughed. I wasn't expecting him to laugh.

"You understand why we stopped after one child?" Dad said.

I rolled my eyes and sat down beside him.

"They used to tell me they wished me luck with finding a husband," I told Cruz.

"Used to? We—" Dad stopped short. "*I* still think that." He squeezed the bridge of his nose between his index finger and thumb.

"Look at that snow," I said, before Dad could break down again. For a while, we all watched the spectacular white downpour in silence. Then I stood up and popped one of Dad's old CDs—the best of Etta James—in our obsolete CD player. The warm, rich voice eased the cold melancholy almost immediately.

"Where are you from?" Dad asked Cruz.

"Originally from Minnesota, but I live on Beaver Island now."

"Beaver Island? Doesn't it belong to this uber-rich family... what's their name?"

"The Woods?" he said. "Yes."

"And they let you live there?" he asked.

"Yes."

"Are you related to them?" I asked.

"Not yet," Cruz said, swirling his wine. He took a sip, and then set it back on the table.

I wanted to ask him what he meant by "not yet," but Dad spoke before I could. "Nova told me her relatives were from Beaver Island but had a falling out with the Woods way back when. Apparently, they cursed her ancestors. She actually believed she would be burned alive if she set foot on that island."

I snorted. "Mom and her curses."

"Show her some respect," Dad said.

My mouth gaped at his reproof. He'd made it sound nonsensical just seconds earlier.

"You're allowed your beliefs, but so was she. So was she..." Dad slipped his hand out from behind me and leaned forward. "Could I ask you for a refill?"

"Of course," Cruz said.

I snapped my jaw shut and kept it closed for a long time. When Cruz asked me a question, I would nod or shake my head, but that was the extent of my participation in their discussion. At some point, I excused myself, placed my empty glass in the kitchen sink, and stared at the terrible paint job I'd done.

Although I'd had every intention of going upstairs, the pull to go downstairs was overwhelming. Quietly, I eased the door handle, flicked on the lights, and walked down the steps. I was curious about the old coffin Cruz had mentioned. How I hadn't noticed it this morning was beyond me, considering it was smack in the middle of the morgue. I circled it, stroked the wood that was rough and knotted, so unlike the modern-day coffins which were varnished and smooth. I grasped the lid and lifted it. It weighed a ton and slammed shut, nearly chopping off my fingers. I tried again, this time prepared for the weight. I heaved it up. Since it didn't have hinges, I slid it over the base until I could see inside.

Rose petals. That's all there was. A lot of them. I pushed the top farther off. Still, I found no bones. I scooped up the petals. They were velvety and fragrant—fresh. Had my mother put them in there?

"You opened it," Cruz said.

I jumped. "Jeez...creep up on people much?"

"I didn't mean to startle you," he said. He was looking at the petals. "Where's the body?"

"Body? There wouldn't be a body anymore."

"I meant the bones."

"Maybe Mom put them in one of the cold chambers," I said.

Pulse battering, I pulled a lever at random. It opened the chamber stuffed with the casseroles. I closed it. My fingers froze on the handle of the next one. It was the one containing my mother. Slowly, I let them glide off. I tore my gaze away from the metal door and continued my frenzied search for the remnants, but all the other chambers were empty.

"They're not anywhere," I said.

"They must have turned to dust, Catori," Cruz said.

I bit the inside of my cheek. "Of course. That's what happened. *Ashes to ashes. Dust to dust,*" I said. I'd been present at my fair share of funerals, whether I'd wanted to or not. Even if I closed my bedroom window, I could still hear the eulogies. "But what's with the rose petals?"

"They're said to preserve the bodies of dead faeries."

Stunned, I blinked. He had to be pulling my leg.

He cracked a smile. "You fell for it."

"No," I said, although I had believed him. But just for a second.

5

SPARKS

*B*efore getting into bed that night, I collected the leather-bound book my mother had ordered. I read well into the night, absorbing facts and stories. As I was about to nod off, I stumbled on a chapter about rose petal burials.

Throughout the ages, bouquets have been deposited on graves to mask the stench of decaying flesh. This tradition was perpetuated by the fae whose use of flowers—particularly roses—originated from a desire to keep dead bodies from decomposing. Instead of laying flowers on top of the casket, though, they would place them around the dead body. This practice was called rhodonpreservation and was widely used by all the fae. But rhodonpreservation was taken to the next level by the faehunters.

After Negongwa's tribe was almost entirely decimated by the woodland faeries, the powerful chief and his surviving relatives filled caskets with rose petals, etched a spell inside the lid, and had humans bury them alive in a circle of rowan trees that no faeries could penetrate. Although being buried alive might sound gruesome to some, to them it was their only means of survival. The longer they lived, the stronger they became. By immobilizing their bodies, they were growing their magic, and when the time came, they would be powerful enough to move the earth and rise again.

My hands shook as I reread the last sentence. And then goose bumps rose over every inch of my skin.

This was completely insane! This book made no sense and yet too much sense. What was I supposed to do with this information? Accept that Mom might have been right? That magical creatures walked the Earth? I shut the book and tossed it at my feet. And then I just stared at it and replayed the rose petals and Cruz's "joke," until my brain throbbed. Massaging my temples to alleviate the ache, I came to the conclusion that Cruz had read this book, and that Mom had researched *rhodonpreservation*.

I thought about the last message she'd left on my phone. "Cat, I discovered something…" She'd sounded breathless. "Something unbelievable. And I'm dying to tell you. Call me back. I love you."

By the time I'd called her back—because I sucked at checking my voicemail—Mom was dead. Is this what she wanted to tell me about? Had she opened the casket? Had there been a body?

"Ugh," I groaned, just as a text message appeared on my phone.

You never called me back. It was from Blake.

I checked the time: 3:40 a.m.

Go to sleep. All's well, I texted back, even though all was not well.

The snow was still falling. Under the light of the moon, it glowed bright. As I went to draw the curtains, something caught my attention. A dark figure with bright skin. The person was circling the rowan trees. I squinted and made out black hair and broad shoulders. What was Cruz doing outside in the middle of the night? I caught the glow of a cell phone, which he raised to his ear. I cracked my window open so that I could hear him. Sure enough, his voice drifted into my room. However, he wasn't speaking English. He was speaking some foreign tongue that sort of sounded like Latin.

I was so busy eavesdropping that I didn't react fast enough when he spun around and looked up. By the time I yanked my curtains shut, I knew I'd been made. I paced my room. The temptation to confront him overwhelmed my desire to hide out. Sliding the thick book underneath my bed, I threw on the red sweater I'd tossed on the back of my desk chair and tiptoed down the stairs. They only creaked once. I checked Dad's door. When it remained shut, I dashed into the living room, slid my boots on, wrapped a scarf around my neck, and threw open the front door.

Cruz was standing right there, ridding his shoes of the excess snow.

"What the hell are you doing outside at this hour?" I hissed.

"I had trouble sleeping," he said, coming in. "Apparently, you too."

"Who were you talking to?"

"Are you training to be a detective or a doctor?" He pulled off his leather jacket and hung it in the closet.

"Answer the question," I said, folding my arms.

"I don't see why I owe you an explanation, Catori."

"Because you're staying under our roof. And it's four o'clock in the morning. And you were lurking outside."

"I called a friend. And I went outside, so that I didn't risk waking you or your father."

"What language were you speaking?"

"Not that I don't enjoy your inquisition, but why are *you* up?"

My cheeks flushed. "I...you...I was reading. And then I heard you."

"What were you reading?"

"A book."

Thankfully he didn't ask which book.

"What did you mean by not being related to the Woods, *yet?*" I asked, untying my arms.

"My parents worked for Linus Wood, so I grew up with his two children."

"You're friends with Ace and Lily?"

Cruz nodded.

The Woods children were like royalty—famous and yet mysterious. Their mother was a famous actress and model who married wealthy and powerful Linus Wood, the man who had a share of every American multibillion-dollar company. Some said he had a keen eye for finding golden opportunities, while others assumed he had a knack for blackmail and persuasion. I sided with the others.

"Are they as obnoxious as they looked in that *Vanity Fair* spread?" I asked.

His lips quirked up in a smile. "More."

"What did your parents do for them?"

"Mom was their nanny. Dad was Linus's right-hand man."

"And you became a medical examiner? What made you want to become *that?*"

"When my parents passed, it was my way of making death less alarming." His gaze roamed over my bare legs. "You do know you're missing pants."

"I have shorts on."

"Is that what those are?"

"They're not extra-large panties."

He laughed softly.

"You should get some sleep, Catori. Tomorrow's going to be a long day for you."

My smile faltered. "The funeral isn't tomorrow."

"Isn't your entire family arriving though?"

"Aren't you well informed?"

"Blake told me I needed to get out of town by Thursday because all the rooms at the inn were reserved. I assumed it was people coming for the funeral."

"You assumed right."

"My friend just told me the ferries to cross back to Beaver Island aren't going to be operational tomorrow. Do you think I can stay an extra night here? I'll make myself scarce."

I bit my lip. "One more night should be okay."

"Thank you."

I was about to return to my room to get some sleep, but thought about the book under my mattress. "Hey, Cruz, could you help me flip the lid of that old casket over?"

He narrowed his eyes. "Why? It was empty."

"I'm not looking for remains."

"What are you looking for then?"

"Just...never mind."

He narrowed his eyes. They looked incandescent in the ray of moonlight hitting the right side of his face, just like his skin.

"What's up with your skin?" I asked.

He tipped his face to the side. "What do you mean, what's wrong with it?"

If I told him it glowed, he would think me certifiable. "You're very pale," I ended up saying. "Are you sick?"

"You're the doctor. You tell me." He took my hand and rested it on his wrist. "How's my pulse?"

My skin burned and then sparks erupted. "Did you see that?" I yelled, yanking my hand away from his.

"Static shock."

I swallowed. "Of course." I tugged on the collar of my sweater that suddenly felt too tight around my throat. "I'm going to try to get some sleep now. I think I really need sleep," I mumbled, giving Cruz a stupid wave as I backed up toward the stairs.

They creaked, but I didn't care. I was too preoccupied by what I had just witnessed. I flipped my hands back and forth. Could static create actual sparks, or was I hallucinating?

6

THE SPELL

*T*he first people to arrive in Rowan were Aylen, her husband, Tony, and her two children. They blustered into the house, carrying several bags in spite of having already checked into Bee's Place.

"Sweetheart," she said, trapping me in a hug. "Sorry it took us so long to get here but this damn snowstorm—"

"You're here. That's all that matters," I said.

My aunt didn't resemble Mom much, but that could have been due to the fact that she colored her hair blonde and used *a lot* of makeup. Mom had barely ever lined her eyes.

"Hi, Cat," Tony said, slinging one fat arm around my shoulder and squeezing. He slugged Dad's shoulder next, mumbled some condolences, and then he picked up the remote control and plopped down on the couch.

"Hi, Sati. Hi, Shy." I tried to hug their nine-year-old twins, but Satyana and Shiloh were too busy playing a game on their electronic tablets to even notice me. They just went to the couch and sat down next to their father.

"Kids these days," Aylen said.

More like *parents* these days.

My aunt was all about not disciplining children because she was a firm believer that they disciplined themselves. I wasn't sure if Tony shared her belief. He worked as a mechanic and when he came home, he sat in front of the TV until bedtime. It was a habit he'd picked up right after the girls were born, which explained the hundred and fifty extra pounds he'd put on. He went from built to fat in nine years.

"How can I—" Aylen stopped midsentence and brushed past me, grinning. "You must be Cat's new boyfriend." She tried to hug Cruz, but he backed away.

My jaw prickled with heat. "No, Aylen. Cruz is the medical examiner," I said.

"But your mom said you had a new boyfriend."

"We broke up."

"Already? How quickly do you go through men?" Aylen said. "Well, anywho, glad to meet you, Cruz." She stuck out her hand.

His Adam's apple bobbed in his throat as he took it. I watched their hands for sparks, but of course, nothing happened. "I'm sorry for your loss. I believe Nova was your only sister?"

Aylen nodded.

"I'm going to retrieve my belongings from the inn," Cruz said, making his way to the front door. "I'll see you all later."

Once the door shut behind him, Aylen whistled. "That's the most handsome medical examiner I've ever seen. Besides you, Derek," she added.

Dad gave her a small smile. "I'm an undertaker. Not the same thing."

"Could I go down to see her?" she asked.

Dad nodded. "I'll get the backhoe up and running."

"Are you going to put her next to Mom and Dad?" Aylen asked.

"That's where she wanted to be. I just never thought I'd be the one who'd have to dig"—he cleared his throat—"dig her resting place."

"Why don't you let Tony do it?" Aylen said.

"It's okay. He's busy," Dad said.

She snorted. "Tony, get your ass off the couch and help Derek."

Tony shot her a sour look, but got up and put his coat back on. After the door closed, she said, "Maybe I should've suggested he shovel by hand. He could do with some exercise." She winked at me. "Girls, behave while I'm gone."

"Yeah, sure," they mumbled without looking up. They just kept tapping on their tablets while we headed to the kitchen. Aylen stared at the white door, and for the first time since she'd walked in, emotion flashed over her face. "Always thought yellow was too loud a color." She dug a tissue from her cardigan sleeve and pressed it against the corners of her eyes. I never understood how people could keep tissues balled under their sleeves. It was weird and probably uncomfortable. "You know, your mom always believed there was an afterlife. Not like reincarnation. More like your soul went on a journey to find the souls of departed relatives."

"I hope she was right," I whispered.

"I hope she was too." Aylen blew her nose, then tucked the wet tissue back into her sleeve.

Slowly, we went through the white door and descended into the morgue. I let Aylen slide Mom out. When she pulled the sheet off her, I gasped.

"Why don't you turn around, sweetie?" Aylen suggested.

When I didn't, she tried to spin me around, but I resisted. "He didn't prepare her!"

Aylen frowned. "What more did you want him to do?"

"Put some clothes on her, for one."

One of Aylen's eyebrows lifted. "Honey, are you feeling okay?"

"Yes. I feel fine."

I pulled the sheet further down. "He didn't even open her up," I exclaimed. "How can he establish cause of death without—"

Aylen clapped her hand on my wrist. The one holding the sheet. "What's going on with you, Cat?"

"What do you mean?"

"The stitches are right there. And she *is* dressed. He even did her makeup. She would've hated it, but hey, the dead can't complain, can they?" She stroked my mother's cheek. "Hey, Nova."

Mom's face resembled marble, white and veined. Not even a drop of makeup had been applied.

"Here, let me take off some of that purple powder," Aylen said with a smile destined for my mother. She swiped the tissue she'd used to blow her nose over my mother's lids.

"Purple powder?" I murmured. I blinked. Was something wrong with my eyes?

"I like the feather he put in her hair."

This time, I didn't ask what feather since clearly my eyesight was defective, or my aunt was crazy.

"Are you going to remove the opal earrings before you put her below ground?" she asked me.

My gaze swung to her earlobes through which were speared her favorite pair of earrings. At least I could see *those*.

"She would've wanted you to have them. They were our grandmother's, you know." She wriggled her fingers in front of my face. "I got the ring; Nova got the earrings. Opal's our family stone."

"I know. Mom told me all about it. How it's supposed to make us invisible to evil beings. Obviously it didn't do her any good."

"She died of a heart attack. Not from an attack," Aylen said. "Your dad told me you were having a tough time accepting this, but you must, Cat. Or you're going to make yourself miserable."

She stared down at my mother, then bent at the waist and placed a kiss on her ashen cheek. She covered her in the sheet again and pressed her back into the dark metal hole.

"This must be that old casket she dug up." Aylen stood next to it. "She told me the ground gave in. Help me lift the lid up, will you, Cat?"

I nodded. Aylen grabbed one side and I grabbed the other, and together we heaved it up and leaned it against the wall.

"What the..." Aylen said. She raked her fingers through the

petals, bringing a handful up. Some fluttered out and landed on top of the others. "Why are there rose petals inside the casket?"

"I was hoping Mom had told you about them."

"No. The last time we talked, she hadn't opened it yet." She sniffed the pink petals. "These are fresh. They'd make an amazing soap."

I wrinkled my nose. How could she entertain the idea of making soap with rose petals from a casket?

Aylen glanced around the sterile room. "Where's the body?"

"There was no body."

She dropped all the petals and rubbed her hands together. "You mean, I was snorting old ashes? Gross."

I started to smile when my gaze settled over the lid. I crouched down in front of it. "What is that? An epitaph?"

Aylen joined me. "Nope. That's a spell."

"A spell?"

"Yes. Your grandmother told me about it way back when. She said that's what our ancestors did. They'd write spells on the inside of their caskets. If it was read out loud by a descendant, they would come back to life."

I blinked up at my aunt.

She squeezed my shoulder and gave a small laugh. "It's just an *adsookin*...a legend, Cat."

"What if it isn't? Mom knew how to read Gottwa."

"Oh come on, Cat." Aylen snorted. "Even *I* don't believe this, and I'm totally gullible, unlike you."

"Can you read it?"

She eyed me, but then she underlined a word with her finger. "This word here is *maahin*. It means 'come forth.'"

"Do you recognize any other words?"

Her brow furrowed in concentration. "This word—*gwe*—means 'woman.'" She scanned the rest of the etching. "That's all I recognize. I should really wash my hands. I was just fondling my ancestor's ashes."

"Use the sink here," I said, dashing up the stairs. "I'll be right back."

I ran into the living room where the twins hadn't moved an inch. As they tapped on their screens, I combed through the huge bookcase around the television until I found the book my grandmother had written. I raced back to the kitchen and hurtled down the stairs. Breathless, I sat down in front of the casket lid, and with the help of Aylen, we deciphered the spell.

> From the past, I, a woman of Negongwa, will come forth to
> avenge my tribe.

"Wow," Aylen said, sitting back on her heels.

I felt as winded as she looked. "That's why there's no body," I whispered, glancing around us to make sure we were still alone.

Aylen gaped at me and then she started laughing. "Sweetie, I will say this one last time. *It's a legend.*" She drew out the last word. "A silly myth."

"But—"

"I wish the dead could walk the Earth. That would mean Mom and Dad and Nova would come back, but you know as well as I that death is final. But if you want to believe—if it can help you get through these hard times—then believe." I'm not sure why but Aylen felt the need to hug me again. "You're using my soap. You smell so good." She smiled, ran her knuckle underneath her eyes, and then stood up. "I just heard the door. Tony and Derek must be done. Let's go make lunch. They'll be hungry."

I closed my grandmother's book and held it against my chest as I trailed Aylen upstairs. While I set the dining room table, all I could think about was the engraving. No, that was a lie. I also thought about the fact that Aylen had seen my mother clothed and embalmed and I hadn't.

7

IRON

"**I**s Cruz at the inn?" I asked Blake the second he came through our front door that evening for the wake.

"Hello to you too, Cat. And no. He came by this morning and then he left. He's done here, isn't he?"

"Um…yes." I peered over Blake's shoulder, at my dad helping Bee out of her long coat. "Sort of."

"Catori?" someone said, grabbing my elbow. It was a very short woman with a wide face and high cheekbones.

"Yes?"

"It is me. Gwenelda." She must have caught the blank expression on my face, because she added, "You probably do not remember me. I am one of your cousins. From Canada." She didn't look much older than I was. If she had a decade on me, that was it. She pushed a long strand of black hair behind her ear.

It still didn't ring a bell. "Of course. Gwenelda. Thank you for coming. It must not have been easy to travel in this weather."

"The weather could not keep me away." She had an accent—Canadian maybe?

"Hi, I'm Blake."

She smiled, but kept her teeth clenched. It was a little weird. "What happened to your face, Blake?"

Color tinged his cheeks. "IED blast."

"What is IED?"

"A sort of bomb."

"Bomb like boom?" she asked, throwing her hands up in the air.

Blake raised the eyebrow that hadn't been singed off. "Yes, like boom." I knew him so well that I could tell he was thinking Gwen-something was a little cuckoo.

"Catori, may you take me to see your mother?"

"She's right through that door." I tipped my chin toward the dining room in which Dad and Tony had placed the open coffin.

Gwen latched onto my arm. "Come with me."

"I—I'd rather not. It's hard."

"I can take you," Blake offered.

She looked up at him and her black eyes seemed to flash. "Someone is calling you."

I hadn't heard anything, but Blake had. He walked toward Cass who was talking with a group of our high school friends. They'd all flown home to be there for me. When they saw me staring, they gestured me over.

"Bring me to her," she said.

How I wished I could go to them. "Fine," I said, dutiful as I was.

Every step was painful, almost more painful than the tight grip Gwen exerted on my forearm. When we arrived in the room, the crowd parted around the coffin to let us through. My gaze fell on Mom's ghostly face. I froze. Her cheeks were completely caved in now and her skin had taken on the sallow tinge of a decomposing body.

"Who prepared her for her slumber?" Gwen asked.

"A coroner that Dad hired."

"He did a lousy job, no?" she asked, keeping her voice low.

"I know," I said absentmindedly, but then jerked my gaze down to Gwen's face. "What do you mean?"

"I mean what I mean," she said cryptically before dragging me back out to the overcrowded living room. Her gaze rested on Aylen for a moment, then lifted back to mine. "Nothing was done to her."

"You can see that?"

"Yes. I have the sight, and apparently you do too."

"The sight?"

"Keep your voice low," she whispered.

"What's the sight?"

"Something that allows you to see through the *gassen*."

My brow furrowed.

"The dust," she translated. "Walk with me."

"What dust?" I asked.

She yanked me past the front door. "You know nothing of our family?" she asked, as we walked down the porch steps.

"I should get my coat," I said.

"You will not freeze."

"Why are we going outside?"

"The conversation we are going to have, it is better we have it out here. I do not want people overhearing it."

I heaved my arm out of her reach. "I lied earlier. I don't recognize you. Who are you?"

"There." She gestured toward the circle of trees. "We will talk there."

"No. This is far enough. No one's around."

She scanned the cemetery. "You are wrong. We are not alone," she murmured. Her eyes glowed like candlewicks as she peered into the night. "I must go, Catori." She reached out for my hand, pulled my fingers open, and pressed something cool inside my palm. "This will keep you safe until I can return to rouse the others."

I spread my fingers and unraveled the long silver chain. A large oval pendant swung from the intricate metal. It was smooth, with milky white, fiery orange, and neon green veins. An opal. Mom's favorite stone. When I looked up to ask Gwen if this was a family heirloom, she was gone.

"What the hell," I murmured to myself. Had she run away? I spun around to survey the graveyard but there was no movement. When I whirled back toward the house, I came face to face with Cruz and shrieked.

He clapped his hand over my mouth to silence me, but yanked it away immediately. Plumes of smoke curled away from his palm. "Fuck," he whispered.

I bounced away from him, keeping my gaze leveled on his still-fuming palm. "Is your hand smoking?"

He glowered at his hand, then at mine, and then at the opal pendant. Slowly, his expression smoothed out, and he held his palm out in the space between us. His skin was pale and glowed, but it wasn't on fire. "Not anymore."

"But it was?"

He didn't answer.

"Static shock can't set fire to skin," I said.

"Can't it?"

I shook my head no, all the while wondering if it could. I was being ridiculous. Of course it couldn't. "What did you do to Mom?"

"I didn't do anything to your mother," he said.

"You're lying!"

"No, Catori, I'm telling you the truth. I didn't do anything to your mother. I didn't prepare her. I don't know the first thing about embalming a corpse. Or about autopsies."

"I knew it!"

Cruz turned his face away, and I was left staring at the pale curves of his profile.

"Why am I the only one who sees it?" I asked.

He returned his gaze to me. "Because I dusted your mother."

"You what?"

"I put magical dust all over her. It creates an illusion."

"Magical?" My skin prickled with goose flesh that wasn't brought on by the frigid air.

"Did your aunt see your mother's real face?"

"No. She saw makeup."

"And your cousins?"

"I have no idea. I didn't ask them." But then I realized the absurdity of our conversation and squashed my lips together.

Cruz was watching the necklace clenched in my hand. "A gift from Gwenelda?"

My mouth unbolted. "You know Gwenelda?"

"I know *about* her. I haven't had the pleasure of meeting her yet."

"She said that it would keep me safe from…" I frowned, trying to remember her exact words.

"From whom?"

"She actually didn't tell me."

"She didn't?"

"No. She didn't have time."

"Do you mind getting rid of it?" he asked me.

"Why?"

"Because if you don't, I'm going to have to leave."

"That wouldn't be such a bad thing."

"That's not very nice."

"Why should I be nice to you? And besides, why would a necklace make you leave? Are you deathly allergic to semiprecious stones or something?" I asked, more as a joke than anything else.

"It's not the stone I'm *allergic* to, it's the metal."

"You're allergic to silver? What are you, a vampire?"

"No. Vampires don't exist."

"Oh good, because I was starting to think I was losing it."

"I'm allergic to iron." He watched me, as though gauging my reaction. "Like all faes."

"Faes?" I croaked.

He smiled, seemingly amused by the disbelief that must have been printed on my face.

"But you look human," I said.

"Faes are humans. On the outside we're the same; on the inside, we're a little different."

"Different how?"

"We have, um…we have powers."

"Like superpowers? Is magic dust one of them?"

"Yes. And this."

Cruz raised his hand that started to glow whiter. Suddenly, blue flames sparked and darted over his palm, making the frigid air ripple with heat. Even though I wasn't standing close to him, I could feel the heat from the fire. Cruz snapped his fingers shut and extinguished the fire.

"Some so-called magicians can do that too," I said, shooting my gaze back to his face. My brain was desperately attempting to remain rational and desperately failing.

"I know it's difficult to believe—that magic exists—but you've seen it with your own eyes. Twice now. Why don't you want to believe it?"

"Because it makes no sense."

"Neither does life on this planet, yet we've accepted this."

"Life here does make sense. There's gravity and water and—"

"Look at my feet."

I gasped. They were levitating over the snow. "You can…you can fly?"

"Now can you please get rid of the necklace?"

I clutched it tighter. "How could you think that seeing you do *that* would reassure me?"

The stone had warmed in my palm. Although Gwen hadn't told me from whom it would protect me, Cruz just had. By admitting he was averse to iron, I deduced the necklace was supposed to protect me from him.

8

THE CORPSE

I gripped the necklace so tightly that the chain links bit into my flesh. "You didn't suggest I take the wind chime down because it would blow away, did you?"

Cruz sighed. The air he expelled came out as a little cloud of fog that dispersed sluggishly. "I couldn't have gone into your house through the front door. Since you don't have a back door, I would have had to climb through a window. It would have looked strange, don't you think?"

"So if I wear the necklace, you just can't come to close to me, right? You're not going to die?"

He nodded, so I unraveled the necklace, held it up, and slipped it on. Cruz scowled.

"What does opal do to you?" I asked as the pendant settled against my rising chest.

"It makes you invisible to us."

"So you can't see me right now?"

"We can see you. We just don't know what you are."

Time, like his breath, seemed suspended. "What I am?" I shivered, as though my skin were just remembering I was outside in the dead of winter in nothing but a long-sleeved black dress. "What am I?" I asked him.

"You're a hunter."

"A hunter?"

"A faehunter."

The trembling stopped, and not because I felt warmer. If anything, the wind was picking up, lifting snowflakes from the ground, and swirling them around the graveyard. "So you're the enemy?" I asked, as my long hair flogged my cheeks.

"You're the enemy."

"Why are you still standing next to me then? Why aren't you... flying off?"

"Because you're powerless."

"But I thought I had the sight."

"Which means you can see me for what I am. That's it."

"But you can't touch me now that I'm wearing the necklace."

"I don't need to touch you to kill you, Catori. Did you not see the flames in my hands?" He shoved his leather sleeve up. Sure enough, his entire forearm glowed. "There's fire underneath my skin. It seethes inside my entire body."

I found myself stepping back, but then I stopped. "If you wanted to kill me, you would have done it already. You want something from me, don't you?" Snow was starting to soak through my leather boots. I could no longer feel my toes. "And it has to do with my mother, doesn't it? That's why you're here."

"I'm here *because* of what your mother did."

"What did she do?"

"She dug up an ancient grave."

"So what? The only thing inside was a bunch of rose petals. Are those lethal to you faeries too?"

Cruz smirked, but then his expression grew somber as he peered beyond me at the burial site surrounded by the rowan trees. "There was a body underneath those rose petals."

My jaw came unhinged. "Where did you put it?"

"By the time I was alerted and sent to retrieve it, it was gone."

"Gone where? Did my mother hide—" I clapped my hand in front of my mouth. "That's why you killed her. Because she wouldn't tell you where she put it."

"I did not kill your mother."

"But—"

"Your mother was already dead when I got here."

"Another faerie then. It was another faerie's fault," I said, my voice pulsing with anger.

"No." The word pierced the night like the tip of an arrow. "What was inside the coffin killed your mother."

"You mean the corpse?"

"Your mother could read Gottwa, couldn't she?"

"What does that have to do with anything?"

"It's a yes or no answer, Catori."

"Yes."

"Then she resurrected the body."

The instrumental music playing inside the house felt like it had gotten louder. "What?"

"Hey, Cat," Blake called out. "I was looking everywhere for you."

I whirled around and almost screamed for him to get back inside, but I'd lost my voice.

"Forgot something, Mason?" Blake asked, walking up to us.

"Yes." The glow of Cruz's exposed skin grew brighter, as though he were about to burst into flames. Or fry Blake with a flick of his fingers. I stumbled toward my friend and latched onto his arm. Cruz couldn't hurt him if I held on to him, right?

"You're as cold as a block of ice, Cat. Here." He draped his jacket over my shoulders, and then squeezed me against him, rubbing my back with his palm. "How long have you been out here?"

"I don't know," I said, through rattling teeth. "Cruz forgot his wallet. He just came to get it."

Cruz's eyes glimmered in the night. Could fire shoot out of his eyes too?

As he treaded past me, he said, "I need you to help me find it, Catori. That's why I'm back."

Blake snorted. "You need help finding your wallet? Come on, man. That's lame."

"I'm sure you'll be able to find it on your own," I told Cruz. "And once you do, please just go away. With *it*."

"Things like to hide from me."

Blake's good eye shifted from me to Cruz. Perhaps if I explained that wallet was code for corpse, he wouldn't be as baffled. Or perhaps he'd be even more so.

"Where's your cousin?" Blake asked as Cruz hopped up the porch steps.

He slowed down.

"She left," I said.

"She was weird," Blake said.

"Very."

"One of the twins has gone berserk inside. She's been telling everyone how gross your—" He paused. "Sorry. You don't need to hear this."

"Telling everyone what?" I asked, pressing away to face him. Cruz still hadn't moved. He was listening.

"I shouldn't have said anything."

"Just spit it out, Blake."

He held my gaze, and then he didn't. He looked away and I knew it was about my mother.

"Shiloh said her body was decomposing. But it's not, Cat. Your mom looks beautiful," Blake said stiffly. Surely paying Cruz a compliment was hard on him. "Aylen brought her upstairs to your bedroom. Everyone has calmed down," Blake said. "So let's go back in. Our friends want to see you."

Before he could try slinging his arm around my shoulder again,

I shot forward, past Cruz, reaching for the doorknob before he could. He bounded backward, yanking his hand as far away as he could. Because of the necklace. For some reason, that made me smile. I raced to the second floor. Everyone watched me. Dad even asked where I'd been. I just climbed those creaky steps before the fae could get to Shiloh. As soon as I was in my bedroom, I slammed the door shut.

Aylen slapped her hand against her heart. "Cat, you just scared the bejeezus out of me."

"Can I talk to Shiloh alone a minute?" I asked, walking over to my window. Was Cruz still outside or had he come in after me?

"Okay, but—is it about—what happened?" Aylen asked in a choppy, hushed voice. Shiloh had her headphones plugged into her tablet and she was watching something. "I just managed to calm her down. Please don't talk to her about...*it.*"

I was about to tell Aylen not to worry, when a knock resounded on the door. She opened the door and grinned at Cruz. I think she even batted her purple mascara-laden eyelashes.

"What?" I snapped.

"Sorry to interrupt, but I need Catori's help with something in the morgue."

I shook my head. "No way," I said.

"It's really urgent," Cruz said.

"You have two minutes," I huffed, walking past my still-smiling aunt and my still-oblivious cousin. When I passed him, he stuck his back flush against the wall. The pendant slammed against my chest as I sprang down the stairs, walked through the packed kitchen. People moved out of my way as I pulled open the white door. Conversations stopped, yet no one followed me downstairs. Not even Blake.

I waited for Cruz with my arms folded tightly over my chest. When the noise from upstairs dimmed and footsteps echoed, I knew he was coming.

"You can't tell anyone what I just told you, Catori."

"I was only going to tell Shiloh. It concerns her now."

"Yes, but knowledge of us…it comes at a price."

"What price?"

"When she finds out what she is, she becomes a hunter."

"She's nine."

"Age plays no role in what you are. As long as she's not aware, she stays off the grid. Do you understand? You can't hunt what you don't know about. And you can't be hunted by what doesn't know about you."

I gulped. "*I'm* going to be hunted?"

Cruz nodded. "But I can protect you from faes if you help me find"—he tipped his chin toward the still open casket with the still very pink rose petals—"her."

"Her? You can read Gottwa?"

"No."

"Then how do you know it's a woman?"

"Those twelve graves, Catori, we've had our eyes on them for two centuries now. We know everything there is to know about your ancestors. And the one your mother brought back…her name was Gwenelda."

My blood felt like it was draining out of my body and pooling at my feet. "I talked to her."

"I know. I saw you."

"Did she kill Mom?" I murmured.

He lowered his gaze. "She had to take a life to come back."

Suddenly, the necklace felt like it was choking me. I wrenched it off and threw it inside the casket. It landed noiselessly on top of the rose petals. Cruz placed his hand on top of mine and the heat from his body invaded mine. I flung his hand away. "Just because I'm choosing not to wear a murderer's gift doesn't mean I trust you. I just hate you less than I hate her."

His Adam's apple bobbed up and down. "Will you help me stop her from waking the others?"

"Yes."

"My people will be grateful to you."

"I'm not doing it for your people. I'm doing it for my mother. But in exchange, your people will forget I exist. *You* will forget I exist. Deal?"

Cruz nodded ever so slowly.

9

THE ARREST

One of Dad's oldest friends was playing his cello as Mom's casket was carried out of the house toward her final resting place. I wanted to tell him to stop as each note made my heart and my head throb.

Through my dark sunglasses and puffy eyes, I could barely make out where I was stepping. Even though it was mid-morning, it looked as though the sun hadn't risen yet. The sky was the sort of muted gray that made everything appear dull and flat. The elements were mourning Mom, along with every single citizen in Rowan. The headstones had disappeared behind the ocean of black-clad bodies. Tissues were clutched in almost every hand. I counted them as I followed the procession. It distracted me from watching the casket gliding over the pallbearers' heads.

Dad wrapped his hand around mine, and held it like he used to when I was a little girl and we'd skip down Morgan Street to buy ice cream from Mrs. Matty's little shop. Mrs. Matty, whose lips Mom had forgotten to sew shut. Mom, whose lips Cruz hadn't sewed shut. A sob broke loose, making me lose count of the tissues. Dad squeezed my hand.

When we arrived in front of the dark hole, he let go. He helped guide the coffin down, and then he stared around the graveyard and took a deep breath. "Our town is like no other," he said, his voice booming, yet weighty with emotion. "It is united and caring and supportive. To call us a town does not do us justice. We are a family. My parents used to say there existed no better place to live than Rowan. It took me leaving to realize this. Unlike Nova. She never felt the need to leave because she knew that this place, that all of you, were irreplaceable." A soft smile settled over Dad's lips that seemed thinner than usual, emaciated like him. "I wish to send Nova off with a reminder." He crouched down and placed his palm over the casket. "You were the most extraordinary woman and wife. Why you ever said yes to a man like me remains a mystery, but how lucky I am that you accepted to marry me all those years ago."

An arm wrapped around me. Blake's. I rested my cheek against his shoulder.

"You were the love of my life, Nova," Dad continued. "You gave me twenty-four years of uninterrupted happiness. And you gave me the most wonderful daughter—with one hell of a personality, I might add. But even for that, I am grateful."

I flicked the tears off my cheeks with my fingertips.

"The day we married, I carried you across the threshold of our house. You laughed and ordered me to put you down right away, and I did, because I could never say no to you. No one could ever say no to you."

Dad's remark elicited smiles from the crowd. It was true. Mom always got her way. Except with me. I could be so tough with her.

"I didn't want to put you down that day, Nova. Today, I carry you across a new threshold, and again, I don't want to put you down, but again, I have no choice." He squeezed his mouth shut for a long, terrible second. "I didn't get a chance to say goodbye," he murmured, contemplating his reflection in the varnished wood.

Then he looked up and held out his hands, and I stepped out of Blake's embrace and into my father's.

As Mom's shaman took over, wishing her a safe journey to the Great Spirit's side, Aylen put her arms around us. Her acrylic nails dug into my neck. When I couldn't take the pinching sensation anymore, I wiggled out from the group hug.

Dad collapsed onto his knees in the snow, raked handfuls of dirt mixed with snow from the mound next to the hole, and cast it over Mom's coffin. His face was streaked with tears and his light eyes were barely slits. He seized more and more dirt and flung it over Mom. I tried laying my hand on his shoulder but he slung it off. Perplexed, I looked around. The music stopped. His friend laid down his instrument and pushed through the crowd. Others followed him. Together, they heaved him up and away, whispering soothing words in his ear.

Bending at the waist, I cupped my hands and scooped cold dirt that I threw in turn. It glimmered as it drifted through the air, but the sparkle blunted when it landed in the dark pit.

Without music, the graveyard was silent, so very silent.

I'll find you, Gwenelda, and I will make you pay, I thought. Maybe she was here. As I looked around, I spotted a familiar face near the property's gate. Cruz was leaning against his fancy car like the first time he'd appeared in my life. I walked toward him. No one was paying attention to me anymore. The attendees were busy taking turns lobbing handfuls of dirt on top of the coffin. Instead of heading inside to shoulder my father, I broke into a slow jog toward Cruz.

"Did you find her?" I asked once I'd reached him.

"No."

"Then why are you here?"

"To pay my respects."

I snorted.

"And to see how you were holding up," he said.

"How kind of you," I said, a tad frostily.

"Will you take a ride with me?" When I made no move toward the passenger door, he said, "There's more I'd like to discuss, and what I have to tell you has to stay private."

Before I could come to my senses, I got in. "Don't lock the doors," I warned him.

"They lock automatically when the car starts, but by all means, keep your fingers on the handle. If you pump it twice, it releases the latch."

"And don't drive too fast."

"Anything else, Miss Price?" he asked, giving me a sidelong glance as he drove away, down the cobbled path that turned into a dirt road.

In the rearview mirror, I spotted Blake watching the car slip away. At least one person knew where I was—in case something happened. My phone vibrated in my coat pocket. Probably Blake. I let it go to voicemail.

Everything was whitewashed around us, as though Rowan had been soaked in bleach, from the rooftops to the tree branches to the fields.

"What is it you want to talk about?" I asked.

"That ancestor of yours, Gwenelda. If we're going to hunt her down together, you need to know a few things about her."

"I'm listening."

"She's powerful."

"I'm guessing you mean more than just having the sight."

He nodded. "She can make people do things. We call it having the influence. It won't work on you, though."

"Why? Because I have the sight?"

"Yes."

"Can she influence faeries?"

"Only the weak-blooded ones."

"Weak-blooded?"

"The ones who have mixed with humans for too many generations. The purer our blood, the more magic we have."

I snorted. "That must be healthy."

Cruz shot me a half-smile.

"What else can she do?" I asked.

"She can control things with her mind."

"Like telekinesis?"

"Yes. But I don't think she's strong enough to do that yet."

"Can I do those things too?"

"No, but I think you might have the influence. Those straight As you got during high school, your perfect SAT score, your freshman year 4.0 GPA…maybe you're smart, but no one is *that* smart."

"How do you know about my grades?"

"I was briefed before coming."

"Faeries have a whole file on me?"

"They keep track of…potential hunters."

I mentally ran over every exam I'd ever taken. My driving test popped up. During the exam, I'd been so nervous that I'd forgotten to turn on my windshield wipers. I had driven with my nose glued to the windshield to see through the torrential downpour. It had only occurred to me to turn them on after I'd bumped into the rear fender of Mr. Hamilton's car. He'd been incensed, slamming his car door and trampling through the mud to pound on my window. I'd apologized profusely, after which he'd told me not to worry. Had I sent him brainwaves to make him forgive me or had he calmed down because of my apology? Considering what a grouch Mr. Hamilton was—still is—I suspected I'd made him forgive me. Just like I suspected I'd made the DMV instructor award me a driving license I hadn't merited.

I squinted at a snow-lined hedge, attempting to shift its branches. Nothing happened. "I can't move things with my mind," I said after some time.

"It's a tough skill to master."

"Can you do it?"

"No."

"Then how do you know it's tough?"

"Don't you want to know what your ancestors' greatest power was?"

I suspected Cruz didn't want to talk about his shortcomings. "Of course I do."

"They could kill us," he said.

"Um…are you, like, immortal?"

"No."

"Then why is that such a feat?"

"Because only old age can kill faeries."

"What? You can't die of cancer? Or in a plane crash?"

He shook his head. "We don't get cancer. And when planes crash, and one of us happens to be on it, we fly out."

"Even if it blows up?"

"We're made of fire, so that doesn't bother us."

"And you can't kill each other?"

"We can, but we try not to."

"How can faehunters kill you?"

"I'd rather not tell you. I wouldn't want to give you any ideas."

"Seriously?"

"Yes, seriously. Anyway, Gwenelda can't fatally harm faeries yet. She's not strong enough, even though she's a hell of a lot stronger than what she should be. Linus thinks—"

"Linus? As in Linus Wood? You told him about—" I didn't bother finishing my question. "He's a faerie, isn't he?"

Cruz glanced at me, then fixed his gaze back on the road. He didn't have to say yes.

"What does Linus Wood think?" I asked.

"He thinks it's because she's been hibernating. Faehunters believed hibernation increased their power. That's why they buried themselves alive underneath rose petals. To grow their power."

I was about to tell him I knew, but clamped my mouth shut. I didn't want to share my mother's book until I'd read every page. In case there were interesting tidbits on faeries—like how to kill them. I kept my gaze fastened to the pale landscape outside, which was becoming brighter now that some sun was leaking through the thick clouds. "What do *you* think?"

"I believe she's strong because she absorbed your mother's life. A relative is like pure heroin versus street heroin."

My gut twisted at the comparison. "So her next move will be to dig up another grave and influence someone to open it. And preferably another relative." Abruptly, I spun toward him. "Shit, Cruz. She's going to go after Aylen, or one of her daughters."

"Shiloh can't be influenced."

"But Satyana and Aylen can. What the hell are we doing driving around? Turn back."

"Gwenelda's not going to do it with that many people around. She'll wait until they leave."

"Which is only a few hours away," I said, taking out my cell phone and scrolling through my contacts for Aylen's number. She needed to leave Rowan immediately.

Cruz seized the phone from my fingers and stuffed it inside his jacket pocket.

"I need to warn them!"

"How exactly were you going to phrase it? Our long-lost ancestor woke up, killed Mom, and is coming after one of us?"

I leaned across the elbow rest and tried to grab my phone from his pocket, but Cruz swerved the car, which pinned me against the door. "Give it back."

"I will once you calm down."

I narrowed my eyes. "Give it back, right away."

He smiled. "You're trying to influence me."

"No, I'm—I am?"

"Yes."

"How do you even know that?"

"I can feel it inside my brain. It tingles."

My forehead unfurrowed. "You can feel it, yet you can't be influenced?"

He nodded.

I was getting sidetracked. "Can I get my phone back?" I asked, my tone cooler but still crisp.

Keeping one hand on the wheel, he fished it out and tossed it on my lap. "No impulsive actions, deal?"

I didn't say deal, but I also didn't try calling my aunt. For now. Instead, I toyed with the small apparatus. "Tell me about the *gassen*."

"I haven't heard that word in nearly a century," he said.

"A century?" I squeaked. "How old are you?"

"Two decades over one hundred. The equivalent of twenty-four human years. Five human years represents one year for us."

"You're a hundred and twenty!"

"Yes."

"You were born before cars," I mused.

"Just before." A smile twitched at the corners of his mouth. "What do you want to know about our *dust*?"

"How does it work?"

He glanced at me. "We cloak things and it creates whatever illusion we have in our mind. I'm sure you've heard those old tales in which faeries played tricks on people, giving them gold coins that turned out to be chicken eggs. Or the mirages of an oasis that certain men saw after days of walking in a desert. Also faerie work. The illusions only last until we need our dust again. One illusion fades to make place for another."

"So now that Mom is underground, you got your *dust* back?"

He dipped his chin into his neck, which I took as a nod.

"Are there others like me and Shiloh?"

"Your tribe was the last one."

"But there were others?"

"Ages ago, yes."

"What happened to them?"

"They died," he said.

"They died, or they were killed?"

His knuckles whitened against the steering wheel. "We trick people; we don't kill them."

"Not even the ones who can end your lives?"

His silence was answer enough.

"So Negongwa's tribe was the only one that…in a way…made it out alive?"

"The Lost Clan."

"What?"

"That's how we refer to them since we never thought they'd wake up."

"Why didn't you set fire to their graves? You know, to make sure they didn't rise?" I asked.

His eyes flashed. "They built their caskets from rowan wood. Faerie fire can't penetrate it."

"Why didn't you ask humans to get rid of the graves?"

"Because only a family member can dig them up, and no family member would ever have betrayed their own to aid us."

"Until now," I said, my voice low.

"You're avenging your mother, Catori. You're not doing this to help me…or any other faerie."

"It still makes me a traitor."

Cruz rested his hand on top of mine. It felt like the fire from underneath his skin was penetrating mine. But there were no sparks this time. Curious, I raised my fingers to his jaw and touched it to see if it was unnaturally hot too.

"What are you doing?" he asked, his voice husky.

"The fire inside, is that what makes your skin so hot?" I glided my hand down to his neck. Goose bumps rose over his skin. "I thought you'd actually burned me the other night. I saw sparks."

He swallowed, the tendons in his neck more taut than the string of a bow.

"How come there are no sparks now?" I asked.

He turned toward me, his eyes the most intense shade of green I'd ever seen. "The other night, I—"

A siren wailed right behind the car.

"Fuck," he growled.

I turned around. A police cruiser was on our tail. "Were you speeding?" I asked, as Cruz slowed down.

"I don't know. I was distracted," he muttered.

"Cat!" Blake yelled, slamming the cruiser door and racing toward me, along with our hefty sheriff.

Blake yanked on my door handle. When it didn't open, he started banging on the window like a maniac. Stunned, I didn't pump the handle. I didn't move. But the doors must have unlocked, because Blake unhooked my seat belt, plucked me from the car seat, and shoved me behind his back.

"He's a murderer, Cat," Blake yelled. "A fucking murderer!"

I blanched. "Y-you got it wrong, Blake," I croaked. "He didn't kill Mom."

Blake frowned so deeply that his eyebrows, which had been tattooed to replace the ones that would never grow back, met on his forehead. "What are you talking about?"

"Cruz Vega, you're under arrest for the murder of Henry Mason," the cop said.

I pushed past Blake just as Sheriff Jones snapped a pair of handcuffs on Cruz's wrists. Where the metal touched his skin, it became orange and smoke curled up. He was melting the metal.

"Vega?" I croaked. "I thought—I thought your last name was Mason."

"Henry Mason was the medical examiner who was supposed to come prepare your mother," Blake explained.

His voice sounded like it was coming from very far away.

"This guy...he's some sick impersonator. To think you were in a car with him. Shit, Cat, I thought—I thought I'd never get you back."

Cruz faced me from the other side of the car. His eyes burned an electric shade of green.

"You killed—" My voice dried up in my throat. I swallowed and shivered. "You killed someone?"

He didn't say no. He didn't say anything. He just kept his eyes locked on mine. He'd said faeries only tricked people, but he'd lied. Faeries killed too.

THE WOODS

*C*ruz had been taken into custody and locked in a cell in Rowan's tiny jail. Sheriff Jones was ecstatic because this was one of the first times his jail was being used, and because arresting Cruz had turned him into an instant, local celebrity.

"Why do you think he impersonated a medical examiner?" Cass asked as she set a cheeseburger in front of me. It glistened with oil.

"I didn't order this," I told her, pushing the plate away.

She thrust it back toward me. "Just pretend to eat it." She moved her eyeballs toward the kitchen. "Blake's been on my case about making sure you didn't leave here on an empty stomach."

The sheriff and Mr. Hamilton, who sat a few tables behind me, were discussing the body that was uncovered in the middle of the woods. "There were burn marks all over it, but the snow kept it in pretty good shape considering."

I pressed my burger away. Definitely not hungry anymore.

"That's sick," Mr. Hamilton said, readjusting his tweed newsboy cap. Apparently, he'd gotten it in Scotland, on the set of one of his movies, but Blake had seen the label inside, and it read *made in Michigan*. "I still don't get what the kid's endgame was. Do you think he was planning on killing more of us?"

"Who knows? I tried interrogating him after I booked him, but he didn't say anything. He just asked for his phone call."

"Who did he call?" Mr. Hamilton asked.

"What can I get you, Sheriff?" Cass asked, wiping down their table. "Another coffee?"

"Nah, I'm good, Cass. I need to get back to the jailhouse."

"I'll take a BLT," Hamilton said. "With extra mayo."

"But you just had a steak," Cass said.

Mr. Hamilton placed his elbows on the table. "Did I ask you for dietary advice, Cassidy, or did I ask for a BLT?"

"Coming right up." As she walked past my table, she whispered, "Sheesh," and blew her bangs out of her eyes.

"So who'd he call?" Hamilton asked, lacing his fingers together.

"He spoke some weird language, so I didn't get a name."

"Probably a lawyer."

"Probably. He said that person would be able to explain. Not sure how anyone can give a good reason for homicidal identity theft." He got up, zipped his jacket over his paunch, and tapped Hamilton's skinny shoulder. "Catch you later, old sport."

As the door of Bee's Place jingled, I shot up and dashed out after the sheriff. "Sheriff Jones," I called out.

"Yes?" He stopped walking.

"Can I talk to him?"

"To the prisoner?"

I nodded.

"I don't think that's a good idea. We're not sure yet what sort of person we're dealing with."

"Please. I just need to ask him something about my mother."

His small eyes ran over my face. "Heard your dad's thinking of pulling her out of the ground. You know...to check that he didn't, um...molest her."

"Cruz wouldn't—"

"You're defending him?"

"He's not a necrophiliac," I said.

"How would you know that?"

"I just know. Please, can I just have a minute with him?"

He tilted his face to the side. "Fine. One minute. Supervised by me. Wouldn't want Derek telling me how irresponsible I was to let you within ten feet of him."

One supervised minute wasn't ideal, but it was better than none. We walked side by side down the dusk-covered main street toward the county jail. When we stepped into the brick building, the cop at the entrance shot out of his seat. It took me a second to realize it was Cass's older brother, Jimmy. He'd changed his hair, or grown, or something.

"Has the prisoner been cooperating?"

"Nothing to report, sir," Jimmy said.

"Buzz us through," Sheriff Jones told him.

The metal door behind the desk unlocked. The sheriff pushed through and I trailed him in. The jail smelled like Lysol and was lit by several strips of neon lights. The cells weren't cozy, but they weren't dank like I'd pictured them.

"He's in the last one," the sheriff told me.

I was nearly surprised to see Cruz. Part of me had imagined he would have broken out already. His thick black lashes swept up over his bright eyes when he spotted me. He couldn't have murdered a man, could he?

"Hi," I said.

"Hi," he said. Cruz was sitting on a cot with a mattress that looked no thicker than a shoe sole. With a sigh, he combed his hand through his wavy black hair, mussing it up. "What are you doing here, Catori?"

I approached the bars, but the sheriff cleared his throat, so I stopped. "Dad wants to exhume Mom's body. He's suffered enough. I don't want him to be shocked by anything. She'll be…visible, right?"

His lips set in a grim twist. "No."

A voice erupted over a speaker above the secure doorway. "Sheriff, the prisoner's visitor is here."

Cruz rose.

The sheriff pointed his finger at him. "Don't you move. Cat, you got your minute. I'm going to have to ask you to leave now."

I wasn't ready to go. "You could've just taken his place without killing him," I whispered.

"I didn't kill him."

"Really? Then who did?"

He hesitated. "I don't know." The hesitation was a dead give-away that he *did* know.

"Cat, now!" The sheriff held the door open for me.

"What do I do if she comes back?" I asked in a hushed voice.

"Just act normal."

I tugged on the hem of my black scarf. "She'll see right through me."

He stepped up to the bars. "No, she won't. She can't."

"I told you not to move, Vega," the sheriff barked. "Step back before I Taser you. And, Cat, don't make me regret allowing you inside. Out!"

Biting my lip, I turned away from Cruz and treaded back down the corridor. Just this morning, we were burying Mom, and now I was visiting him in jail. When I emerged from the short corridor, I looked up and stumbled, catching myself on the edge of the front desk. Standing right there was America's elusive heartthrob. The sheriff didn't make a fool of himself like I had just done, but he did freeze at the sight of Cruz's visitor.

"M-Mr. Wood?" he stammered. "You're"—he turned toward Cruz's cell—"You're here for the suspect?"

"Yes," Ace said, eyes on me. He tilted his head to the side.

He was more handsome than in the *Vanity Fair* article. Too handsome with his dark blond hair which he wore cropped on the sides and longer on the top, and his afternoon shadow that made his pretty boy face look rugged.

"I flew over as quickly as I could. Pleasure to meet you, officer," he said with a smile.

It took me a second to realize he meant me. "Oh, I'm not a cop."

"Then who are you?" he asked.

"I-I'm Catori Price."

"Ah."

"What, *ah?*"

"You're prettier than in the pictures," he said, extending his hand.

I fed my fingers through his, expecting his skin to be hot like Cruz's, and it was. "What pictures?"

His smile faltered. "The ones on your Facebook wall."

"My Facebook profile is set on private," I said, yanking my hand back and stuffing it inside my coat pocket.

Ace wasn't smiling anymore. "Interesting."

Had he felt I was a faehunter's descendant? Is that what he meant by interesting?

"So, Sheriff, where are you keeping the big bad prisoner?" Ace asked.

Sheriff Jones's round cheeks reddened and sweat beaded on his upper lip. "I-In here. After you." The door buzzed again.

As soon as both disappeared behind it, Jimmy took out his cell phone. "I can't believe Ace Wood is here. I need to call Cass. She's going to flip. She's had a crush on him since junior high."

"When did this happen?" I pointed at the badge hooked onto his belt.

"I completed my training during the fall. Cass didn't tell you? I suppose with everything that's happened, she didn't think to mention it. I'm really sorry about your mom, Cat. I was at the wake and the funeral, but there were so many people that I don't think you saw me."

I strained to hear voices beyond the door. "Is Sheriff Jones treating you well?"

"He's cool. But I'm still on desk duty. I was hoping for some field jobs."

"This is Rowan, Jimmy. You should move to Detroit for some field jobs."

"Maybe. You know, when I saw Cruz at Bee's Place the night he got into town, I told Blake and Cass something was off."

I nearly laughed and told him, *No shit, he's a faerie*, but obviously I kept that to myself.

"Why do you think Ace Wood is here?" Jimmy asked.

"Cruz grew up with his family," I said.

"That is dope. Apparently their island is like the most insane place to live. You know, that's on my bucket list of places to visit before I croak."

"I didn't know." Metal clanked beyond the door. Had the sheriff set Cruz free? "I don't think they allow visitors."

"Still, how cool would it be to go?" he asked, just as the door buzzed behind him. He jumped to his feet to hold it open.

As Ace and Cruz walked out, Jimmy blinked. Then his gaze, like mine, darted to Cruz's unshackled wrists, and an eyebrow lifted on his large forehead.

"You wanted field work, Jimmy? I got something for you," Jones said, cheeks even brighter than before. He slapped a piece of paper into Jimmy's hands. "Mr. Wood was kind enough to hire a private detective to find out who Mr. Mason's true killer was. Mr. Vega, I am deeply sorry for my rash conviction. I hadn't realized Mr. Mason had called on you to replace him."

I shot Cruz an incredulous glance.

He smiled at the sheriff, but I suspected it was intended for me. "Don't mention it, Sheriff. You couldn't have known." He turned to go. "Catori, I owe your father an apology. Would you mind terribly if we came home with you?"

"We?"

"Ace would like to meet him."

"I could drive you over," Jimmy offered, "if you need an extra vehicle."

"Jimmy," the sheriff snapped. "I just handed you an assignment. Shoo."

"Yes, sir. Right away, sir," he said, quickly shrugging into his khaki winter jacket. He scuttled past me, but then doubled back. "I forgot the car keys." He grabbed them from his desk drawer and dashed out of the station.

"Sheriff, it was a pleasure doing business with you," Ace said.

As they shook hands, Sheriff Jones's beady eyes darted toward me. "I phoned Derek and briefly explained things. He's expecting you."

"You have yourself a good evening, Sheriff," Ace said as he pulled the front door open. "Ladies first."

I walked out into the cold evening and stuffed my hands inside my pockets. Cruz and Ace joined me seconds later. Even though I expected Ace to glow like Cruz, when I saw that he did, it was still odd to witness.

"Where's your car, Cruz?" Ace asked.

I tipped my chin to the wide alley that led to the jail parking lot. "Blake parked it right behind the station."

After the sheriff had cuffed Cruz and dragged him to the cruiser, Blake had driven the sports car back. During the entire ride, he told me how lucky I was that they'd found me in time. I'd been too dazed to feel lucky.

"It's a two-seater," Cruz said.

"Right. I can get a ride back with…" I couldn't ask Blake, because he would hang around, and I didn't want him to. And Cass had just started her shift. And Bee didn't drive. Maybe Mr. Hamilton? "With someone."

"Nonsense. You go with Cruz. It's such a clear night. Perfect for a little…promenade."

"It's far," I said. "You can't walk—"

"Who said anything about walking?" Ace winked at me, checked the alley, then levitated and shot upward like a human rocket. I snapped my neck back to watch his ascent. In seconds, he was as high up as a fugitive helium balloon, and then he whizzed through the darkness like a shooting star.

"He's going to get there before us, isn't he?" I asked stupidly.

"Most probably. Let's not subject your poor father to too much time alone in Ace's company."

I nodded, gaze still turned upward. My hair blew around my face, and I raked it back. Besides a few stars, the sky was pitch-black. "I wish I could do that," I said. "I can drive your car back if you also want to, you know…fly."

"I'd rather drive."

"Why would anyone rather drive?"

His green eyes looked dark against his shiny skin.

"You don't trust me with your car, is that it?"

"I don't care about the car," he said, his voice low. "I just thought you'd still have questions for me."

"A few."

"You have the keys?"

I blanched. "No. Blake has them. Shoot. You want me to go—"

"Why don't you try starting it with your mind?"

"Huh? What?"

He tapped his temple.

"Oh. Uh. How—Do I just focus on it?"

"I heard that's how your ancestors did it back in the day. They concentrated on what they wanted to happen and it happened."

I swallowed, then turned my gaze to the car, and thought about the ignition button. Nothing happened. I squinted. Still nothing. I focused harder. Suddenly the car beeped and flashed.

"I did it," I whispered in disbelief. Then I flung my gaze onto Cruz. "I did—" My excitement dwindled when I spied a small keypad in his hand and a grin on his face. "I didn't do it, did I?"

"The sheriff gave them back to me."

I was so embarrassed that my eyes fogged up. It was silly, and the tears were surely brought on by my exhaustion, but it didn't change the fact that I felt like a massive fool.

"Oh, Catori, I didn't mean to upset you."

He stepped toward me but I held my palm out. I kept my eyes on the shimmery gray pavement, too mortified to look at him. "Just get me home."

"Catori…"

"Please." I walked to his car, listening to the quiet echo of my boot heels. I opened the door and dropped inside, pulling the seat belt across my chest. Cruz swung his door open and got in. I kept my face turned away from him. He didn't start the car. I tapped my foot. He reached out and turned my face toward him. The heat from his skin shocked my cold skin…shocked me.

"Don't cry," he said gently.

I sniffled. "I'm not."

His thumb whisked a tear off my cheek. And then he tugged my face closer until I could feel his hot breath on my nose. "In time, I'm sure you'll be able to do it."

I hooked my fingers around his hand and hauled it off my cheek. "If doing it means becoming someone like Gwenelda, then I don't want to." I exhaled a shaky breath. "I don't want any of this. I didn't ask for any of this."

"You could never be like Gwenelda."

"How can you know that, Cruz?" I asked, scanning his eyes. He was so close that I could see all the different shades of green thrum around his black pupil.

"Because your heart doesn't beat with hate. Your life doesn't revolve around destroying us. And"—he pushed a stray lock of hair behind my ear—"I would never let you."

"Never letting me would mean sticking around," I told him. "Once you get Gwenelda, you'll go home."

"It depends," he said, hand settling on the nape of my neck. He drew me closer.

"We had a deal. No staying," I said, pulse quickening.

"I don't like that deal," he murmured, right before pressing his lips against mine.

Although I should have pushed him away, I couldn't. The sparks that had erupted over my skin the first night he touched me exploded inside my body. His hands brushed against my arms. Through my jacket sleeves, I felt the heat, but I still trembled because the tremors had nothing to do with my internal temperature. His hands rose back to my neck, then glided down the curve of my shoulders again. His tongue explored my mouth while his hands caressed my spine.

I pulled away, breathless. "What are we doing?"

"Faeries call it kissing."

I smiled, and then I didn't. "That's not what I meant, Cruz."

"I don't know what we're doing," he said, his voice now grave. "I don't know." He looked at the brick wall in front of us, and stayed silent for so long that it exacerbated my anxiety. Without glancing my way, he started the car. "And we should probably not do it again," he said as he pulled out of his parking space. Halfway home, he added, "Don't tell Ace."

As if I would blab about kissing a guy to a perfect stranger. I didn't even kiss and tell my friends. I stuck my elbow on the armrest and stared out the window at the nearly full moon.

11

THE OFFER

The frostiness that had settled over Cruz and me in the car pursued us into the house. Dad and Ace were sitting on the couch talking. When we walked in, both looked up. Ace cocked an eyebrow, while my father shot up and wrapped his arms around me.

"What a day," he whispered into my hair. "What a day..." He smelled like stale beer.

"Is everyone gone?" I asked.

"Yes."

"Even Aylen?"

He nodded.

"For good?"

"No, just for the night. She'll be back tomorrow. She offered to bring breakfast. Not that we need any more food." He gestured to the coffee table that was laden with bowls of chips, nuts, raw veggies, and candy. "I was thinking of driving some of this food over to the local shelter. They need it more than we do. Remember all those food drives we organized at your school?"

Ace cleared his throat. "Mr. Price, will you accept our offer?"

"What offer?" I asked, flinging my attention to Ace.

"This nice young man offered to buy our property—"

"It's not on the market," I said, glaring at Ace.

Dad frowned. "I thought this would make you ecstatic."

"Mom's buried here. We're not leaving her."

"I'll let you talk this over," Ace said, standing up. "We'll be back in the morning. You can give us your final answer then."

"This *is* our final answer," I said.

"Then I guess we have no more business here." He walked over to the front door and pulled it open. "Let's go home, brother."

Brother?

Cruz glanced at me, rubbed the back of his neck, then glanced at Ace. "I'm exhausted, Ace. I'd like to stay overnight in Rowan"—he looked at Dad—"not in your house, of course, Mr. Price. We'll get a room at Bee's."

"She doesn't have any available rooms," I said.

"You can stay in the guest room," Dad offered.

"No. They can't. I don't want anyone in the house. Can you respect that, Dad?"

A frown gusted over Ace's face. "Clearly, we've overstayed our welcome, Cruz."

"What if Gwenelda comes back?" Cruz said, staring at me intensely.

My eyes widened.

"I have a shotgun," Dad said.

I swung my face from the two faeries to my father. "They told you about Gwenelda?"

"She was at the wake, honey," Dad said. "And apparently she talked with you."

My jaw dropped a little. How much had they told him?

"Mr. Mason mentioned marital problems when he asked Cruz to replace him," he continued.

"You don't say." My sarcasm was lost on Dad, who'd apparently had no trouble swallowing Ace's lies.

"You hear about husbands abusing wives all the time, but wives abusing husbands…that's rare." Dad shook his head. "Poor man. Poor, poor man."

"Huh?"

"Gwenelda was Mr. Mason's wife. She killed him," Dad said very matter-of-factly.

I glowered at Cruz. "What a story."

"To think she came all the way here to find out if he'd confessed the abuse to Cruz." Dad shook his head. "Perhaps you *should* get out of here, Cruz. Just in case she isn't apprehended tonight. I would hate for anything bad to happen to you."

"Thank you for your consideration toward my future brother-in-law, Mr. Price," Ace said.

"Brother-in-law?" I said.

"He's engaged to my sister." He slugged Cruz's shoulder. "Wedding's this summer. Anyway, we should go. I'll wait for you in the car." He strolled over to our front door and swung it open. As it closed behind him, cool air blasted through the warm living room, but it wasn't cool enough to make the blush recede from my cheeks.

Engaged! I released my lip as I looked at Cruz and he looked at me. With Dad there, I couldn't call him all the choice words that popped into my mind, so I spun around and tore up the stairs to my bedroom. When the front door banged shut a moment later, I walked up to my window and peered down. Cruz treaded across the snow toward his car. Right before getting in, he glanced up and held my gaze. Perhaps I should have turned away, but I didn't. I couldn't.

He broke our eye contact, his gaze sweeping the perimeter. I scanned the dark graveyard for Gwenelda. Had she returned? Had Jimmy found her? *God, Jimmy.* She could kill him in a second. Apprehending my ancestor was a suicide mission.

As the car glided off the property, I pulled my phone out of my pocket and dialed Cass. She didn't answer. Blake would have Jimmy's number, but Blake would want to know why I wanted

Jimmy's number. I logged on to my Facebook account and combed through my friend list until I came upon Jimmy's name.

Call me, I typed in a private message. *It's urgent.*

I paced my bedroom floor waiting for my phone to ping with an answer, but no ping came. Sighing, I phoned Aylen next. I wanted to tell her to get out of town. She too didn't answer. *Agh*! I was about to call Bee's Place and have them transfer me to Aylen's room, when there was a knock on my door.

Dad poked his head in. "Can I come in, sweetie?"

I nodded.

"I'm worried about you."

"About me? Why?"

"You've been acting strange. I know it was easier for you to speak to your mother, but now that she's—" He hooked his thumbs through his belt loops and shifted in his boots. "Now that she's not here, well, you can talk to me," he said choppily.

"I never talked to Mom about private stuff. At least not willing-ly," I added with a smile.

"She could worm anything out of anyone."

"That she could."

He shifted again. "By the way, I'm glad you didn't want to sell this place. I know it's odd living over a cemetery, but—"

"How much did he offer?"

Dad blanched.

"I don't want to sell it, Dad, I just want to know what this place is worth to him."

"Seven million dollars."

"Seven million?"

"We might never get an offer like that again."

"This place is priceless." To me, and to my father, but also to every faerie out there.

"I should get some sleep."

Relieved I was dismissing him, Dad's face smoothed out and he quit shifting.

"Goodnight, Dad."

"Goodnight, sweetheart. Sleep tight."

I nodded. Although I was tired, I wouldn't be able to sleep until I'd heard back from Jimmy. Just as Dad shut my door, my phone pinged. I swiped my finger over the screen and read the message. The phone slipped from my fingers and bounced on the hardwood floor.

I will let him go once you come here, Catori. Meet me at the old cabin. Apparently you will know which one I mean.

Gwenelda had Jimmy.

And she was holding him in the middle of the woods.

12

THE CABIN

I stood in front of the abandoned ranger's cabin, arms wrapped tightly around my chest. There was no light inside and no movement. I strained to hear voices, but the only sounds came from the dark forest. I approached slowly, heart thumping inside my ribcage. I raised my fist to knock, but the door swept open before my knuckles met the worm-eaten wood.

"You came," Gwenelda said. There was a hint of surprise in her voice.

"Where's Jimmy?"

A grunt emanated from one of the dusky corners. Jimmy was curled onto himself with his knees rammed into his chest.

"What did you do to him?"

"Nothing."

Jimmy looked up, his large forehead as pale as a corpse.

"That doesn't look like nothing," I said, pointing to the ropes tied around his wrists and ankles. I was about to go free him, when I realized turning my back on Gwenelda was unwise. "Release him right now."

Gwenelda nodded. She didn't move, though.

"I said *now*."

"He is already unbound."

Sure enough, Jimmy scrambled to his feet.

"How did you do that?" I asked.

She touched her palm to her forehead.

As the young cop raced toward the door, Gwenelda locked her fingers around his arm, her eyes glowing like prism reflectors. "You will forget about tonight. You will forget about me."

Jimmy didn't blink. Not once. He stared at Gwenelda, and then, trance-like, he slid past me and hopped into the cruiser that was parked next to the cabin. "Is he okay to drive?" Perhaps it was a silly concern, but I couldn't help it.

"I am hoping."

"You're hoping?" I exclaimed.

I ran after the car, waving my hands over my head to stop him, but the taillights grew fainter and then vanished. "If anything happens to him, I'll—"

"You will kill me? I would like that, but it is impossible."

"What do you mean?"

"Come inside and I will tell you, child."

"Child?"

"You are two hundred years younger than I. That makes you a child." When I still didn't budge, she said, "It is not in my interest to kill you, Catori." She fixed me with her dark eyes. "Your name is not Gottwa. Do you know?"

"Dad chose it. He liked the sound of it and he liked its meaning. If you have a problem with it, take it up with him."

Gwenelda smiled. "You are indeed a lively one."

"Mom used to say that, but you wouldn't know. You killed her."

The rustling of pine needles became deafening as Gwenelda stared at me. "You do not know what you are talking about, little girl."

"Then tell me."

"Not out here." She glanced into the night. "It is not safe in these woods. I placed a spell on the cabin. No faerie can penetrate it. Please, enter inside."

"I'm not scared of faeries."

"That is because you do not know what they are capable of."

"I'm sure they're not perfect, but *they* didn't kill my mother." My voice seemed to resonate against the bark of the pines, or perhaps it was my thrumming pulse that made it sound louder.

"Just because your heart beats for one does not mean their species is good."

"My heart beats for no one."

She smirked. "You struck me as an intelligent girl the first time we met, but perhaps I was mistaken."

I glowered at her. "If I come inside, you'll tell me everything?"

She nodded. "Everything."

Bracing myself, I went in, and she shut the door. There was no furniture inside, so I stood in the middle of the room with my arms crossed tightly in front of my chest. "Talk."

"Would you like to sit?"

"Where?"

"On the floor."

"Not really. It's dirty."

"Dirt will not kill you," she said.

"Apparently," I said sarcastically. From the way she furrowed her square forehead, I doubted she got my insinuation.

"Two hundred years ago, Catori, our tribe was decimated by the fae. They wanted to eradicate us because we represented a threat to them. We were the only ones with the power to kill them."

Although I knew all this already, I didn't want to interrupt. A cloud passed over the moon, which was the only source of light inside the cabin. Darkness slid over Gwen's face, and then glided off.

"Faes are wicked creatures. They kill and pillage and trick people. Their wickedness went unpunished for centuries. But one night, the Great Spirit came to the Gottwa people and asked us to become the protectors of humans. The Great Spirit entrusted us with the power to control them. We became what you call today, a police. When faeries committed a crime, we tracked them and chastised them."

"Chastised?" I snorted. "What a pretty word for murder."

"We rarely killed them. We reprimanded them by seizing their *gassen*. Their dust. If they behaved properly, we would return their magic."

"You can confiscate magic?"

"Yes. But we cannot use it. It is stored inside of us. You see these marks on me?" She hiked up the back of her blue sweater. Intricate tattoos ran up her spine. "Each etching holds the magic of one fae." I counted four tattoos. "One day, the faes came after us. They sliced through our skin, tortured so many of us, to retrieve their magic." Darkness passed over her face again, but not because of any clouds this time. "When they realized that slaughtering us freed the magic from our bodies and replaced it in theirs, they massacred us. The Great Spirit came to my father in his sleep and told him we had to slumber in coffins made of rowan wood underneath spelled rose petals. We did not know if we would survive, but here I stand today. My father, Negongwa, was right. The Great Spirit has protected us."

Gwenelda sounded so genuine that my stance had loosened, from surprise and fascination. But then I thought about Mom and drew my arms tight again. "He didn't protect my mother."

"She is with her, I am sure."

"Her?"

"For the Gottwa people, the Great Spirit was *gwe*. Female."

"I know what *gwe* means. It was in the spell. The one that brought you back, but took my mother."

Gwenelda narrowed her eyes. "I did not take the life of your mother, Catori."

"Then who did?"

"When I awakened, she was lying on the floor beside my coffin.

I believe a fae learned she had raised a casket from the earth and killed her to make sure she could not do it again."

"Then why didn't they kill you at the same time?"

"Because I was still surrounded by rowan. Their magic does not penetrate it."

"I know that."

"Or..."

"Or what?"

"Or the spell took her," she said, in a low voice. "But I do not know that for sure." Suddenly, she frowned and turned toward one of the dusty windowpanes. "Did you hear something?"

"No."

Cautiously, she approached the cracked window. Most people wanted to rehabilitate the cabin, but not the mayor. He wanted to build a landscaped park with a playground and a community center that would cost taxpayers a bunch of money and maim the natural beauty of Manistee Forest.

"The Woods were quick to come to Rowan," she said, dragging her gaze to me. "I heard they even killed a man on their way."

"What are you implying?"

"You are not wearing your necklace."

My coat was zipped all the way up to my neck. "How can you tell?"

"I can feel the presence of opal. It hums to me."

Of course it does...because you're a lunatic.

"Although I cannot force you to wear it, it will protect you from them."

"Maybe two centuries ago, it would have. But now, I can bet you that every faerie knows what I look like. Haven't you heard of the Internet?"

"I am learning about it. But there are so many clans of faes. Hundreds. They spread like smallpox when we were gone, onto every continent. And they do not get along, Catori. The Woods might all know about you, but they would not have warned the Fiori or the Rios. Faeries are selfish and only care for themselves."

I ran my fingers across my neck. "If they're all over the world, there must be other hunters."

"I have not seen any indication of others. For now, it is only you and I."

"I'm not a hunter."

"You are, child. The Great Spirit has bestowed the sight upon you, which makes you one of us. It is a glorious gift."

"You have to stop calling me child. It's weird, Gwen. You look thirty."

"Twenty-nine. I was twenty-nine when they placed me in the ground."

"My point exactly."

Her gaze shot over to the cracked window again.

"You said killing you is impossible. You're not immortal, so why is that?"

"Only faes can kill me. They asphyxiate us hunters with their dust. It is the worst form of death. One I hope you will never feel." Suddenly, she hissed. "They have come."

Against the blackness, two figures glowed bright white, Cruz and Ace. I wasn't sure whether to feel relieved or alarmed by their presence.

"Let her go, Gwenelda, and no one will get hurt." Ace's voice seeped through the fissures in the glass and the holes in the rotten wood.

Gwenelda snarled. "I do not trust Woods."

"And I do not trust Gottwas," Ace continued, "but this girl has nothing to do with our feud. If you leave Rowan tonight, we will not warn the others that you have returned. If you don't—"

"You will kill me? Like you killed that poor medical examining man and blamed me for it."

Ace snorted. "Did those rose petals fry your brain?" He shook his head. "Your people always blamed faeries for everything. I'm not saying we're perfect, but come on, Gwenelda, you just came back from the dead. You have no clue how the world works nowadays."

Ace and Cruz seemed like they'd moved closer to the cabin, yet their legs hadn't shifted. I stared down at their feet. They weren't touching the ground.

"There is hatred everywhere," Gwenelda said. "Perhaps it was not only the doing of your people, Ace, but I am certain faeries did not try to better the world."

Cruz and Ace were right in front of the broken glass. I jerked backward whereas Gwenelda stood her ground.

"Do not threaten us," she said.

"Oh." Ace smiled, a wicked smile. "We're not threatening Catori. Just you."

"Stop it!" My voice rang out in the small cabin, surprising everyone including myself. "For your information, Ace, Gwenelda's not holding me hostage. I came here of my own will, just like I'll leave...of my own will. And, Gwen, don't bother asking me to wake the others, because I won't do it. I don't want to propagate...this." I gestured between the faeries and the hunter. "I'll be on my way now."

I backed away slowly, my gaze cemented to Gwenelda's. There was no animosity, but there was some other emotion drifting over her face. Despair? Disappointment? I almost apologized. What exactly would I be apologizing for? Refusing to dig up old graves and wake vengeful relatives? My heels knocked into the wall. I spun around and unlatched the door. It creaked as it opened. And then I ran out. I was halfway home when Cruz flew right in front of me. I just managed to stop before colliding into him. I lost my footing and toppled into the snow.

"Leave me alone." Shakily, I got back up.

"I don't want to leave you alone," he said.

I brushed the snow off my jeans. My fingertips were as white as Cruz's skin, although there was no magic in them, only raw cold.

Keeping my eyes on him, I circled around his floating body and started up again, slower, because my legs trembled as furiously as my hands. Cruz didn't stop me this time, but he followed me all the way back to my house. I could feel his blazing presence behind me, a beacon in the harsh obscurity, one that would never lead me to safety.

Just before I vanished inside my house, I heard him say, "Guards have been called. They'll patrol the property. For your safety."

"How stupid do you think I am?" I asked, spinning around.

He'd landed, probably worried Dad might spot him floating around.

"It's not for *my* safety; it's for yours…your people's safety."

I waited for him to dispute this—to prove that faes weren't completely selfish—but the words I lingered for in my doorway never came.

13

THE GUARDS

I looked out through my window that night for the faerie guards Cruz had spoken of but didn't see them. The only thing out there was a swarm of fireflies. They bobbed over the headstones and twirled around the blackened tree trunks. The spectacle was enthralling, so much so that I spent a long time looking at the creatures' dance, and when I slept that night, I dreamt of them.

It was nearly noon when I woke up to banging on my door. When I grumbled that I was awake, Dad came in and drew my curtains open.

"I need to get out of this house," he said.

I sat up in bed and stretched. "What are you thinking?"

"I made a reservation at Bee's Place."

"Oh." There went hoping for a road trip. "I doubt you needed to make a reservation." Bee would throw out customers to accommodate us.

"I'm starving, so get ready quick, okay?" he said, then left my bedroom and closed the door.

The dangling yellow feathers of my dream catcher fluttered, reminding me of the fireflies' nocturnal dance. Come to think of it, weren't they warm weather insects? After I brushed my teeth and pulled on a fresh pair of jeans and a sweater, I went downstairs to the hearse and slid in next to Dad. The air was frigid inside the car.

"Dad, have you ever seen fireflies in the winter?"

"No." He spun the dials of the temperature to the maximum. "Why?"

"I saw some last night."

"I think you need some more sleep, honey." He shot me a smile. "I'm sorry I woke you, but I wanted to spend time with you before —" His voice cracked, but then he cleared his throat. "Before you leave."

I forgot all about the lightning bugs then. "I'll stay as long as you need me," I said, placing my hand on top of his.

"Do you think there would ever come a time when I wouldn't need you?"

I squeezed his hand and he squeezed back. "I can take a semester off."

He turned his face toward me, his eyes bright, but then the sparkle blunted. "Your mother would be so angry with me if I held you back. You need to return to Boston and live your life."

The reasons to leave Rowan weren't lacking, but what would happen to Gwenelda, to her family, to the people of this town? Would the faeries retreat back to their island and leave us all alone or would they stay until they'd slaughtered their slumbering enemies?

"I'm taking a semester off," I said resolutely.

Silence hung in the car as Dad checked and rechecked the expression on my face. As we passed the ancient sand dune, he smiled at me, and then he smiled at the road and the trees and the squirrels. I'd made him happy.

The snow had melted over the sand, just like it was thawing out in patches over most of Rowan. It was by no means warm, but the sun was bright and the sky cloudless. People were out today. Most were on their way to lunch. The bakery and coffee shop had long lines of students snaking out of them. Although high school was a year and a half ago, it felt like it had happened in another lifetime. Watching them gossip and share laughs made me think of Boston. I hadn't really made any friends there—acquaintances, sure, but not close friends. No one from Boston University had attended the funeral, and yet almost everyone from Rowan High had.

But that was my own fault. I'd so wanted to prove to my parents that their money wasn't wasted that I spent every waking minute studying. The person I was closest to was my Goth roommate Cora, and saying we were close was an exaggeration. It just felt that way because her boyfriend, Duke, was always hanging around our dorm room making eyes at her. She'd probably be thrilled to have the room to herself.

"I'll need to fly back to get my stuff. And my car," I told Dad who slowed down in front of the police station, then backed into a parking spot. "I'm pretty sure there's closer parking."

"I wanted to ask Sheriff Jones if he'd apprehended the criminal."

"Oh. Um. Probably not," I said, taking off my seat belt and getting out of the car.

Dad rounded the front of the hearse while tightening his belt. It bunched up the waistband of his jeans. He'd lost a ton of weight in the past three days. "What makes you think that?"

"I just imagine she's left town."

"Well, if you don't mind, since we're here, I'd like to go and check."

I nodded and followed him into the precinct. Jimmy was at the front desk, tapping on his phone with such fervor that he had to be playing a game. Or he was sending a very hateful text message. When he looked up, I was expecting surprise or recognition for last night, but instead his face became pink and he stashed his phone in the drawer.

"I was checking the police radar. See if there was any spotting of that suspect we're looking for," he said.

I frowned. Had he really forgotten about last night?

"You can do that from a cell phone?" Dad asked.

He jerked his head up and down, clearly lying.

Dad let out a heavy sigh. "So that means you haven't caught her yet."

"No, sir. But we will. I have no doubt that we will. Sheriff Jones is on a conference call with the other police departments in the region. He wants us to join forces. The more of us, the better, right?"

"I hope so," Dad said. "Well, anyway, we're off to lunch."

"*Bon apuetiti*, Mr. Price." Not sure what language he was aiming for.

Once Dad had stepped out of the precinct, I asked, "Were you out last night, Jimmy?"

"Nope. I stayed in with Momma. We watched *The Reverence*. Do you follow that show? It's so freaky."

"No, I don't. And after that? Did you leave the house?"

His eyebrows hiked up on his forehead, drawing his lids along until his eyes were unnaturally round. He dropped his voice to a whisper, "Why? Did you see me?"

"I thought—"

"I have a history of sleepwalking." He checked the precinct door. "Was I...was I wearing clothes?"

"Yes." I wrinkled my nose at the thought of seeing Jimmy in his birthday suit. "Definitely clothed."

He breathed the heaviest sigh I'd ever heard. I could nearly see it drop out of his mouth. "I'm always sleepwalking naked. I've been taking meds for that. I thought it was getting better. I should phone the doctor." He fiddled with the drawer handle, dragged it open, and plucked his phone out.

I debated whether to reassure him that I hadn't seen him, but he was already on the line with his doctor. As I left, I wondered how Cass had turned out so differently than Jimmy. Where he was attached to his mother's hip at age twenty-two, she was independent. It probably had to do with their father leaving their mother for another woman ten years back. It had been tougher on him than on her.

"I'm so happy the sheriff hired Jimmy. That boy needed a real job," Dad said once I'd caught up to him. He offered me his arm and I took it.

"Selling cell phone plans was a real job."

Dad glanced at me. "He needed a purpose, and negotiating data packages wasn't it."

"Don't go shouting that at the mall or we'll become *persona non grata*," I said.

"I just think that he needed a role model, and Sheriff Jones is a great one."

"You don't have to explain yourself, Dad. I was just joking."

"I'm so glad you didn't become a cop. I don't think I would've been cool with my little girl willingly exposing herself to danger."

"I'm not so little anymore," I said.

His eyes got all shiny. "Don't remind me."

"Aw, Dad. Don't cry. I'll always be your little girl."

He smiled, which creased the lines around his eyes and mouth.

When we pushed through the doors of Bee's a moment later, Aylen hopped out from one of the booths that lined the brick wall. Over the din, she yelled, "Derek!" She swung her arms in the air. "Cat!"

"I'll get you some chairs," Aylen said, already shoving two people off their seats.

"There goes our quiet lunch," Dad whispered in my ear. "You think we can pretend we didn't see her?"

"We can try, but I'm not sure we'll make it out in one piece," I whispered back.

As we walked over to the booth, we stopped to say hello to people. Cass deposited a hefty helping of mac and cheese on one of the tables, which reminded me of the casseroles stashed in the cold chamber. I'd have to get rid of them soon or they would go bad.

When we finally reached the booth, Aylen scooted back next to one of her daughters. "We got some nachos with spinach dip for the table." She gestured to a bowl in which only a green smear remained. Her gaze lifted to her husband's and then returned to the bowl.

Tony blushed. "I said I'd go on a diet when we got home. We're not home," he mumbled.

Aylen didn't look up from the bowl.

"Hey, Tony. Hi, girls," Dad said, sitting down next to me.

Satyana and Shiloh didn't react. Then again, they probably couldn't hear Dad over the videogame soundtrack blasting from their candy-colored headphones. While Dad engaged a still red-cheeked Tony in small talk, I spoke to Aylen about her naturopath business.

"Cat, Mr. Price, what can I get you?" Cass asked, swinging by our table, balancing a round platter on her hip. She deposited melted cheese sandwiches in front of the twins and a salad in front of Aylen.

"Here, let me help you with that." Dad grabbed an enormous platter of ribs and grilled corn glistening with butter. "Tony, I suppose this is yours."

"Whose else would it be?" Aylen muttered.

A whole bunch of tension ensued.

"I'll take the roast chicken," I said.

"Me too." Dad handed his menu back to Cass. "Thanks, honey."

Cass smiled and bustled away.

"So when are you all heading home?" I asked.

"I booked us tickets on the six o'clock flight," she said, spearing a green leaf. "But if you need us, we could stay longer. Or *I* can stay longer. Tony can take the girls home and I can stay," she repeated so hopefully that it pained me to tell her that we didn't need her.

"We could use an extra hand to pack Nova's personal items. I know you already went through her closet, but there are a bunch of boxes in the attic. I wouldn't know the first thing about what to keep and what to throw," Dad said.

Aylen perked up. She even sat straighter and looked at Tony again, unknotting the tautness that had settled between them. She even ordered an extra bowl of spinach dip. Tony didn't touch her peace offering. After polishing off his rack of ribs, he was probably not hungry anymore. But then he ordered an ice cream sundae when Cass came back with our roast chicken.

We ate in uncomfortable silence. At some point, Aylen lifted her napkin to blot the corners of her eyes, smudging some of her heavy black eyeliner in the process.

Dad shoveled in his food so he could get away. I sped up too.

When he was done, he placed his paper napkin on top of his neat, little pile of chicken bones, and rose. "I'm going to say hi to Bee. I'll be right back." I could wager a lot of money that he wouldn't be *right back*. He was going to work the room until my extended family went to pack.

Swallowing one last forkful of green beans, I scooted back, my chair legs scraping the floor. "I need to go to the bathroom." I couldn't take another minute of the strained atmosphere. Plus, I thought they could use some time alone to talk things out.

Since I didn't really need to go, I washed my hands and checked my reflection. The little bit of mascara I'd applied looked clumpy. I tried to scratch some of it off, but instead, I yanked out one of my lashes. "Ouch."

When I was seven, Mom had told me that wishes made on eyelashes always came true. She said that it was because you were giving Mother Earth a piece of yourself, which was the sincerest offering. I'd asked her if nail clippings were also considered offerings—because then I would have had a bunch of wishes—but she'd said no. *Only what involuntarily falls away from your body.* Baby teeth counted. I'd wished on all the ones I hadn't swallowed.

The eyelash stuck to my thumb hadn't fallen out voluntarily, so I flicked it into the sink where it stuck to the white porcelain before slithering down like a minuscule snail leaving an inky trail.

I'd believed wishes came true as a kid, but not anymore. If

wishes came true, then Mom would still be here, because one of my wishes had been that I would be happy forever. How could I be happy without her? Before tears could spring into my eyes, I walked out of the bathroom, bumping into a girl with blonde hair down to her waist. I did a double-take as the door swung shut behind me. There was something familiar about her, but what? I spotted Cass filling a pitcher with water behind the bar and traipsed over to her.

"Did you see who walked in here?" she asked, voice lilting with excitement.

"Was she in school with us?" I asked.

Cass snorted. "I wish."

I swung my gaze back toward the bathroom, but the girl was inside, and besides blonde hair and a pointy nose, I couldn't recollect what she looked like. "Well, are you going to tell me who it is?"

"Really? You don't recognize her?"

"No, I don't. Tell me already."

"Lily Wood."

"Lil—" *Oh.* "Oh!"

"I can't believe we have a celebrity in the house." She blew on her bangs. "Do you think I should ask her for her autograph? Or maybe she'll pose on a picture with me?"

"Is she here alone?"

"Nope. She came with that cute medical examiner. The one who —I should learn to shut up. Sorry."

Cruz had his back to me. "Is her brother here too?" I scanned the room, but couldn't see him.

"Would I be standing here, talking with you if he were?"

"Hey, Cass, did you go to the well to get my water?" Mr. Hamilton asked, grumpy as always. He lifted his tweed cap, smoothed his thinning white hair, and then put the hat back on.

"Coming," Cass said.

My coat was still draped over the chair. If I went to retrieve it, Aylen would rope me into the quiet argument she and Tony were having. Or Cruz would spot me. Since neither option suited me, I sat on one of the burgundy leather bar stools to wait for Dad to finish his conversation with his musician friend. What was his name? As I attempted to conjure it up, a hand settled over my shoulder. I twirled around, dislodging Cruz's hand in the process.

"Did you come back to introduce me to your fiancée?" I asked sourly.

"*I* don't want to meet her," I said.

"Why not?"

"Because," I muttered.

"That's not an answer, Catori."

"Are you trying to torture me?" I whispered.

"You'll like her."

"I'm not looking to make a friend. I don't need friends. I have plenty here," I said, gesturing toward Blake and Cass. "And if she's anything like her brother—"

"She's nothing like Ace. Nothing," he said, somewhat protectively.

Lily stepped out of the bathroom then, long hair swishing around her bare shoulders. Who wore a sleeveless turtleneck in winter? When her gaze landed on Cruz's unoccupied chair, color drained from her face, but then she saw him, and her composure returned. Shoulders squared, she walked back to her table, the heels of her black suede boots clicking with each step. They came up over her knee and looked exorbitantly expensive and uncomfortable, but really pretty. I bet her closet was chock-full of pretty and pricey stuff.

When she sat, she pulled her hair out from behind her ear and let it drape around her face. Maybe it was her unexpected shyness, or maybe it was because Cruz wouldn't let it go, but I ended up sighing and accepting to meet her. I felt gazes on me as I trailed Cruz through the restaurant, particularly Blake's. He was glowering, elbows rigidly planted on the counter of the kitchen hole. I focused on the back of Cruz's leather jacket to avoid my friend's glare.

As we made our way across the room, Cruz glanced back at me a few times, as though checking that I was really following him. Lily looked up when we reached the table. Her eyes were cartoonishly large and gray. They shone silver in the ray of sun falling across her face. When they alighted on me, I expected them to narrow but they didn't. She stuck out her hand. I felt obliged to shake it. She inhaled sharply when our fingers touched, and jerked her large eyes toward Cruz. I wondered if it was as painful for her as it was for me. Holding her hand was like touching a porcelain bowl that had been left too long in the microwave.

As quickly as was acceptable, I let go. "Well, it was nice to meet you. I should go now."

Lily caught my wrist and shook her head. I stared at her fingers and she released me. Then she tipped her head toward one of the chairs.

"She'd like you to join us," Cruz explained.

"I'd rather not. I have errands—"

"You don't have errands," Cruz said.

"How would you know?"

"Tell me what errands," he said.

"I...uh. I have to pick up some groceries."

He grinned. "I'm pretty sure the supermarket will be open this afternoon."

"But not the post office. It closes at"—I pretended to look at my watch, which I'd forgotten to put on—"two. And it's one-thirty."

"Catori, sit," Cruz said, smile still in place. "Please."

Grumbling, I dropped into the chair opposite Lily. After a few painfully quiet seconds, I asked, "Is this your first time in Rowan?"

Lily shook her head no.

"You've come here before?"

She nodded.

"Why?"

She shot her gaze to Cruz.

The rose petal graves. I was certain that was the purpose of her trip. Maybe it was a mandatory class trip in faerie school: *visit the graveyard where our mortal enemies lie.* Did they even have a faerie school?

"Pretty boring town. I wouldn't suggest staying too long," I said. "I hear the weather's supposed to get bad again tonight so you should probably leave."

Lily didn't say anything. She just stared at me with those doll-like eyes of hers. I heaved in a breath and tried to strike up a conversation with her again, but it was like striking a match to paper. No words flared out of her mouth. She was trying to make me uncomfortable. That was it. She knew what had happened last night in the car. Giving me the silent treatment was her punishment. She was going to stand up on her chair and wag her finger at me and proclaim I was a slut. And I wouldn't deny it, because she'd be right.

Cruz placed his hand on my knee. I hadn't realized I was bouncing it up and down. "Breathe," he said.

I glued the soles of my shoes to the wooden floor. "Look, Lily, I imagine Cruz told you about last night, and that's why you're treating me funny, but in my defense I had no idea you two were engaged."

I must have spoken my apology louder than I imagined because *a lot* of people gawked, and then glass shattered and Cass's platter spun like a top. Blake backed away from the kitchen hole. And it wasn't to help Cass sweep up the broken glass. He just retreated deep into the kitchen while Cass swore and dropped to her knees to pick up the broken pieces. It took a while for conversations to start up again.

I leaned forward in my chair. "Best of luck with your engagement." I attempted to stand up but Cruz's agonizingly hot hand returned to my knee, pinning me in place.

"Can I tell her, Lily?" he asked.

"Tell me what?"

Lily nodded, her hair rippling around her pale cheeks.

"We've been engaged for several dec—years now. It was an arrangement between my parents and Linus. Ace is also engaged to someone of Linus's choosing. You see, weddings for us are strategic. They're not romantic." He collected Lily's hand in his. "I adore Lily, but she's like my sister."

Her gaze flickered up to him and then to their linked hands, and her cheeks, which were pink, turned darker. Lily liked Cruz, and not as a brother. I wasn't particularly intuitive, but it didn't take a medium to realize this.

Dad came by our table. He shook Cruz's hand, then turned toward Lily. "Hello, dear. I'm Catori's father."

She stood up and took Dad's extended hand. Once she released it, she placed both her hands on her heart and pressed her lips together.

"She's offering her condolences for the passing of your wife, Mr. Price," Cruz explained.

"Do you always talk for her?" I said.

The flushed patches on Lily's skin joined together like puzzle pieces until her entire face was cherry-red.

"Do you know sign language, Catori?" Cruz asked.

I blinked. "She's—She can't—"

"Lily's mute."

"Mute?" I wasn't sure why I felt the need to repeat the word. It felt like a bad word. One that should never be spoken out loud. I raised my gaze to Lily's. "But I read that article about you, and it wasn't mentioned."

"Because it's nobody's business," Cruz said.

Dad made some hand gestures and Lily smiled, and then she wriggled her hands, and he smiled.

"You know how to sign?" I asked my father.

"I had a friend who was deaf. So I learned a few words." He looked at Lily who spun her hands and tapped them together.

"That means, *I'm really hungry. I could eat like a cow*," Dad explained.

Lily laughed. It was a strange, hiccuppy laugh. When she saw me staring, she stopped abruptly.

"I could eat *a cow*, not *like a cow*," Cruz said, also chuckling.

"My sign language skills are a little rusty. Anyway, I didn't want to crash your get-together. I just came by to tell Cat I was leaving."

"I'm ready to go," I said, soaring out of my chair faster than the puck on a high striker. "I'll go get my coat."

"Will you come by later for a drink, or are you heading back to Beaver Island tonight?" I heard Dad ask just as I reached the booth.

Tony had left but Aylen was still there. She placed her hand on my arm. "That's Lily Wood, isn't it?" she whispered. "I didn't want to interrupt, but I really did want to interrupt." Her eyes moved toward Lily then back toward me.

"Go introduce yourself if you want to," I said.

She started hyperventilating with excitement. "Satyana, Shiloh, do you want to go meet Lily Wood?" They looked up from their tablets.

"She's here?" one of them asked, dragging her headphones down to her neck.

Aylen nodded and—unfortunately—pointed straight at Lily.

"Could you be any more obvious, Mom?" the other twin grumbled.

"Yeah, you're embarrassing us."

"Could you try being nice to your mom, for a change," I said.

"Please, Cat, don't get involved," Aylen said.

"Don't what? Tell them they act like brats? That they take their mother for granted? You have no idea what I would give to get my mother back. No idea." My voice was so low that it vibrated inside my chest.

"Don't talk to my girls like that," Aylen snapped, wrapping a protective arm around Shiloh's shoulders. Or maybe it was her other devil-daughter.

I blinked.

"I've decided to go home with my family. They need me," Aylen said.

"Fine."

"I didn't mean to—" She took a deep breath. "I'm sorry I raised my voice."

"It's fine. Have a safe trip." I walked back over to my father. "I'm ready."

He slung his arm around my shoulder and kissed the top of my head. "See you both later."

Lily nodded while Cruz just sat there, observing me.

As we walked out of Bee's Place, Dad said, "Isn't it nice that they're coming over? Lily is such a sweet girl, and she's only a year younger than you. And—"

"I'm not three, Dad. I don't need you to organize playdates for me," I said, stepping out of his reach. "I don't want to be friends with that girl. Or with Cruz."

"Why not?"

"Because I just don't," I said after we'd stepped out of the restaurant. "Mom would have understood."

Dad's face whitened.

It was a mean thing to say, and I wanted to take it back, but I also wanted him to stop treating me like a little girl who didn't know her own mind. I knew my own mind. Only too well.

I twirled around and walked up the street instead of toward the hearse. "I'll see you at home," I called out, my voice choked up with tears. I had no right to cry, and yet the stress from meeting Lily, Aylen's rebuke…it made everything pour out of me.

I stuffed my hands inside my pockets and walked, and walked, through the sand dunes and down a snaking forest trail. The wind licked my cheeks and the cold made my eardrums ache, and yet I kept walking. I took the trail that wound around the sand dunes and cut across the fields tended by Rowan's oldest gardener, an eighty-something-year-old woman named Holly. We'd had a class outing to her greenhouse where she'd explained how to nurture soil to grow plants. I remembered how she'd touched a bud and it had cracked open and blossomed before my very eyes. I'd told my father about it, and he'd said it was probably a magic trick. Now I wondered if it wasn't just magic.

Snow started falling. I looked up. Cold flakes landed in my open eyes. I blinked and looked down at the uneven ground that swelled underneath my boots. Everything would be white again. I kicked a pinecone out of the way and followed its trajectory with my eyes. It smacked right into something bright red. With the falling snow, it took me a second to realize it was a boot.

It moved. And then there were two boots. And two legs sticking out of the boots. And then the two legs bent and the body collapsed.

"Gwenelda," I whispered, or shrieked. I wasn't quite sure. I fell to my knees next to her.

She didn't move. She didn't speak.

I sucked in a breath and placed a hand on her back, against the flimsy black sweater she wore, to feel for a sign of life. When her back rose and fell, I let the trapped breath whoosh out of my mouth. I lifted my hand off of her and tried to roll her onto her back, but my hands slipped. I tried a second time, but again, they glided right off. That's when I noticed that my skin was stained red, the same red as Gwenelda's rubber boots. I twirled my hands in front of my eyes, attempting to connect the dots.

"You're bleeding?" I asked stupidly.

I dragged her sweater up a few inches. The white T-shirt underneath was soaked in blood. It had even started to seep into the snow, turning it pink, like the strawberry shaved ice I bought at the fair each summer.

"I'm going to call an ambulance," I said, pulling the sweater back down. "It's going to be all right."

"No ambulance," she whispered, her voice hoarse.

"Why not?"

"Because doctors"—she planted one hand on the snow and pressed down hard; her fingers vanished in the white—"will not know"—she gritted her teeth and squeezed her eyes shut—"how to close wounds inflicted by—" She flipped herself onto her back, letting out a deafening cry.

"Inflicted by what?"

She stared into my face. "By faeries," she said, before losing consciousness.

"Shit, shit, shit," I muttered. "Gwenelda?" I shook her. I stopped when I saw more blood leaking out of her. Maybe I'd angered the wound. I placed my palm on her cheek and tapped slowly. "Gwenelda, wake up."

She didn't so I yanked my cell phone out my coat pocket, but it slipped through my fingers, disappearing into the pink snow besides Gwen's body. I bent over and grabbed it. I was going to call my dad. No, wait, I couldn't call him. He thought she was a madwoman, which she was—in a way. But I couldn't just let her die. With shaky fingers, I dialed Blake's number.

He didn't pick up. I tried him again.

"What?" he huffed.

"I need your help."

"My help?" The pitch of his voice changed then, becoming almost strident when he spoke next, "Are you okay? Did something happen? I heard you walked back—"

"I'm okay. Remember my aunt?"

"The wacky lady from Canada?"

"Yeah. That one. Well, she's in really bad shape."

"How bad?"

"There's so much blood," I whispered.

She wasn't moving. Had she died? She said she could die of faerie wounds. Would it be so terrible if she had?

"Catori!" Blake sounded pissed. "Where are you?"

This woman could have killed my mother.

"Where are you?" I heard Blake shout.

Could have. Those two magic words jolted me out of my wicked deliberations. I looked around me, but there was so much snow falling that I couldn't see anything. I squeezed my eyes shut and tried to remember where I was when I bumped into Gwenelda.

"Holly's field," I said, lids flying open. "I'm in Holly's field, by the woods."

15

FIREFLIES

$\mathcal{I}$ took off my coat and placed it on top of Gwenelda's unresponsive body. I shivered, so I walked briskly around, attempting to stay warm. Blake would be here in a few minutes.

"Catori?"

I snapped my neck in the direction of the voice. The grayish sketch of a body filled with color. "Cruz?"

"Are you all right?"

"*I* am, but she's not." I pointed to Gwenelda whose small body was slowly becoming invisible underneath the heavy snowfall.

"Who's she?"

"Gwenelda," I said. "How did you find me?"

"I...I went to your house and you weren't there. You're shaking. Where's your coat?"

I tipped my head toward Gwen.

"You're going to get sick," he said, shrugging out of his leather jacket and wrapping it around my shoulders.

The silk lining was so warm that I pulled it tighter around me, and the leather crackled.

"What happened to her?" he asked, kneeling beside her.

"Faeries."

"Are you sure?"

"Only faes can inflict mortal wounds on hunters, right?"

"That's how it used to be, but maybe—"

"Maybe she did it to herself? Is that what you were about to say?"

"It's a possibility."

"Oh, come on." I stepped away from him. "Look at the wound! No one does that to herself. The faeries were probably trying to get their magic back or maybe they were just trying to get rid of her. She doesn't want me to call an ambulance, but I have no clue what to do."

"Do you want her to live, Catori?" he asked, glancing up at me with those magnificent green eyes of his.

"Well, I don't want her to die."

He turned his attention back to the prostrate body and peeled my coat off of her. Then he exposed her back and placed his hands on the wounds. As he mumbled words in that language I didn't understand, his fingers began sparkling with gold flames. Slowly, magically, the large cuts mended, the torn pieces of skin reattaching. She was still covered in blood, but there wasn't even the hint of a scar. There were also no more tattoos.

"Is she...Did she die?" I asked, crouching down beside Cruz.

"She did. But her spirit wasn't far."

"Her spirit? You mean, you can resuscitate people?"

"Yes."

"Why didn't you bring my mother back then?"

Cruz pulled down Gwen's sweater, draped my coat over her still body, and then turned toward me. Tiny snowflakes drifted between us. They tangled in my long hair but evaporated when they touched Cruz. "She'd been gone too long. Her spirit was no longer next to her body."

He unfurled his long body and stuck out his hand to help me up. I took it, even though I didn't need his help.

"Thank you," I said.

Many thoughts slipped in and out of my mind. From the intensity of his gaze, I could tell that his mind was crowded with contemplations of his own. Tentatively, he raised his free hand toward my cheek. He let it hover in the air, millimeters away from my skin. Even from that distance, I could feel the heat of his palm.

"What about Lily, Cruz?"

"What about Lily?"

"You say the marriage is arranged, that your relationship with Lily is fraternal, but that's not the way she feels about you."

He frowned. "I spend every day with her. Lily is my best friend. I can assure you that I'm not attracted to her in the way I'm attracted to you."

"Which you really shouldn't be."

"Which I really shouldn't be," he repeated, softly cupping my cheek.

I should have insisted that we were all wrong for each other, but I simply didn't want to. As intrepid, or perhaps as idiotic as a moth drawn to the sun, I tilted my face up toward Cruz.

He moved closer to me, which made my body temperature soar, a combination of the fire raging underneath his skin and the wild thumping of my heart. I waited—for what felt like an eternity but lasted only a second—for him to press his lips against mine. My mouth tingled, my nose, my ears, and slowly every inch of me was consumed by Cruz's fire. The heat was startling at first, but soon it became deliciously bearable, like basking in the sun on a gloriously hot day. He spread my fingers with his, all the while exploring my mouth with his tongue, alternating the pressure of his lips from hard to gentle, obliterating the memory of the kiss we'd shared in his car. I'm not sure if it was because he was magical that his embrace was too, but I was sure I'd never been kissed like this before.

"Ahem."

I spun away from Cruz so fast I lost my balance. His arms shot out, circling my waist to hold me up. He didn't let go when I'd regained my footing, which made Blake's jaw flush.

I pushed his arm off, and took a step toward my friend, but he backed away.

"Why did you call me if you had him?" Blake's voice vibrated with irritation.

"Cruz just got here. I didn't know he was coming."

Blake's legs were planted wide, and he held his chin up. "He's engaged, Cat. I thought you were a better person." He shook his head. "Your mother would've been so disappointed."

Heat filled my eyes. "Don't you dare bring Mom into this."

Cruz's chest pressed against my back and his hands wrapped around my upper arms. "Don't let him get to you," he murmured in my ear.

Blake's good eye darkened. "If you have something to say to me, man up and say it!"

"What you just witnessed, buddy, is none of your business."

"It's your fiancée's business. Maybe I should go inform her—"

"By all means, tell her. She won't care," Cruz said.

She would care.

"Is that really the sort of guy you want to be with, Cat? One with no morals, no respect."

"You better stop talking now," Cruz warned.

"Or what? You're going to punch me? Go ahead. Break some more bones in my face. I've had so much worse."

Cruz's body warmed up, as though the fire had pooled into his skin. I jumped away from him, and stared at my sweater sleeves that had started smoking. I grabbed handfuls of snow and rubbed it against the smoke.

"I'm sorry," Cruz said, when he realized what he'd done.

Blake's brow furrowed. There was no more smoke but Cruz had burned a hole through one of the sleeves.

"It's okay," I murmured. "It's nothing."

Cruz curled his fingers into tight fists.

"Did you just set fire to Cat?"

"He just squeezed my arms a bit hard," I said, hoping Blake would swallow my lie.

"But I saw—"

Blake was interrupted by loud sputtering. Gwenelda writhed on the floor next to us, emerging from the snow. I crouched by her side and caught hold of her arm to ease her up.

She swiped her bloodied fingers against her back, then brought them in front of her face. "I no longer bleed. You healed me, Catori. Thank you."

"It isn't me you should be thanking. It's Cruz. He's the one who saved you."

"Cruz?" She let her hand collapse against her waist as she took in the fae standing a few feet away from her. "*You* saved *me*? Isn't that—"

He cut her off. "Who attacked you, Gwenelda?"

Her breathing was slow, grating. "The *golwinim.*"

"*Golwinim?*" I asked.

Cruz and Gwenelda held each other's gazes for so long that Blake and I exchanged a look. As though remembering he was angry with me, Blake dropped my gaze.

"I'll go find them," Cruz said. "In the meantime, Catori and Blake will take you somewhere safe to rest."

"Who are the *golwinim?*" I asked, but Cruz had started running. Or perhaps he'd started flying. I'd lost sight of him in the snowstorm.

"The guards," Gwenelda said.

"What guards?" Blake asked.

"The Woods's guards." She dropped her voice. "The fireflies." Over the blowing wind, I could barely make out her words.

"You call them fireflies?" Blake asked, arching an eyebrow.

"Yes."

The fireflies flitting through the graveyard last night weren't insects; they were faeries.

16

FRIENDS AND FOES

*E*ven though Gwenelda was healed, she limped when she walked, so Blake, being the gentleman that he was, picked her up and carried her to his navy Jeep. He set her down on the backseat.

"Thanks for letting us come to your place," I said, glancing at his profile.

His lips stayed pressed together as he started the car and plowed fast through the snowy field.

"You're driving too fast," I said, watching the needle on the speedometer reach seventy. Most of Rowan was limited to forty-five miles an hour. "With the snow—"

"You don't get to tell me what to do," he didn't yell this, but his voice was loud and clipped.

I sucked in a breath. "I know you don't approve, but don't be mad at me."

"I'm not mad."

"Well, you're acting like it."

"I'm disappointed that you chose him."

"Why? Because of Lily?"

He kept his eyes on the road beyond the windshield.

"It's a strategic match, not a love—"

"Are you hearing yourself?" he shouted this time. "You're making excuses for him, for yourself."

"I'm not," I mumbled, peering into the backseat. Gwenelda had her eyes closed as though she were sleeping. I hoped she was.

"Catori, the dude's creepy. He passed himself off for a medical examiner, for God's sake. Who does that?"

"It's the guy's wife who killed him," I said, propagating a story which I knew was untrue, but it beat admitting that Cruz might have had a hand in the man's death.

Blake slapped his steering wheel. "Bull crap!"

A tomblike silence invaded the car.

He had no right to be pissed at me. "I didn't ask for your blessing *or* your opinion," I said, trying to keep my voice calm, but doing a shit job.

Blake sighed and it rumbled like the warm air blasting out of the car's heater. "Are you trying to destroy the only part of me that wasn't damaged in the blast?"

"What?"

"Nothing," he grumbled.

"No. Not nothing. What do you mean?"

"You really need me to spell it out?" His anger had deflated like the bouncy castle his mom had salvaged when we were kids. We'd jumped on that thing until the hole she'd duct-taped ripped further.

"Oh…Blake."

"Don't, Cat. Don't pity me. Pity's emasculating, and right now, I don't need to feel like even less of a man."

Although I wanted to reach out to touch his arm, I sat on my hands for the rest of the ride and watched the snowflakes drift down against the car window like the single tear that rolled out of Blake's eye. He didn't wipe it away. He was probably hoping I hadn't noticed it.

When we parked in front of his one-story, flat-roofed house, which he'd bought with his disability severance pay, he got out of the car and unlocked his front door. Then he came back for Gwenelda who was apparently not pretending to be asleep.

I traipsed behind them into the dark house. He brought Gwen to his bedroom and closed his door, then he turned on the lights in the tiny living room and pulled a beer from his fridge.

"You want one?" He had his back to me. His shoulders strained the fabric of his sweater.

"Sure."

He grabbed another bottle and flipped the cap off with his bare fingers, then handed it to me. "Why couldn't we go to your place?"

"Because Dad thinks she's a murderer. He doesn't know she's related to us."

"Is she family?"

"Sort of."

"Is she a murderer?"

"She didn't murder the medical examiner. She hadn't...*arrived* yet."

Either Blake could read me too well, or my hesitation came through. "Did she murder anyone else?"

I raked my hands through my damp hair. "I don't know."

"So what *do* you know?" He took a swig of beer and sat in his dark-green armchair.

I plopped down on the couch facing him. "She is related to me, that I know for sure. I also know that she and the Woods hate each other."

"Why?"

"Bad blood between them. She claims the Woods had a hand in the death of her friend." I didn't make the word plural, although it should have been.

"Wouldn't surprise me," he muttered.

A cell phone rang. I was so surprised by the interruption that it took me a few seconds to realize that the ringing was coming from my jeans. I swiped my finger against the screen when I read my father's name.

"I've been worried sick. Where are you?" he shouted.

"I'm at Blake's, Dad. Everything's fine. I'm fine."

"Still, you could've texted me back. I sent you tons of messages! I left you a voicemail."

"I never check those."

"That's not the point, Cat. You can't do this to me. Not after... not after what happened."

"I'm sorry. I'm going to come straight home." But how would I get there? I couldn't just take Blake's car. If only I could fly. "Can you pick me up?"

"Yes," he said, and it sounded as though all of his pent-up stress released in time with the word. "I'm leaving right now." I could hear his heavy boots pound against the porch steps. "I'll honk when I'm in front."

When he disconnected, I stared at my phone's screen until it went dark, then I lifted my gaze to my friend's face. "I want you to forgive me, Blake. I can't leave here with you mad at me."

His jaw tightened.

"Please." I begged him with my eyes. I loved Blake, just not the way he loved me.

Blake sighed. "As if I could ever refuse you anything."

I leaped off the couch to hug him, and while I held him and he held me, a tiny part of me wondered if he'd forgiven me because I had the influence. I breathed him in, wishing I could return his feelings.

Some time later, Dad honked. Blake didn't walk me to the door. He stayed sitting in the green armchair, rigid. "Call me when she wakes up," I said. All I could see was the back of his head that dipped in a stiff nod. "I'll come back." And like that, I was gone, leaving him alone with a woman I probably shouldn't have left him alone with.

DECEPTION

The phone rang while I was clearing dinner. Dad had gone to the living room to find us something to watch, so I was alone in the kitchen. The second I saw it was Blake, I picked up.

"She's awake?" I asked, before he even had time to talk.

"She's gone." There was something mechanic in the way he said it, or perhaps it was the blood rushing into my eardrums that made his voice sound funny.

"Where? When?"

"She left a note. Something about meeting you at the old cabin. I can go there now."

"No," I said. "I'll go. It's right next to the house. You've done enough."

"Okay," he said, and hung up. He was still angry with me. The old Blake would never have given me a choice. He would have come.

Going out in the middle of the night alone to see Gwenelda worried me, but I couldn't involve my father, and I had no way of reaching Cruz. After lying to my father about going to Bee's Place, I took the hearse and drove, not because it was far, but because if I didn't, Dad would see straight through my lie. It took three minutes to get to the cabin, and five for me to turn off the ignition and dare step out into the freezing woods. The snow had eased up, but it still fell, making everything a bit prettier but also much colder. I shivered with each step. When I stood in front of the cabin, I knocked.

There was no answer.

I knocked again. I even called out, "Hello?" Still nothing. I pressed my fingertip to the old wood and pushed the door open. It creaked, heightening the speed of the blood coursing through my veins. For a second, I saw dots in front of my eyes, as though I were about to pass out. "Gwenelda," I tried again. The moon brightened the dim interior, but still I used my phone's flashlight to peer into the corners. They were all empty. Gwen wasn't here.

A clicking sound made me jump. I whirled around, mouth full with the taste of metal and muscles thrumming with adrenaline. "Gwen?" I repeated hoarsely.

A little rock struck the broken, dusty window. *Click.* Sucking in a lungful of courage, I approached the door and scanned the darkness below. When I saw who was throwing the little rocks, I stayed in the archway of the cabin, just in case it could still repel faeries.

"What are you guys doing here?" I asked Ace and Lily. I was trying to get my pulse under control, but Cruz wasn't with them. I trusted him; I didn't trust them.

"Cruz sent us," Ace said.

"Why didn't he come?" I asked.

Lily's large eyes seem to slant.

"He didn't come because you got him in trouble with your little plea to save a hunter. That's punishable by death in our world."

"What?"

"He willingly turned himself in. Hopefully that will help his case."

My stomach tightened. "Death?"

"Yeah. Death. Just so we're clear, if he hangs, you hang, got that?"

I gulped. "Take me to Beaver Island. I'll tell them it was my fault."

"Take a faehunter to the Isle? I'd be signing my own death sentence." He snorted. "Now, what's going on here? What's got you so flummoxed?"

"Gwenelda said she would meet me here, but she hasn't shown up."

Lily was so petite compared to her brother, but she didn't look like the shy waif of a girl I'd interacted with only hours before. I supposed resentment trumped diffidence.

"Why did Cruz send you?" I asked suddenly. "How did he know where I was?"

"He marked you, so he can track you. He can also track your heartbeats, your moods. It's a pretty useful trick we faes possess to keep tabs on our enemy. Turns you into easy prey. In this case, although *we* believe you're the enemy," he said, pointing at his sister and himself, "I don't think *he* sees it. Although, apparently prison changes people, so he'll come around. Your *influence* on him will go *poof*." Ace lifted his hands in opposite directions.

"He told me the influence doesn't work on him."

Lily snorted.

"And you fell for it?" Ace said.

Four fireflies zipped past the cottony snowflakes, and buzzed around Ace's face. One of them expanded until it was no longer bug-sized, but nearly as tall as Ace. He glowed brighter than brother and sister, gilt instead of moon-white. Speaking in that language of theirs, he informed Ace of something that made his smirk vanish. He swore, then walked past his guard, toward me.

"They've found Gwenelda."

"Did they hurt her again?" I asked.

"She was too quick for them this time, thanks to that lame boyfriend of yours."

"What boyfriend?"

"The dude whose face was blasted off."

"Blake?" Goose bumps scattered over my entire body.

"My guard tells me he drove right up to the rowan grove. And guess what they're doing?"

I started running back home, forgetting I had a car, forgetting there were deadly faeries flying right beside me. A firefly droned around my face. I swiped it away and it burned my hand.

I didn't yelp; I just kept running. I needed to get to the grave-yard before Blake and Gwen could wake up another clan member. Snow slapped my face and cooled the welt rising on my hand. The chilling wind howled around me, and a branch slapped my face stinging almost more than my hand. My eyes watered. My nose ran. My toes became numb. If it weren't for the crunching of pinecones and fresh snow, I would have thought I was flying.

When I burst out of the woods, I froze. All of me froze. I was still at a distance but I could see a coffin resting on the snow. I could see hands scooping inside, pink rose petals fluttering out, glimmering, and falling. I could smell their cloying aroma. A torso appeared, and then arms and hands that pressed against the side of the wooden box, revealing legs and feet. It was like looking at someone emerging from the lake after a midnight dip.

I couldn't get closer. My legs wouldn't move, so I squinted, not to make out the new arrival but to see if there were three bodies.

I only saw two. And they saw me.

PART II
HUNTERS

THE NEW ONE

I trembled as I advanced toward the ring of rowan trees that protected the sacred piece of land in which my ancestors were buried. The cold wind and thick snowflakes stung my cheeks, but cooled the welt the faerie guards had exacted on my hand. I spun around to see if the faeries had remained, but no bodies lit up the cold night. They probably fled back to their island to inform their fellow fae that another hunter had risen.

The wind blew Gwenelda's waist-long black hair against a long, broad, bare torso that ended in a face so chiseled it looked carved from stone. I trailed my eyes down the man's chest, over the inked arabesques tattooed on his skin, over the animal-hide loincloth that covered so little of him, down his muscular legs, to my friend's slumped body.

I hoped Blake was immobile because they'd rid him of energy, and not of life. As I approached, Gwenelda and the hunter didn't back away to make room for me. They simply stood over Blake. Gwenelda's eyes flashed with guilt that increased the slow tearing inside my chest.

The man went very still when I dropped to my knees. I placed my ear against Blake's still-warm chest, but nothing beat. I shut my eyes and pressed my forehead against his still-warm flannel shirt. "You killed him," I whispered. "You *deliberately* killed him, Gwenelda."

"I regret his death."

I jerked my head back to stare at the huntress. "Regret? I saved you, and this is how you repay me? You murder my best friend? My best friend! Which means"—the confirmation sucked me under like a groundswell, carrying me out into a sea of absolute, frenzied fury —"which means that *you* murdered my mother!" I shook my head. "I...hate...you." I injected each word with venom, hoping they'd poison her cruel heart, but they weren't magical, unlike the spell she'd just read to wake the hunter. "I hate him, too. I hate every single one of you."

The hunter's eyes widened and gleamed, and his lips parted with a soundless gasp.

"You are the worst thing that has ever happened to me." Angry, chilling tears dripped off my chin. I tipped my face down toward Blake. "Get out of here. Before—Before..." My voice cracked. My threat of destroying the rest of their family became stuck in my swollen throat.

Neither moved.

I jumped to my feet. "Leave!"

My scream might wake my father, but I didn't care. I just didn't care anymore...if he came out of our house, I would admit everything to him, from the existence of faeries to that of faehunters. I would tell him Mom didn't die of a heart attack. I would tell him she died because her heart was stopped to jumpstart another.

Movement jolted me out of my thoughts. Gwen wound her fingers around the newcomer's wrist and tugged him as she began to back away. "We will give you time to process the passing of your friend."

"If you come back, Gwen, I'll torch the rest of the graves."

"You will not."

"Try me," I growled.

"They are your people, too."

"*My* people?" I spat out. "I don't have a people. Because of you, I have a person. Just one. My father. You destroyed the rest of *my* people. You killed my mother. You killed my best friend." Like a shroud, white snowflakes settled over the uneven planes of Blake's face.

"You still have Aylen and—"

"You leave Aylen out of this," I growled.

Gwenelda nodded. "But if you demolish these graves, Catori, you allow the faeries to win."

I lifted my gaze to hers. "Maybe I want them to win."

"They are dangerous—"

"A *faerie* saved you! Yet you're still so intent on destroying them. I'm sorry, but I fail to see how letting them win would be such a terrible thing."

Gwenelda shook her head and her hair flapped around her torn black sweater. "He saved me for a reason, Catori. He did not resuscitate me simply because you asked him to. He had a motive."

I snorted. "Really? And what is that motive?"

"I will share my thoughts with you once you calm down."

Distorted by my tears, Gwen looked so much like my mother, so much like me. "I'm calm."

"You are anything but tranquil. Grieve, Catori, then come and find us," she said, retreating.

"I will *not* come and find you," I called out.

Gwenelda lowered her chin, then turned away from me, while the man kept his gaze on me until the shadows of the trees enveloped them both. And even then, I could feel his piercing eyes. I rocked back on my heels and pounded my balled fists into the frozen ground until my knuckles throbbed as fiercely as my heart.

Like a revolving door, memories of Blake whooshed through me. The afternoons spent together as kids, jumping in the salvaged bouncy castle. The hours of videogames we played when his parents would come over for dinner and the adults would go on and on talking and drinking wine. The movie house we'd sneak into on rainy afternoons without paying. The time he'd defended me in the town playground when Cass's cousin, Faith Sakar, bullied me about my height. And then I remembered the summer I turned thirteen when I'd cycled to his house to complain about my parents not allowing me to go to school parties. We'd climbed into the tree house he'd built with his father. As the sun set over the sand dunes, he'd kissed me. And I'd let him, because he was Blake, my best friend in the entire world, the boy I trusted with my life and my heart.

Then the image of the plane crash that killed both his parents spilled into my mind. It had been everywhere. In every newspaper, all over the Internet. A freak accident, they'd called it. His father, a decorated air force pilot, flew charter planes for a living. He'd taken his wife on a trip to celebrate their anniversary. The small aircraft was hit by a storm and plummeted thousands of feet. Investigators deemed the accident a pilot error, but Blake was convinced it was a fabricated ploy so he couldn't sue the insurance company. Broken and broke, he moved in with his grandmother, and then he enlisted in the army.

"Oh...Bee..." Terror filled me. And sorrow. And overpowering desolation. Could she survive her grandson's death after having lost her son and daughter-in-law?

"Catori?"

I craned my neck, but couldn't see anything through the tumbling snow.

"Oh my God, honey, what happened? Did you get into a car accident?"

Dad. Dad was here. Relief mingled with dread. "Car accident?" I whispered.

He dropped to his knees next to me, next to Blake, seized my friend's lifeless shoulders, and shook him. "Was he projected from the car?"

I frowned. "What?"

"Was he drunk?" Dad leaned over and sniffed Blake's mouth. "I smell alcohol." He tapped Blake's cheek. When he didn't get a reaction, he pressed two fingers into his neck to feel for a pulse. He wouldn't find one. "Where is all this blood coming from?"

I looked at the spot Dad stared at. It was red. Pink and red and white, like a Pollock painting. Goosebumps scattered over my skin. He lifted Blake's arm, pulled up his sleeve. An angry gash oozed blood.

Dad's face transformed into a ghost's face, pallid, with sunken sockets where his eyes should've been. "Oh, Blake," he whispered. "Oh, no, no, no. Not you too..."

I yanked on my scarf and wrapped it frenziedly around Blake's forearm. It was senseless. Forcing the blood to stay inside his body wouldn't make his heart beat again.

Dad placed a steadying palm on my hands. "We need to call 9-1-1. Report the crash."

My hands froze. "What *crash*?"

Dad's face contorted into an odd grimace. "Honey, his car is totaled. He wrapped it around one of the tree trunks."

I swung my gaze to the Jeep, which looked...fine.

"That's probably where he got his injury," my father said.

"He didn't get this in the...crash."

"Were you in the car with him?"

I looked at the Jeep, searching for a dent I just couldn't see. "No."

As he rushed back into the house to call for help, my gaze caught the pale glimmer of a hovering body with flowing blonde hair. Lily. She floated, bobbing like a buoy on a frenzied ocean, her body swathed by the falling snow.

"Bring him back," I hollered. "Call him back!"

She didn't say anything...because she couldn't. But she could've nodded or approached, and she did neither.

"I'll give you anything. Please. Lily, please," I called out just as footfalls disturbed the snow beside me.

Dad yammered on his cell phone, oblivious to my plea, oblivious to the faerie. Even though I didn't point her out, I kept my eyes locked on hers. And she kept her eyes locked on mine. When sirens wailed in the distance, she shot upward. I followed her flight. Snowflakes hit my eyes, made them burn.

A hand scrubbed against my back. It was Dad. "Go inside, Catori. You're freezing. I'll take care of Blake."

"It's too late," I murmured.

"I know."

I didn't move. I couldn't move, too anesthetized with cold and pain.

Like he used to do when I was a little girl and I'd fall asleep on the couch in front of a cartoon, Dad picked me up and cradled me in his arms. Carefully he walked me back home. I snuggled against his chest, searching for warmth and comfort. I found warmth, but I found no comfort.

My Blake was gone.

19

FAULTY GENE

*A*n ambulance parked in front of the house, followed by the sheriff's patrol car. I watched from the living room window, shaking, even though Dad had wrapped a thick, wool cover around my shoulders before returning to Blake.

The clattering of my teeth and the low hiss of the radiator were the only noises in the house. Outside, though...outside was filled with noise—strident voices, clicking metal, scraping shovels, howling wind. Bright flashlights made the night look like dappled gray velvet. I tried to pick out voices to know what was being said but couldn't.

At some point, Dad and Sheriff Jones meandered back toward the house and I shifted in my cocoon to face them.

The sheriff rubbed his small eyes that seemed smaller still from the late hour. "What a night. What a night."

Dad came to sit next to me, placing his hand against my back. His long fingers kneaded my back. "Honey, George has some questions for you."

I swallowed and then I nodded.

Heaving a heavy sigh, he asked, "Can you walk me through what happened tonight, Cat?"

While I watched them, I came up with a story that would protect the people I hated. Perhaps I should've told my father and Sheriff Jones the truth, but what if they didn't believe me? Or worse. What if they did, and spread the word that faeries walked amongst humans? That two-hundred-year-old dead hunters had risen? What then?

"I was clearing dinner when Blake called from the inn. He was speaking, but his words were all jumbled, so I took the hearse and drove over to Bee's Place. He wasn't there, so I went to his house. He wasn't there either. I called him back, and he told me to meet him at the old cabin. When I arrived there, I heard a loud bang."

"You heard it all the way from the cabin?" George asked.

I nodded, neck so stiff the movement was jerky.

"That's a mile away," he said.

"Outside, sound carries."

"But *you* heard nothing, Derek?"

Dad shook his head. "But like I told you, George, I was listening to the TV pretty loudly."

"Since there's no car, I assume you ran back. How long did it take?"

"I don't know. Five minutes." I hoisted my shoulders. "I don't remember."

"An entire mile?"

"Maybe it was ten."

The sheriff took notes on a narrow leather-bound notebook. "What I still fail to understand—and I've paced the cemetery back and forth—is how Blake managed to slalom through the graveyard without hitting a single tombstone, yet managed to hit a tree?" He looked up at me then.

I felt the blood desert my face and pool into my heart. "I don't know...I was at the cabin."

The sheriff pursed his fat lips. "But don't you find it strange, Cat?"

"I do." I bobbed my head up and down to add weight to my deceitful concurrence. "Maybe there *is* damage. With all the snow falling, you could've missed it."

George turned his dime-sized eyes on me. "It's a possibility. I plan on canvassing the area tomorrow. The snow's supposed to stop by noon." He tapped the ink tip of his blue pen against the lined paper. It was the same blue as Blake's Jeep. The same blue as his good eye. The same blue as his glass eye.

"I hope he didn't suffer," I said.

George eyed Dad and Dad eyed him.

"What?" I croaked.

Dad's arm tightened around me. "I'm pretty sure he died on impact. We'll know tomorrow. Cruz said he'd be back by then."

I pressed away from him. "You spoke to him?"

"I did. He's a medical examiner."

"And he said he'd be back?"

"Yes."

I narrowed my eyes, not because I didn't believe my father, but because I couldn't understand how Cruz had used a phone in prison. Either faerie jail was the laxest system, or Ace had lied when he said Cruz had been imprisoned. "Can you give me his number?"

Dad arched an eyebrow. "Why?"

"I just want to ask him something."

"You promise you're not going to convince him not to come?"

"I promise."

Dad slid his phone out of his jeans and tapped the screen a few times. "There. I sent it." He heaved a long sigh. "Have you informed Bee yet, George?"

"I didn't want to give her the news over the phone. I wanted to do it in person."

"You mind if I do it?"

"Of course not. Want company?"

Dad shook his head, dislodging tears from his red eyes. They leaked when he blinked. "Ugh…" He scraped a hand over his face, then reached over for a tissue and blew his nose loudly. "Shit, George. Two deaths in a week."

"I know," the sheriff said, his lips pressed in a tight, straight line. "And both on your property, Derek. If I didn't know you and Cat better, I'd have some serious questions. I do have one last thing to ask the both of you, though. Why did you dig up that old grave?"

I startled at his question, but collected myself. "The ground started caving in around it. Mom said that if that ever happened, we should lift the caskets out and repack the earth."

"The ground's frozen stiff, Catori. How can it have caved in?"

"It caved in before the blizzard."

"And you dug it out when?" He poised the pen over his paper while I damned Gwenelda for leaving me in this mess, and Lily for not having thought to make it vanish with her dust. Although, technically she'd been quite helpful.

"This afternoon. After lunch."

I felt Dad's eyes on me. Thankfully, he didn't tell the sheriff I was lying.

"Blake helped me," I added. "And then we went over to his house. And then Dad came to pick me up from there." I twisted my fingers in my lap.

"Did you have an argument? At his house?" the sheriff asked.

"An argument?" I said a bit too loudly.

"George, please. Don't." Dad's eyes looked larger, pleading almost.

Had someone heard us argue? We'd talked, but we hadn't raised our voices, had we?

"And the petals, Catori? What's with the rose petals? And why aren't there any bones inside the casket?"

I stopped trying to remember my last moments with Blake as lying took up every firing synapse and functioning neuron in my brain. "It was a family superstition. After a body decomposes fully the spirit is left unguarded. Grandma Woni told me that empty coffins must be filled with rose petals to appease lurking spirits. I'd forgotten about it until I found the other casket Mom had unearthed. She'd filled it with petals."

"So that's why she did that," Dad mused.

"Yeah." I nodded to validate my lie. "It could be a harebrained tale, but since Mom did it, I thought I should too."

I had no clue if Dad believed me, but he squeezed me harder and smiled down at me, as though proud I'd upheld one of Mom's traditions. "And here I thought you were angry at her for being so woo-woo."

"Angry?"

"You took down her wind chime."

"I...I *was* angry. But not at her."

His gaze drifted to the formerly-yellow door. "Well I'm glad you're not angry anymore." Dad squeezed me once more, then he stood up. "George, can you drop me off by the hearse?"

"Sure thing."

Dad walked to the two little hooks nailed by the door. Only one set of house keys hung there. Mom's. She'd made a tassel out of brown leather and turquoise beads. She'd been so good at crafts. Dad fingered the tassel. Heaving a deep breath, he let his fingers slide off of it. "You have the car keys, honey?"

I patted my pockets. "No. I left them inside the hearse."

The sheriff opened the front door, and snowdrifts gusted in like wandering souls.

"How the heck am I supposed to tell Bee her baby boy is gone?" Dad whispered, voice catching. "It'll destroy her."

The sheriff patted Dad's arm. They'd gone to school together way back when. Although George had always looked older, the tables had turned after Mom passed.

"Want me to come with you, Dad?" I asked, already shedding the thick blanket like a butterfly emerging from a cocoon. I was no butterfly, though. Butterflies weren't venomous. Blake's death was on me. If I hadn't begged him for help earlier, out in Holly's field, he'd still be alive.

"No, Cat." It took me a second to understand that Dad was answering my question and not comforting me like I so wished he would. But would he comfort me if I explained everything to him? "I want you to stay put. Run yourself a bath to warm up, or better yet, get into bed and just try to get some sleep."

I didn't think I would sleep that night.

Dad hugged me before leaving.

"It's so unfair, Daddy."

He stroked my hair as I trembled. He squashed me harder as though trying to squeeze the night out of me. "I know. I know…" Finally, Dad let his arms fall away from my body and walked toward the sheriff, who was speaking with someone outside.

"The paramedics want to bring him in, Derek. Lay him out downstairs in one of the cold chambers."

Wasn't Blake cold enough?

"I'll take them downstairs," Dad offered. "I'll be a minute."

A man and woman dressed in matching navy uniforms and puffer jackets wheeled in the stretcher bearing the body bag. I swallowed hard, making the thick, jagged ball of grief dip and rise in my raw throat.

Dad tried to block my view by stepping in front of me. "Go upstairs, Cat."

I whirled around and ran away, up to my bedroom. I shut the door, then slid against the frame and shut my swollen eyes. I didn't move as the metal wheels of the stretcher clanged against the cement stairs. I didn't move as Dad exchanged hushed words with the paramedics; I still didn't move when the car engines rumbled loud and then petered out. When it was quiet, I opened my eyes and stared at the dark, snow-mottled sky outside my bedroom window. I was alone now.

Blake was downstairs, but I was alone.

The wind whistled outside, penetrating the old walls of our house, pulsing against the slate shingles of our snow-crested roof. My granddaddy had installed the roof, like he'd erected the walls and put in the floorboards. He'd worked in construction until he could no longer climb a ladder and lift a block of cement. He'd built many houses in Rowan, which had made him a much-admired member of the community.

My stiff fingers crawled over my jeans until they came in contact with my phone. On the screen, there was Dad's message. And several missed calls from Cass. Did she know? I read one of her texts: **Is Blake with you?**

"Yes," I whispered out loud. I didn't write back, though. My dad had probably reached the inn by then.

I saved Cruz's digital card to my contact list, then dialed him. The phone rang and rang until the call was dropped. I tried again. And again the call was dropped. I did this eight times. On the ninth, someone picked up.

It wasn't Cruz.

"What can I do for you, Catori?" It was Ace's voice, crisp and rushed, as though I'd interrupted him in the middle of something important. I hoped I had.

"Cruz is coming to my house tomorrow? I thought he was in jail."

"*He* won't be coming."

"But someone will?"

"I will."

"And what?" I snorted. "You're going to pretend to be a medical examiner?"

"Cruz did."

"Dad will never fall for it."

"I'm dusting myself, so he'll see Cruz."

"What about the way you sound? Can you *dust* your voice too?"

"Yes."

"Of course you can."

"Well, if that's all—"

"Is Cruz really in jail?"

"Yes, Catori. He's really in jail."

"Why did he save Gwenelda?"

"Because you influenced him to do so."

"You keep saying that."

"You know that noxious gas released by a dead body? I bet you know the one, what with living in a funeral home. Anyway, that's how hunters smell to us. Your scent, your touch, your presence... they make the hairs on the back of our necks rise and our stomachs heave. But for some reason, Cruz didn't pass out in your presence, and the only explanation I have is that you influenced him to stick around."

I couldn't help myself. I sniffed my arm. My skin smelled like nothing. I dropped it back alongside my body, feeling utterly stupid for listening to Ace. "I hope I repel you, Ace," I said. "I hope I repel all faeries. You've brought me nothing but hell."

"Your hunters are a bit to blame too, don't you think?"

"They're not *my* hunters. I want nothing to do with them."

"You have the gene. Even if you choose not to persecute us, we'll remain wary of you. It's nature. Your nature; our nature. My condolences, by the way." There was a lilt to his voice, as though he was more amused than saddened by what happened to Blake.

Telling him to go eff himself would be childish, but it was so damn tempting. "Is Lily with you?"

"I'm in the middle of something I wouldn't want my little sister to witness. Something I'd really like to get back to."

"Ask her to come tomorrow. I need to speak with her."

"I'll ask if she's interested. Bye now, Kitty Cat."

"Do *not*"—the dial tone rang in my ear—"call me that."

Incensed, I tossed my phone on the bed and stared daggers at it, wishing I could use my influence—if I had any—to piggyback on the radio waves and ruin Ace's booty call.

I yanked my curtains closed, realizing that at some point during the conversation I'd gotten up to prowl my room like an angry beast. I still trembled, but it wasn't from sadness. It was from rage. Rage against the hunters and the fae. I needed to find a way out. And the solution came to me as I peeled off my dank clothes: I would eradicate the faulty hunter gene from my body.

20

MYTHS

woke up long before my father. I pulled on gray leggings, a black sweater, and the thick woolen socks Mom had knitted for me two winters before. They were scratchy, so I rarely wore them, but I wanted to wear them as a tribute to Mom. Just like I wanted to reattach the iron wind chime. I was tempted to hook it up before Ace and Lily showed up, to humble the brother and sister by making them crawl into our house through a window, but that would alert Dad and possibly endanger him. As long as he remained oblivious to the existence of faeries, he was safe. I hoped.

It was still pouring snow outside, so I pulled on a thick coat and shearling boots to walk over to the dumpster. As I lifted the lid, readying myself to dig through week-old trash, I was met by something worse than rotting food and dirty tissues. Emptiness. My fingers fumbled off the plastic lid, which snapped shut, dispersing the unpleasant smell of garbage past. In spite of the crazy weather, the trash collectors had stopped by our house!

I checked again, just in case the wind chime had magically stayed put, but it hadn't. I trudged back to the house, kicked off my snow-crusted boots by the door, and went to the kitchen to wash my hands. As soap and water slipped through my fingers, I thought of the leather-bound book hidden underneath my mattress. Perhaps *The Wytchen Tree* held instructions on how to build another wind chime. I hopped up the creaking stairs. Once inside my bedroom, I locked the door.

There was no table of contents, which made the task of finding a specific passage tedious. Careful not to rip the fine, silken paper, I flicked through the pages, hoping for a sketch of a wind chime. By page 150, I'd found three mentions of the word "iron," but nothing on wind chimes. One particular passage caught my attention.

Averse to iron, faeries were believed to possess a great love for other metals such as gold, bronze, and silver. They mined the metals and gathered them in airtight caverns only accessible through faerie portals. Negongwa claimed that one of these caverns was on Beaver Island. Invisible to the human eye, he described it as an extra-dimensional baseetogan, a globe where faeries reveled and socialized among themselves. Considered folklore by most, several fishermen from the Great Lakes have claimed that when navigating close to Beaver Island, they could hear music and voices.

Another myth that closely joins that of the baseetogan is the existence of mishipeshu, a mythical aquatic monster with the head of a panther and the body of a dragon. Most natives believed mishipeshu to be malevolent beings guarding Lake Superior's underwater copper mines; some whispered the water monster was made of copper, and if killed, turned into solid metal that could lead to great wealth.

Negongwa's view on the mishipeshu differed slightly. According to him, mishipeshu were shape-shifting faeries ordered to distract ill-intentioned humans with offerings of

sparkling gold treasure that would turn into underwater sediment once the human returned home.

Now, this remains an ambiguous myth as faerie caverns were deemed inaccessible to humans. Which leads to the question: What true role do the mishipeshu play?

Even though there was no mention of wind chimes, I found myself reading on. I discovered that the Bella Point Light, the oldest lighthouse in Michigan, was supposedly a faerie portal. I typed the name in my phone and discovered it was in Traverse City, forty-five miles away from Rowan. I saved the search, and then resumed flipping through the extensive volume.

Drawings inked on a page made me stop again. They were so precise they resembled photographs, but photography had yet to be invented when the hunters were buried. Without having to read the captions, I guessed whom the twelve faces belonged to: Negong-wa's tribe. I found Gwenelda's face in an instant, squarish and sharp with dark, thin eyes and a long black braid woven through with feathers, lips set in a serious line. She seemed as friendly back then as she did now. Briefly I wondered where she could be hiding with her new buddy. But then I pushed that thought away. I didn't care where she was hiding since I had no plans of seeking her out.

I scanned the other faces on the page, pausing twice. As opposed to the other ten, the faces I studied were narrower, with hooded eyes, angular jaws, and shiny, dark hair. The hunter Gwenelda had awakened was one of them. I read the captions: *Kajika* and *Menawa*. I was curious as to why they looked so different from the others. Not that all members of a family had to resemble each other. I didn't look much like Saty and Shiloh, but their eyes, like mine, sloped upward a bit, and our lips were all quite full. Maybe Kajika and Menawa were distant cousins of the tribe.

A knock on the door made me jump.

"Cat?" came Dad's voice.

I shut the book and shoved it underneath my mattress, pulling the edge of my comforter over it.

"You awake, honey?"

"Yeah."

"Have you had lunch yet?"

"Lunch?" I checked the time on my phone to discover that it was already noon. Where had the morning gone? How long had I been reading? "No. You want me to whip something up?"

"I pulled the casseroles from the cold chamber and brought everything up to the kitchen."

As I unlocked the door, my stomach sank and twisted. My disgust must have shown because Dad grimaced.

"I should probably throw those away, huh?" He scrunched up his nose.

"Yeah. Do we have any eggs? I could make an omelet."

"We might. I should go to the supermarket, though."

"I can go."

Dad's face was colorless. Even his undereye circles were gray instead of purple. As we went downstairs together, I thought of Blake another floor below and asked my father how it had gone with Bee.

"It was awful, Cat. Just awful. She wants to see him, and I told her I'd let her come over once Cruz was done making him up."

Cruz wouldn't make him up. Ace would sprinkle him with his dust or Lily would use hers again, and make Blake look tanned and somnolent instead of bloody and bashed.

"How many blows can one woman withstand?" Dad croaked as we entered the kitchen.

He'd piled the casseroles high on the table. I counted three layers of porcelain plates and glass dishes. I ripped a garbage bag from the roll underneath the sink and puffed it open.

As I handed it to Dad, I said, "Bee's a...she's an optimistic person so maybe...maybe she'll get through this." I didn't believe a word I said, but it didn't matter that I believed it. What mattered was that Dad believed it. "Here, hold this."

As I dumped and scraped crusty food, I attempted to breathe only through my mouth. Nothing was covered in mold, but the dishes had been stored next to two corpses, and however much I loved the people those bodies had belonged to, I wasn't keen on eating food that had been kept in the same room.

We filled up the entire bag. While Dad carried it outside, I loaded the dishwasher and filled the sink with the empty receptacles. And then I peered inside the fridge and took out a half-full carton of eggs and a tub of butter. I cooked up a frothy, golden omelet. I'd been tempted to add cheese to it, but the pack I found in our refrigerator drawer was already expired. I moved the supermarket trip to the top of my to-do list, right under speaking with Ace and Lily.

We ate fast and in silence, both shoveling the food into our mouths, hoping that it could fill some of the cracks inside. The omelet was unsatisfying. I pressed away and checked the cupboards for cans of something edible. Instead, I found a packet of pasta. It was frilly and green.

"Basil fettuccini," I read aloud. "You want some?"

Dad, who was still scraping the tines of his fork against his empty plate, blanched.

"What?"

"I bought those to surprise your mother. She loved pesto so much, so I thought...I thought that with some toasted pine nuts, she would—" He closed his still puffy eyes, then reopened them. For once, they were dry. Red but dry. "I thought she would love them. There should be a packet of pine nuts somewhere in there too."

I turned back toward the cupboard and shifted a half-empty box of sugar cubes and a tub of instant coffee until I found the nuts. As I warmed up some water for the pasta, I pulled out a pan and toasted the fragrant nuts in olive oil.

Mom used to grow basil by the fence around the cemetery, next to the blackberry and blueberry bushes. When I was nine, I told her I wouldn't eat anything that was in contact with graveyard soil, so she'd bought a special planter…just for me.

Gosh, I was such a brat.

"Do you think your mom's spirit could still be around? Watching over us? Or do you think it's really traveling to the next world?"

I tossed the pasta inside the pot and watched it thicken as it absorbed the salted water. A few days before, I might have told him that wandering spirits and lingering souls were a religious fabrication, that death wasn't some connecting flight to another dimension. But now, with Gwenelda's appearance, everything I'd staunchly believed had capsized. "I hope she's still around."

"I dreamt of her last night," Dad said. "I dreamt she was pushing you on a swing attached to one of the branches of those trees we have in the cemetery, except this one was huge. So huge, it vanished into the clouds. And there was this boy. And he was standing opposite your mother, and she was swinging you toward him. But your mother didn't really look like your mother. She looked like that crazy woman who came to the wake. The one who murdered the medical examiner." He shot me a coy smile. "I'm not known for predicting the future, so you shouldn't worry."

"About being swung by Gwenelda? Yeah…I don't see that happening." I mirrored his smile even though deep down, his dream irked me. "What did the boy look like?"

"Handsome, I suppose. With lots of tattoos. But his eyes were strange, almost like glass. Like Blake's." His cheek dimpled as he paused to revisit his dream. "You're not going to run away with a tattooed boy, right?"

"Nah. I'm into piercings," I teased. Tattoos belonged to hunters. And hunters were on my shitlist.

Dad's complexion turned as light green as the pasta in the pot. *The pasta!* I grabbed the strainer from a bottom drawer and flung it into the sink, then I seized the scorching pot and poured it out, burning my fingers on the steel handles. I hoped I hadn't over-cooked the noodles. Thankfully, I'd taken the pine nuts off the heat. In a shallow ceramic bowl, I tossed the pasta with the nuts and some extra-virgin olive oil.

As I brought it to the table, I asked Dad what had made him think of tattoos.

"The Great Spirit only knows," he said.

Great Spirit. When had Dad gone so native? "Aren't you Catholic, Dad?"

"Me? I'm not anything anymore. I *was* Catholic, dragged to church on Sundays like most kids around here. I remember having to wear these shiny leather loafers that were so stiff they always gave me blisters. And every time my feet grew, I thought that would be it. I'd finally be rid of them, but my mother, in her far-sightedness, had bought every size available when they'd gone on sale." His earlier smile morphed into a large grin. "I think I might actually have a pair left in my closet. Dear old Mom."

I'd never get to use that expression for my mother. She'd died too young. "Do you miss Grams?"

"You always miss people you've loved. Missing them means they meant something to you. The pain dulls with time. One day, honey, you'll be able to think of your mother without your heart breaking."

"Will you ever be able to think of her without your heart breaking?"

The smile weakened, before blinking off his face. "I'm not sure my heart will ever mend."

Hunched over, he served himself a heaping amount of pasta and ate in silence. I spied a tear dripping into the fragrant, oily mess. I went around to him and hugged him because I couldn't think of anything more to say that hadn't already been said.

"Do you know that Blake wanted to ask you to marry him?" Dad said, after some time.

I stiffened, then pulled back.

"Bee told me he spoke to her about it. He asked her if he should give you his mother's ring or if you'd find it unlucky."

My heart swelled.

"He loved you very, very much."

"I loved him too," I murmured.

Dad tucked a loose strand of hair behind my ear. "But not in the same way."

"Do two people ever love each other the same way? I mean, besides you and Mom."

"I loved your mother far more than she ever loved me."

I stood ramrod straight. "What are you talking about?"

"*I* was struck by lightning, but your mother...she fell in love with me over time. You'll think I'm crazy if I tell you this, but it was like I could see it happen. One morning, she'd look over at me, and get this twinkle in her eye, and this smile...she had such a beautiful smile"—the corners of Dad's lips lifted ever so gradually, like a sun rising over a horizon—"and when she looked at me like that, I knew she'd just fallen a little bit more in love with me. I think it was the same for Blake."

I bit my lip, and my heart swelled a little more.

"Bee told him to wait. She was worried you wouldn't have been able to overlook his disfigurement. He would've made a great husband, though."

I sighed. "I wouldn't have wanted to marry him. At least not now. Not at nineteen."

"Your mother was twenty when we got married."

"But that was in the olden days, Dad," I said, which elicited laughter.

The sound seemed foreign after all these days of mourning. My father was one of those people who always laughed, and he had this great big, contagious, belly laugh—even though he had no belly to speak of.

I grinned and would have laughed too had the doorbell not rung at that exact moment—Ace and Lily. As I walked to open the door, I reminded myself to call Ace, Cruz. Or not to use his name at all. That would probably be safer.

I swung the front door open just as Dad walked up behind me.

"Thank you for coming back on such short notice," Dad said to Ace. They shook hands while I stared at Lily and she stared right back.

21

THE TRADE

*W*hile Dad brought Ace, whom he believed was Cruz, downstairs, I stood in the entryway beholding his blonde waif-of-a-sister.

When I was certain Dad was far enough not to overhear my voice, I asked, "Why did you help your enemies?"

Lily pursed her lips, then moved toward the coffee table where she found a pen and a boating magazine. Dad loved boats. He was always speaking of purchasing one with two cabins so that we could travel the Great Lakes. But that was when Mom was alive. Now that he was alone, I didn't think he'd want a boat anymore.

I crossed my arms as she flipped through the magazine and ripped a page with an ad on it. Using the thick magazine as backing, she jotted words on it. Her writing was loopy and harmonious, as though she were trained in the art of calligraphy. Perhaps she was. I supposed fae packed their very long lives with trivial things, such as learning pretty handwriting. What else did they have to do, besides torment humans and keep an eye on dead hunters...and now live ones?

She flipped the paper toward me so I could read it. **We don't want humans learning about us.**

"Of course not."

Dad's voice drifted from downstairs. I couldn't make out all his words but I did catch "analyze the vitreous humor," and I didn't like the implication. Blake's death wasn't a result of drunk driving, even though we *had* shared a beer. The only positive outcome of having Ace as a medical examiner is that he surely had no clue how to run a tox screen on the gel-like substance from Blake's good eye.

Blake no longer had a good eye or a bad one.

Pushing that thought away, I asked, "Why didn't you hide the casket?"

She spun the paper back toward her and wrote. **My dust does not work on rowan wood.**

Right. "Why did you make it look like an accident?"

Easier to explain than another heart attack, no?

I swallowed. "It is, but it also makes his death seem like his fault when it wasn't."

Wasn't it? she wrote.

I shook my head no.

Right...it was your fault.

That knocked the breath right out of my lungs. "I didn't ask Gwenelda to wake another hunter!" I said way too loudly.

Lily narrowed her large gray eyes. **Aren't you pleased there's one more of you?**

"No, Lily, I'm not. Because I'm *not* a hunter."

Lily tipped her head to the side and gave me a look. I recognized that look. It was the same one my organic chemistry teacher back at BU gave me when I misanalysed molecular formulas.

"How's Cruz?"

She frowned, then started to sign, but remembered I couldn't understand sign language, so she wrote instead. **He's angry about being locked up.**

"Is he really locked up?"

She nodded.

"What's prison like back where you live? Jail cells and barbed wire fences?"

Lily shook her head and her long, straight blonde hair rippled around her ribbed sky-blue turtleneck. She pressed the tip of the pen against the paper again. **There are no cells. He just can't leave.**

"What happens if he leaves?"

The wariff has taken away his key to the portals so he just can't.

Checking the basement door for movement, I asked, "Wariff?" There were still streaks of white paint on the metal doorknob, but no more traces of cheery yellow. Yet if I let my eyes go unfocused, I could still see the shade of sunshine my mother had chosen.

It's like a chief of police. Every century or so, a faerie is elected to control our people. After my father, they're the most powerful fae.

"If your father's more powerful," I whisper, "then why doesn't he overrule the wariff?"

Because he has no jurisdiction over wariff ruling.

Curiosity about their political system animated me, but the name Gwenelda drifted up from the basement, and eavesdropping took precedence over learning about the fae world. *Fae world.* How did I come to accept the existence of such a world?

"Do you know where Gwenelda's hiding?"

Lily frowned. **Don't you?**

"No. Have they left Rowan?"

What do you think?

"No."

Lily gave me a thumbs-up. Her nails were painted the same light blue as her top.

Footsteps on the staircase resounded. I was about to yank the paper from Lily's hand when it caught fire. In seconds, it was reduced to shimmering ashes, which she blew off the palm of her hand.

"What are you girls doing still standing?" Dad asked. "Have you even offered our guest something to drink, Cat?"

"Not yet." Although I didn't feel like catering to Lily, I asked her what she wanted.

She signed something to my father.

"Hot water," Dad says.

Lily gave him a smile and shook her head, then signed again.

"Tea! She means tea. Black tea. Correct?"

Lily clapped and nodded, while Dad shot her a proud, goofy grin.

"Coming right up," I said, making my way to the kitchen. I filled the electric kettle with water and turned it on. As I waited for it to boil, I looked through our tea drawer. We had no more black tea—one more thing to add to my supermarket list—but we had some fancy, immune-boosting tea. One of Mom's, surely. She loved herbal medicine.

"If I'd lived during the heyday of our Gottwa tribe, I would've been a healer," she'd once told me.

"You can't treat everything with herbs and spices," my younger self had told her.

"You can cure a lot with roots and incantations. Most natives vanquished diseases the settlers thought incurable."

"Well, I'd rather be a doctor."

I remembered the disappointed gleam in my mother's eyes when I'd told her that. Even though I recognized the benefits of plants—like aloe vera on burns and comfrey for sore throats—I was also a great advocate of modern medicine. Mom never had me inoculated with any vaccine, not because she thought they led to autism, but because she was certain that she could cure whatever ailed me with homemade ointments and brews. I read the news, and was much less certain. Anyway, to attend college, I needed immunizations, so that was that.

I took out the navy mug that said, "Planet's Best Mom" in a pretty white script. I stroked the curly letters, remembering the day

I'd bought it for her with my pocket money. I was nine and mighty proud. I smiled sadly at it before placing it back in the cupboard and selecting a plain, clear mug for Lily's tea.

After pouring hot water over the tea bag, I brought it back out to the living room where she and Dad were conducting an animated, silent conversation. She thanked me with a nod. Concentrating on Dad's flailing hands, she took a sip, sputtered, then gasped. Eyes watering, she turned toward me. Plumes of smoke, like the ones that had erupted from Cruz's palm the night he touched my iron necklace, coiled through her parted lips, which had turned stone-gray. The grayness had crawled over her chin and down her throat. She fanned herself, but it wasn't to cool down. Sparkling dust burst from her palm and settled over her skin like face powder.

I was too startled by her physical reaction to move.

"How hot did you make the tea, Cat?" Dad all but shouted at me, lumbering into the kitchen. I heard the clink of ice cubes in a glass. And then he was back, brandishing the glass in front of Lily.

"Here," Dad said, trying to give her the glass. "Suck on these."

She leaned away from him, as though allergic to the ice also, but I knew why she didn't take it from Dad, why she gestured for him to set it on the table...if she touched the glass, the ice would melt. I didn't think her faerie dust could mask that. As Dad walked back to the armchair, I went to the kitchen and checked the box from which I'd taken the teabag. When I read iron-fortified, I blanched. I'd just slipped Lily faerie poison.

I strode back into the living room, wondering what I could give her to fix my mistake. She couldn't die of iron poisoning, could she? She blinked her large gray eyes at me, then signed something.

"Aloe vera could help," Dad suggested. "Let me go check if we still have some."

Although Lily nodded, I doubted aloe vera would do her much good.

Her eyes were still wet when Ace poked his head out of the

basement door. "Mr. Price, could I speak to you a second?" When he noticed his sister's expression, his eyes slid to me.

Dad interrupted his rummaging in one of our kitchen drawers and followed Ace downstairs.

"I'll be right back," he called out.

When their footsteps dimmed, I turned toward Lily. She grabbed the glass of ice from the table. The cubes melted instantly. She chugged the water down, then replaced it on the table.

"I'm sorry. I didn't know there was iron inside the tea."

Her eyes darted toward me accusingly as she nestled into the couch and folded her arms.

"I swear I didn't know."

This time, when she looked over at me, her gaze stayed on mine. Her eyes still gleamed with tears, which made them resemble the reflective strips on my running clothes.

"Trust me, if I was out to poison anyone, it would be your brother."

Her lips curved a little. They were becoming pinker and her skin returned to its peachy color.

"Is he a good brother at least?"

She nodded, then tipped her head from side to side. I gathered she meant he had his moments.

Finally, she untangled her arms, pointed to me, fashioned the letter C with the fingers from one hand, then used both her hands to draw a heart. The shape stayed invisibly suspended in midair between us.

"Do I love Cruz?" I asked tentatively. I hoped that wasn't her question. I really didn't want to discuss Cruz with Lily.

Unfortunately, she nodded.

"He was nice to me, Lily. With everything that happened, I was glad for some kindness. And a distraction. But do I love him? No. He's very handsome, but you can't love someone after a few days. At least, I can't." I wasn't my father. "I wanted to feel something other than misery. And Cruz provided me with that something."

Remorse flared behind my breastbone. "That makes me a pretty sucky person for what I did to you."

Lily nodded, and I found myself smiling. She didn't smile back. Why would she? I wasn't a sucky person...I was a terrible person. Sure, I wasn't the only one to blame. Cruz had kissed me too—he'd flirted with *me*—but I should've kept my distance once I knew about Lily.

I sank down in the armchair opposite the one my father had occupied and knotted my fingers in my lap. "I promise you that if Cruz ever comes back—"

"I'll get you the results tomorrow," Ace said loudly.

I closed my mouth, hoping Dad hadn't heard the beginning of my aborted sentence.

"Are you already done?" I asked.

"Not yet. I have to get my makeup kit from the car." Ace gave me a pointed stare as he reached the front door.

"I'm going to Bee's to get the suit she wants him to wear," Dad said.

"I can go, Dad. I haven't seen Bee yet."

"She'll come over tonight. You'll see her then. Besides, I'm sure Lily would rather you keep her company than me."

I almost laughed when he said that. Lily's lips also contorted, but in a grimace.

"I'll be back in thirty." Dad kissed my forehead before leaving.

Once the hearse's engine rumbled away, Ace carved his fingers through the longer strands of hair atop his head. "I don't appreciate you torturing my little sister, Catori."

Lily reached out and touched the back of Ace's white dress shirt. He glanced her way. She signed something. He glanced back at me.

I looked down at my thick woolen socks. "It was an accident."

"Sure."

"It was," I insisted.

"Well don't ever do it again, or I'll think up ways to hurt someone *you* love."

I stood up, so that I was about his height. "Don't you dare do anything to my father!"

"He's a kind man, Catori. I would regret harming him, but you hurt one of mine again, I hurt one of yours. You're lucky I didn't seek vengeance for what you did to Cruz," he added, peeking behind him at Lily.

"What I did to Cruz?"

"Making him save a hunter."

"*He* offered to save Gwenelda. I didn't even know he could."

Ace grunted.

"Maybe he didn't even do it for me," I said.

Ace's eyes widened a little, which led me to believe I'd struck a nerve. Could Gwen have been right? Could Cruz have had a motive?

"There isn't a single valid reason to save an enemy, Catori, so please do keep your conspiracy theories to yourself."

He was being awfully defensive.

"Lil, can you dust Blake again? I need to keep mine handy." Lily wrinkled her nose but stood up. "Make him look pretty. Apparently his grandma wants an open casket. And don't forget to add a little ridge on his forehead where he *injured* it. For the keen observers."

After nodding, she latched on to my wrist and tipped her head toward the open white door.

"I won't play any tricks on her while you're gone," Ace said.

Disregarding him, she applied pressure to my wrist again.

"I do want to see him one last time," I said.

"You'll see him at the wake. His grandma's throwing a big party at the inn. Your dad invited us."

I didn't bother telling him a wake was not a party. He wasn't worth my time or my breath. Instead I spun away and walked ahead of Lily.

My friend was laid out in the middle of the room, fully exposed. I realized I'd never seen him naked and suddenly felt ill at ease. I took Mom's old robe and draped it over the lower half of his rigid body. And then I moved up to his face and caressed his cheek, drawing my fingers across the hollow dip that several surgeries hadn't been able to correct. My fingers journeyed over his jaw, in which had been grafted a small piece of his hipbone, down his sinewy shoulder to his forearm where he'd slashed open his pale skin. For the briefest moment, I wondered if Gwenelda had done that to him to make it look like suicide. Slowly, I slid my hands off his body and settled them on the cold autopsy table.

"When I was eight, Blake saw me sitting on a swing in the school playground all by myself. He was two grades above me, but we went to such a small school that every grade had their breaks at the same time. Anyway, he sat on the swing next to mine, and pointed to the Tupperware of carrot sticks on my lap," I told Lily, remembering my swaying toothpick legs and my grumbling stomach. "It was a Wednesday. I know this because Mondays were celery sticks; Tuesdays, cherry tomatoes; and Wednesdays, carrots. That morning, I'd dared ask for something else…something good… something not too wholesome, but Mom refused. 'We eat only what the earth gives us, Catori,' she'd say. 'Feeding yourself well must be learned young.'" I wasn't sure why I was telling her this story. Maybe it was so that she could picture Blake as a person instead of just a task.

I lifted my gaze to Lily's. She was watching me, eyebrows pulled together.

"You know what Blake did that day? He told me he'd like to trade snacks. Apparently, he was bored of chips. And every day after that, he traded whatever he'd brought against my Tupperware of vegetables. When I told this story at a Thanksgiving dinner at his grandmother's house years later, Bee said she'd never seen Blake eat any vegetable beside a potato. He turned so red, and then he left the table." I smiled down at Blake. And then a tear dripped into my mouth. It was salty, like his chips. "I'm going to miss you so damn much," I whispered, my voice breaking.

Another tear dripped off my chin. Slowly, I backed away from the metal table. My lower back collided with another table. I spun around and found myself staring into the rowan wood casket, at gray, bone-dry rose petals. My gaze locked on the opal and iron necklace Gwen had given me. I felt Lily's eyes on me as I retrieved it. I saw her take a small step back. I wasn't planning on hurting her with it. I wasn't even planning on wearing it, but I wanted to put it away. Clutching the opal, I left the basement.

Ace called out to me right as I reached the second-floor landing. "Did you hear who Gwenelda brought back?"

"No." Even though I didn't want to strike up a conversation with him, I couldn't help asking, "Who?"

His eyes trailed down my arm to the swaying necklace. "Her mate. She must've had an itch only he could scratch," he said, looking up at me from the bottom of the stairs.

"You're a real pig."

He winked. "On the upside, you might not see much of them for a long time. I imagine they have tons to catch up on."

I didn't think anything could make me angrier with Gwen, but this…this infuriated me! She'd taken someone I loved to revive her husband. I shoved myself away from the railing and went into my bedroom, shutting the door behind me.

I locked it, even though I doubted a lock would keep a faerie out. Unless it was made of iron. I hoped it was. I thought about hanging the necklace on my door, but I had two windows in my room. Fae could use those to come inside. In the end, I placed it next to the book underneath my mattress. At least, it would keep a faerie from touching it. And what had Cruz told me about opal again?

Yes. When worn, it made hunters invisible to fae. Maybe it worked on objects too.

THE SUPERMARKET

I waited for Dad to come home with Blake's suit, and then I waited some more for Ace and Lily to leave. After Dad settled on the couch with a beer in front of a hockey game, I grabbed two fabric bags from the pile Mom stored in the broom closet and headed to the supermarket. The sky was already dimming by the time I parked in front of The Earth Market. In winter, night crept over Michigan too early.

With no written list, I decided to go aisle by aisle. I started in the dry goods section and loaded up on dried pasta and rice, ready-made tomato sauces, and cans of beans and corn. I moved along, peering at each label and each expiration date.

"Catori!"

I looked up from the neat row of colorful cereal boxes to find Rowan's most exasperating citizen hobbling down the aisle toward me, a cane in one hand and a neon-orange basket in the other.

"Hi, Mr. Hamilton."

"I just heard the news." He dropped his basket and squashed me against him in the most awkward hug I'd gotten since slow-dancing with Harry Spence during prom. He'd been a whole head shorter than me, with out-of-control acne. "I loved that boy so much." It took me a millisecond to remember he wasn't speaking of my prom date. His cane's curved top poked my bottom—hopefully by mistake. "How did it happen?"

"He hit a tree." I hated perpetuating a lie, but the truth was unexplainable.

After he finally released me, he took my hand and squeezed it. "I'll be there tomorrow. For the wake."

I nodded.

"Blake was the grandson I never had. Such a nice boy. Such a shame." Grief often magnified people's memory of the departed. Maybe, in Mr. Hamilton's case, it magnified the memory of his relationship with Blake. He let go of my hand, bent over to pick up his basket, but almost toppled over. I steadied him, then crouched down and seized the basket. Raw egg dribbled out from the carton and onto the shiny floor.

"I think your eggs might've cracked," I said, brandishing the basket.

"Replaceable."

I dug a tissue from my pocket and cleaned the yellow slime next to my boots, then tossed the tissue into my cart.

"Only people are irreplaceable." His wrinkly face moved closer to mine. "Was it really an accident?" he whispered loudly, sending spittle flying against my chin.

I startled at the insinuation.

"Or was it suicide?" he whispered loudly. "Bee told me he was having a lot of trouble accepting his disfigurement."

"It was an accident."

He shook his head. "Such a shame. See you tomorrow night, Catori." Leaning on his cane, he marched away, stopping in the baking section to stuff his carton of eggs behind the all-purpose flour bags.

Shaking my head at the old man's impudence, I continued my shopping. Two more people came up to me to ask about Blake, about what *really* happened. I was stunned by how everyone thought he'd committed suicide. Had Blake been so unwell that he'd contemplated ending his life? I wondered what Cass thought. She knew him best. After all, she'd been working at Bee's alongside him for over a year now.

Chewing on the corner of my thumbnail, I stared at the display of instant soups in front of me. I grabbed some at random and dropped them in the cart. In the milk section, I selected cheese and butter and yogurts—strawberry for Dad and vanilla for me. I reached for a carton of plain, organic yogurt and froze. Only Mom ate plain yogurt. I yanked my fingers back and slid the fridge door closed. As I turned the corner, I almost rammed my cart into the back of a guy wearing a baggy shirt and ankle-cropped jeans. Even though the jeans looked odd on him, what struck me most were his bare feet. Who walked around without shoes in the middle of winter?

While his hands shuffled through a rack of organic clothing, he kept checking his surroundings. I backed away. It was probably a silly reaction, but there was something worrisome about him, a tension in his neck that made the ligaments within strain like dock lines.

He yanked a plain black hoodie off a hanger, held it up to measure its size, and then pulled it on. He'd forgotten to remove the price tag, as well as the security tag, which would surely ring on his way out. I debated whether to alert a sales clerk of the looming theft as I watched him go through another rack, this time of sweatpants. He grabbed a pair, and like he'd done for the hoodie, he pulled it on.

I expected him to walk to the shoe aisle to steal a pair of orthopedic sandals, which were the only ones The Earth Market sold, but instead he spun around. The instant his eyes met mine, I stumbled backward, which made my cart bump into a display of toilet paper. The pyramid crumbled. The thief used the distraction to run away with his stolen loot.

I watched him leave through the entrance, heard the alarm of his tags go off, saw one of the girls behind the register ask him to step back inside. I thought he would run, but he didn't. He stopped and spoke to her. The girl nodded, then waved him off without so much as a reprimand. If I'd had any doubts as to who he was, watching him leave without having to return the merchandise confirmed his identity.

He was Gwenelda's husband.

Blake's killer.

Abandoning the cart, I jogged to the exit. But then I stopped, wondering why the hell I was chasing after him. There was nothing I wanted from him or from Gwen. Nothing.

I returned to my cart and stalked off down aisles, tossing random things inside. My two bags could barely contain my shopping, and when I picked them up, the scratchy fabric handles dug into my skin. I heaved them back into my cart and walked back to the hearse.

God, I missed my car. It seemed stupid to miss a chunk of metal after everything, but it was *my* chunk of metal. After the wake, I would fly back to Boston to pack up, and then I'd make the ten-hour road trip back, singing along to every song that played on the radio. I didn't sing well, but boy did I love singing when no one could hear me.

I opened the trunk and grabbed the first bag. Pinching my shoulder blades together, I hauled it out of the cart and lobbed it inside. As I turned to grab the other one, I found myself nose to neck with *him*. I jolted backward and slid my car key between my index and middle fingers.

His face looked younger than Gwen's. Not babyish, but smooth, with sharp angles and long eyebrows that cast shadows over his already dark eyes. Even though there were a great many things I longed to say to him, I kept silent.

I brandished my makeshift weapon in front of me, praying that the new hunter couldn't see my arm tremble. "Go away."

A quick sweep of the parking lot proved I was alone. Maybe if I yelled loud enough the people inside The Earth Market would hear the commotion.

He smiled. He freaking smiled!

My heart thumped fiercely inside my chest and inside my arm, making the key quiver.

"I mean you no harm, Catori." His voice had a depth I'd never heard in any voice before, as though his vocal cords were wrapped in both chainmail and velvet.

"You don't get it." My own voice shook. "*I* will harm you if you and Gwen don't leave me alone." I hoped I sounded threatening. "Please, leave Rowan."

His smile faltered. "We cannot leave," he said, his voice rumbling like the "T" back in Boston.

"Well you can't stay either."

"I'm sorry I took the life of the boy you loved."

His comment defused my anger, replacing it with shock. "Did Gwenelda make you come and apologize?"

"No one makes me apologize."

I stepped further back. "How do you even know English?" I realized I'd never asked Gwenelda.

The smile flickered off his face. "When I was brought back, I absorbed Blake's mind and spirit. I know everything he knew."

I swallowed. "Everything?"

He nodded.

That was impossible. "How did his parents die?"

"In a plane crash."

He could have read about that. "How many surgeries did he have?"

"Three."

"Wrong," I snapped.

He tilted his face to the side. "I'm not wrong."

"You are. He only had two surgeries for his face."

"And an ap-pen-dec-tomy"—he emphasized each syllable like a child learning a new word—"at six years old."

My outstretched arm wavered. He was right. Blake had told me about it one day in school when I had complained of stomach pains. Turned out, it was the wrong side of my body that hurt. "Who was Bee to him?"

"His grandmother. He loved her very much. But he loved you more."

I swallowed hard.

"He was going to ask you to marry him," he added. "But he believed...he believed..."

My eyesight blurred. "What did he believe?"

"He believed you would turn him down."

My arm collapsed against my side and the keys clinked against the metal keychain. Blake had died thinking I didn't love him enough...*knowing* I didn't love him enough. A tear rolled off my cheek. I brushed it away. "Does Gwenelda"—my voice was hoarse— "does she have my mother's memories?"

He nodded.

"All of them?" I murmured.

Again, he nodded.

A part of Mom, a part of Blake had survived. "She never told me that."

"You did not give her much time."

Our eyes locked as this new information settled like silt in my mind. I squeezed my eyes shut, then reopened them. The hunter hadn't shifted. Even his eyes had stayed fixed on mine.

"Doesn't give you a right to stay," I finally said. I didn't want just a part of Mom and Blake; I wanted the whole of them, and that was something no one could ever give me back. "You better take those magnetic tags off or you'll beep during your next burglary."

He frowned. I pointed to the security tag attached to the hem. He fingered it, flipped over the hem, and observed the mechanism.

"You'll need pliers to take it off, or you could probably just go back inside and *influence* them to take them off. You should steal a pair of shoes while you're at it," I added remonstratively.

His eyes flicked back up to mine. "I needed clothes," he said, before looking back down. Pinching it on both sides, he pulled. I was about to tell him that would never work, when it did.

"At least you stole them in your size this time."

"I didn't steal the others. I borrowed them."

"Sure," I said, but he was no longer listening, too busy scanning the parking lot. Suddenly, he stepped back, and then further back, until he became one with the darkness.

Headlights glistened next to me. I blinked as they grew brighter and closer. I blinked again when I realized that the light wasn't emanating from a car but from a person. No, not a person. A faerie. Gosh, could no one just leave me alone?

"I was wrong," Ace said, coming to stand next to me. Too close for comfort.

I folded my arms.

Ace frowned at the dark space the hunter's body had occupied only minutes before. "That's not Menawa."

"Menawa?"

"Gwen's mate. That's not him."

"Who is it then?"

His forehead furrowed with a frown. "It's his little brother."

"You think she misread the headstone?"

"No. Gwen was reputedly the shrewdest of all."

"Why would she wake up"—I rifled through my memory for his name—"Kaji...?"

"Ka," Ace finished the word for me. "Kajika." He narrowed his eyes. "How did you know his name?"

My heart felt as though it were crackling, like those wooden-wicked candles Aylen had made last summer for Independence Day. "Gwen told me about him. Why would she wake *him* up?"

"To get you on their side."

"What? How?"

One side of his mouth kicked up with half-grin. "He's the only one not related to you."

"How's that supposed to sway me?"

His right eyebrow arched high. "You're easy—"

My palm flew right into his cheek. "Don't even finish that thought."

He chuckled. "I was going to say, 'to sway.'"

"No, you weren't."

"Fine, I wasn't. But you did ask me what I thought."

I went to grab the last bag, but it was already in the car. Had I put it in there? Or had Kajika done that? I eyed the darkness, wondering if I was losing my mind.

I shut the trunk and brought my cart back to the row of trolleys. "Why are you even here?" I asked Ace over my shoulder.

"Your pulse. Every time it speeds up, it lights up Cruz's hand."

The cart clicked into place. "Maybe he should unmark me then. Would spare you the trouble of flying to my rescue." I made sure my voice was extra crisp.

Ace grinned. "Only way to get rid of a mark is to get rid of the person it's linked to. Since I'm not authorized to kill you, my poor friend's stuck sponging your emotions."

I squeezed my temples with my fingertips, then let them slide down the sides of my face. "Ugh!"

"Yeah. Ugh," he mimicked.

"Just stop coming."

"I would, but apparently it burns like a bitch until I ascertain there's no danger to his prey."

My eyes widened in horror at being called someone's prey again. "Well, call ahead next time. You have my number. And tell Cruz—since he surely has plenty of time on his hands now—to find a way of getting rid of his stupid mark."

"Will convey your disgruntlement, Kitty Cat."

"Don't call me that!"

But Ace had already shot upward, vanishing into the sky among the stars. I stood there, staring heavenward for a long moment, weighing the odds of Gwen being so calculating against the pleasure Ace got in riling me up.

Dad's dream returned to me: Gwen swinging me toward Blake but it wasn't Blake. It was a boy with tattoos. Kajika had tattoos. I'd seen them when he'd stood in front of me the night he rose.

Oh, God or Great Spirit or whatever was up there. I closed my eyes and breathed. Just breathed. Could it have been premonitory after all? Was Gwen trying to push me toward Kajika? What the hell was the huntress's endgame?

23

THE FIGHTING RING

*B*ee had been a mess when she'd stopped by our house to visit her grandson's body after I returned from the supermarket. The following evening, though, she was calm and composed, holding court like a sovereign in her little inn that had been lit with so many candles it glowed like my mother's last birthday cake.

I hugged her, but instead of returning my hug, she stood rigid until my arms glided off of her. I peered into her face, but her eyes wouldn't meet mine.

She knew.

She knew I was the reason her baby had been taken away from her.

"Bee?" I asked. "Are you mad at me?"

She raised her eyes to mine. They were red, and blue—like Blake's.

"Why did you have to involve him?" she asked me in a raucous voice.

"Involve him?"

Dad shifted uncomfortably next to me. "Didn't he help you dig up that grave?"

I almost said it was Blake's idea, but it was neither his, nor mine. Even though that's what I'd told the sheriff and my father. My gaze sank down to my black leather boots. "I didn't think he would try to finish the job in the middle of the night."

"Catori, my grandson would've done anything for you. Anything."

"But I didn't ask—"

"You never had to ask him to do anything."

"Oh, Bee, please. Don't blame me," I whispered.

"Bee. You promised not to hold it against her," Dad said.

She craned her neck to look into Dad's face. After a long moment, she looked back at me. "I'm sorry, Cat. I was looking for someone to blame. Being angry beats being miserable."

"Then blame me," I said. "If it can alleviate any of the pain, blame me. Just don't hate me. Please."

"I could never hate you." She gave me a desolate smile, then stepped toward another mourner while Dad pulled me aside.

"I'm sorry I told her about the old grave," he told me.

"It's okay."

I spotted Cass and was about to go to her when Dad asked, "Cat, why did you really dig it up?"

"Because the ground was caving—"

"Honey, I might've been a little out of it these past few days, but I'm not stupid."

I held Dad's gaze. "Blake read somewhere that there was buried treasure in the graves. I told him it was a legend, but he wouldn't leave it alone, so…so to prove it, I showed him the casket in the basement." Lying came too easily to me.

"There were only rose petals in that one."

"Exactly."

"You think there could've been treasure in it before she filled it with petals? You think Nova"—Dad's face whitened—"you think she found something inside?" His voice had dropped to a whisper. "Do you think that someone killed her for it?"

My eyes grew as wide as the mushroom tartlets arranged on the table next to us. "No!" I lied, incredulous at how close my father was to the truth.

Although Gwenelda was no treasure.

"You questioned her heart attack."

"Yes, but—"

"What if you were right to doubt it?"

"No. I wasn't right."

Dad's eyes glazed. He was mulling everything over. I didn't want him mulling this over.

"Hi, Mr. Price, Catori." Ace and Lily stood right in front of us. I hadn't even seen them approach. Both were dressed in black, but their clothes looked nothing like the clothes the rest of us were wearing. Ace's tuxedo, which he wore without the bowtie, was made-to-measure, making his lean torso seem broader. Lily's knee-length dress was a mix of silk and lace, all at once girlish and womanly. I tried to find fault in it, but there was no fault to be found. As I stared at her, I decided that Cruz had used me, because there was no way he could've found me prettier than his fiancée.

"Cruz," Dad began, making me snap to attention. I expected to see him, but then remembered Ace had dusted himself to resemble his future brother-in-law. "Could you settle something for me? Did my wife die of a heart attack?"

Ace held my Dad's gaze as he said, "Yes."

"You're sure?" Dad asked.

Ace frowned and his eyes gusted over mine. I gave the teeniest nod, hoping he'd get the message. "Yes."

"I was wrong to question the way she died, Dad. Like Bee, I was looking for someone to blame."

Dad sighed and his Adam's apple bobbed in his clean-shaven throat. "And in the other grave? The one you dug up with Blake... did you find treasure?"

"Treasure?" Ace asked with great interest.

I shot him a warning look. "No."

"Do you know where Blake read about this legend?" Dad asked.

Lily's eyebrows writhed, as though they had a life of their own. First in surprise, then in question.

"Online."

"Well, send me the link. I want to have it shut down before others come rooting around our backyard."

I nodded. "I'll contact the website first thing tomorrow."

Dad kissed my forehead. "I'll leave you with your friends." Before I could reiterate that they weren't my friends, he'd left.

"I can't believe you came," I told them. "You don't have to accept all the invitations thrown your way."

"And turn down free food and free wine? Now, why would we do that?"

"Don't they feed you in the *baseetogan?*"

"Excuse me?"

My face warmed. "Isn't that where you live?"

"Gwenelda teaching you Gottwa?"

Lily eyed me, but her expression was unreadable. Or maybe I was tired of trying to read it.

"No," I finally said.

Instead of hounding me, Ace said, "*Baseetogan* means bubble in Gottwa. We most definitely do not inhabit a bubble."

"What do you call it then?"

"*Neverra* or the Isle, or even Beaver Island. Take your pick."

"*Neverra* sounds like Neverland."

"Fitting," Ace said, with a wily smile. His eyes drifted to someone next to me.

"Hi, I'm Cass. We met that one time you two came over for lunch." Her long face was lit by a smile that was downright inappropriate for a wake.

Ace's smile widened. "I remember." He couldn't remember since he wasn't the one there.

"Lily, right?" Cass extended her hand. "I'm Cass."

"You just said that," I whispered in her ear.

"I'm a bit flummoxed. We don't get many celebrities around here."

"Flummoxed?" I said with a soft snort.

She squeezed my arm harder, smile still hewn into her pretty oval face. "I've been reading."

"Didn't think tabloids used such big words."

"I read books, Cat," she said with a good-natured laugh. "I've just finished *All the Absent Luminaries*. It was incredible."

Lily's face brightened, and then she signed something.

Ace translated. "She loves it, too, apparently."

"What do you mean 'apparently'? Don't you know everything about your sister?" I asked Ace.

His eyes widened, and so did Lily's, but it was less noticeable on her since her eyes were already outrageously large.

"Sister? I thought you two were engaged?" Cass said.

Right... "Didn't I say fiancée? I meant fiancée," I said.

"Is your brother planning on joining you later, Lily?" Cass asked, hopeful.

"Probably not," I said, at the same time as Ace said, "He might stop by."

I gave him a dirty look.

"What's happening later?" he asked Cass.

"Well, yesterday, I was invited to this ultra-private party. I wasn't going to go...with what happened"—her smile faltered as she looked at me—"but I thought about it all day, and I decided that I needed to clear my mind of...of everything, and I thought that maybe you would need that too, Cat."

"I'm not really a party person—"

"It's not really a party. It's more of an event."

"What sort of event?" I asked.

"An ultimate fighting match."

"Ultimate fighting?" Ace grinned. "Ace is a huge fan of that."

"I'm sure Ace is a huge fan, but Ace is not invited," I said through gritted teeth.

"Don't listen to her. Ace can absolutely come," Cass said.

Damn. Why did she have to have a crush on the most annoying faerie out there?

"Let me text him. See where he is. What time are you thinking of going?"

"Like, now," she said.

I was desperate to make an excuse to stay behind, but I couldn't leave Cass alone with a faerie.

"He's actually right outside," Ace said.

"Will you both be coming then?" I asked sweetly.

My snarky comment earned me a smile from Lily.

"My intended hasn't been feeling well, so I'm going to get her back home, but Ace will accompany you. After all, two pretty girls like you shouldn't go to these sorts of events without a chaperone. Men can be animals."

I narrowed my eyes at him. "Finally, something we agree on."

Cass's face whipped around like windshield wipers on a stormy day.

Ace shot me a wicked smile, then he took his sister's hand and pulled her toward the exit. "He'll meet you outside in five."

When the door closed, Cass asked, "Bad blood between the two of you, huh?"

"It's complicated."

"You don't mind Ace coming along, do you?"

Oh, I minded. "Of course not. Why would I?"

"Good. Because he's really, really, really handsome."

"He's engaged."

"Didn't stop you."

"It should've stopped me."

"It doesn't seem to have affected Lily and Cruz too much. Maybe they're even into open relationships. I mean, how old is she? Seventeen? Eighteen?"

"Eighteen."

"Well that's way too young to be engaged, if you ask me. It's probably not that serious between them."

"It's serious," I said before Cass went to grab her coat.

I located my father to tell him I was going to hang out with her. I didn't specify where. Besides, he didn't even ask.

As we turned the corner toward the employee lot, we found Ace shining like a glow-stick in the dark night.

"Hi," she gushed, combing her bangs out of her eyes with her fingerless-gloved hands. "Do you need a ride or did you drive here?"

"I parked a couple streets down."

Yeah, right.

"But I'd rather not drink and drive. Would you have space in your car? If not, I can call a cab."

"Better come with us, because one, you won't find many cabs around here, and two, it's quite a ways away," Cass told him.

I smirked. I couldn't help it. Not only was Cass's car on the compact side, but it was pink. To my great regret, Ace didn't even flinch when he saw it.

"Catori, you mind riding in the back? I don't think Ace will fit back there." She shot me a pleading look.

I wanted to point out that Ace wasn't much taller than I was, but one look at the backseat told me this wasn't about legroom. "Sure." After she reclined the front seat, I climbed in and pushed around the old magazines and candy wrappers. Cass was a neat freak when it came to her home, which she still shared with her mother and brother, but apparently she didn't extend this courtesy to her car. Dried crumbs prickled the back of my stockinged thighs.

"Nice color," Ace said as he clicked his seatbelt into place. For show, obviously. A car crash would unfortunately not kill him.

"I think so too, even though I picked it for the price. Apparently no one of driving age wants a pink car."

"No kidding," I said sarcastically.

As she backed up, she grinned. "Beats a hearse."

"Not quite sure. Hearses get preferential treatment. No one *ever* honks or tailgates."

"They're probably frightened of ending up in the trunk," Ace teased, which earned him a laugh from Cass. Not from me. Although the corners of my lips did quirk up. "Nice to see you finally letting loose, Catori," he added.

I forced the corners back down.

Ace chuckled. "So how'd you get these tickets, Cass?"

"Someone dropped them off yesterday."

"Who?"

"I don't know."

"What did the person look like?"

"Big guy with a blond ponytail. He was just driving through Rowan. I think he was one of the UFC competitors."

"Are you sure this is a legit game?" Ace asked.

Cass's blue eyes traveled over to his face. "What do you mean?"

"Maybe they're just recruiting pretty girls to make guys come into their club."

I snorted. "This is an ultimate fighting match. Since when do they need girls to get boys to watch a fight?"

"Can I see the tickets?" Ace asked.

"They're in my bag. Cat, can you grab them?"

I unzipped her raspberry-pink suede purse and located the envelope. I gave it to Ace without opening it.

He plucked the tickets out and studied them a moment. "Says here you're allowed to invite an unlimited amount of people. Either it's one dull club or the guy's hoping you bring along all of Rowan with you."

She shrugged.

As we drove past our town border, I started regretting coming along. I didn't mind the sight of blood—minding it would've been pitiful considering my future profession—but I was neither a fan of rowdy crowds nor of fighting. Unfortunately, though, it was way too late to turn back.

Cass maneuvered her little car down a dirt road that led to another dirt road, and then another. Grabbing on to the two front headrests, I pulled myself forward. "How can you find this place without a GPS?"

"He explained how to get there," she said.

Ace and I exchanged a look.

"It's right after the broken fence, in the old barn," she said, keeping her eyes cemented to the moonlit road.

Soon the car's high beams landed on a splintered wooden fence. She drove right over it, careless about blowing a tire on the frayed wire that had once upon a time linked the wooden posts.

After veering one last time onto a thinner dirt road, a red clapboard building surrounded by dozens of cars and trucks came into view.

"What is this place?" I whispered, as Cass pulled in behind a black truck with monster wheels. The person could probably just drive over Cass's car without scraping the rooftop.

Bodies moved within. I couldn't see them since the windows were perched right beneath the wooden rafters, but I could hear them shouting, cursing, laughing, yelling.

I clicked off my seatbelt and stepped out after Cass, tugging down my tight black dress that didn't feel appropriate for the place I was about to enter. Ace walked ahead of us, seemingly impatient and excited for what was going down inside.

When he swung the door open, I was hit by the stench of warm sweat and spilled beer. My gaze surfed over the teeming heads and pumping fists crushing green dollar bills, toward the elevated octagonal ring, to the two writhing, bare-chested males. One had a blond ponytail. The other had cropped black hair and was covered in intricate tattoos.

Heartbeat rivaling the boisterous crowd, I moved closer and closer to the woven rope fence and waited for the boy to turn.

Willed him to turn. The tattoos rippled with each punch, gleaming with beads of perspiration in the glowing barn. When Ponytail buckled, landing cheek first on the black mat, the referee grabbed the boy's wrist and pivoted him toward the roaring crowd.

Toward me.

24

HIS STORY

*A*lthough my muscles felt rigid, I managed to take a step back. I bumped into someone. Thick, sweaty palms steadied me. I brushed the stranger's hands off, then started backing away again, eyes locked on Kajika's.

His mouth, which had curved when the referee announced he was the winner, flattened. He glanced beyond me. I twisted around to see what he was looking at.

Ace and Cass.

I wondered if he knew what Ace was since inside the barn, he didn't glow. From the intensity of their glares, I suspected he did. I turned and walked over to them. Kajika might think I was choosing camps, but really, I was looking for a quick ride home.

"The blond guy in the ring gave Cass the tickets," Ace said.

"Yeah. I guessed. Um…Cass, I'm feeling a little agoraphobic. Could we go home?"

"But we just got here," she said, sticking out her lower lip. "Let's at least catch one match. How about I get us some drinks?"

"I don't want…" My voice trailed off since Cass was already making her way across the room toward a keg.

"Want me to fly you back?" Ace asked, typing out a message on his cell phone.

"I trust you less than I trust a drunken stranger in this room."

"Ouch." He was still typing.

"Calling your faerie squad for backup?"

He snorted, then finally looked up. "Loverboy was worried. Apparently, his hand lit up like a firecracker."

I disregarded the title he'd just given Cruz. I had other things to worry about, like the glowering hunter marching straight for us.

"Looking for trouble, Woodland-boy?" he growled.

"Woodland-boy?" Ace smirked. "Now, I've been a called a lot of things, but that's a first. I'm not too fond of the ring it has to it. Makes me sound like a forest pixie, doesn't it?"

"Your blond adversary"—I shifted to place myself between the two males before they could start a fight outside the ring—"invited us." Spectators who'd followed Kajika's trajectory circled around us.

"I never met him before tonight," Kajika said, spearing me with his dark eyes. I noticed they were a few shades lighter than black. Like charred caramel. If I could tell what color they were, I was standing way too close, but backing up meant getting nearer to Ace.

"Where's Gwen?" I asked. "I'm sure she knows how the invitations—"

"You were amazing out there!" Cass gushed, balancing three Solo cups in one hand.

Kajika's stance loosened at the interruption.

Cass handed me a cup, which I took mechanically.

"You two know each other?" she asked.

"No," I said, while Kajika said, "Yes."

I widened my eyes.

"Not well," he added, gaze traveling down my body, lingering on the short hem of my dress, before rising back up to my face. "You should go home with Cass. Girls shouldn't hang around here."

I crossed my arms. "Girls can do whatever they want these days."

"We're not totally alone." Cass gestured toward Ace.

"You shouldn't be hanging out with him, Catori," Kajika said in a low, rough voice.

"Hey, buddy, if I wanted to watch a domestic disturbance, I would've stayed home with the wife. I came to watch a fight," some guy shouted behind us. "*We* came to watch a fight!"

Several others voiced gruff agreements. And then the barn filled with a chant of, "Fight, fight, fight!"

Kajika's sharp jaw pulsed. "Wait for me. We'll go find Gwen together."

Ace puffed his cheeks out. "She doesn't take orders well. Trust me. I tried."

"Shut up, Ace," I said. "And I have no desire to see Gwen. So we'll just be leaving."

"Not with him," Kajika said, in a barely audible voice.

"I came with *him*."

"Well, you shouldn't have." Kajika stared hard at me; I stared back even harder. The referee grabbed Kajika's wrist, but the hunter swung it right out of his grasp. "I'm coming."

"By the way, Kaji, Mommy dearest says hi. She's thrilled you're back," Ace said.

Kajika jerked his gaze over the top of my head, eyes gleaming like starlit puddles of ice. Slowly, he moved backward, returning to the ring.

"Your mom knows him?" Cass asked Ace once the hunter had entered the octagonal cage.

"Yes. Very well."

I turned away from the elevated platform, clutching my cup so tight the plastic crinkled.

Cass wrinkled her nose. "Don't tell me they had an affair."

Ace's gaze slid to Kajika. "No. Mom has higher standards."

"Is she divorced from your dad?" Cass asked.

"No."

"But she sleeps around with other people?" my friend asked, taking a sip of beer.

"Yeah. It's no big deal in our family."

"Are you Mormon?"

He smiled. "Nope. Just polyamorous."

"Really?" I asked.

"Yes. Life's too long to spend it with just one person."

"I totally agree," Cass said. "On *The Reverence*, marriage is a fixed-term contract. It makes so much sense. If people were married for only five years, or ten, they'd enjoy each other way more. I bet my parents would've parted ways amiably instead of my dad running out on us."

"I like the way you think," Ace said, just as a whistle was blown.

"I know you want to go, Cat, but just one match. Pretty please?" Cass asked.

"Fine. One."

Cass squealed, pigtails flopping left and right. For as long as I'd known her, her hairstyle of choice had been pigtails. For prom, she'd twirled and pinned her pigtails into symmetrical buns, Princess Leia-style.

She blew her long bangs out of her eyes and sucked at her teeth. "Ooh. That's got to hurt."

I hadn't turned around. Over my shoulder, I snuck a glance at the ring. Kajika was straddling his adversary, pummeling his head with punches. His fists flew, blurring like hummingbird wings in flight. How was Ponytail not dead?

Finally the guy stopped raising his head…stopped flailing his legs. He lay so still I worried Kajika had killed him, but the referee didn't seem overly worried as he watched his chronometer. When he blew his whistle, Kajika stood up and spat out his tooth guard. He watched his fallen adversary until the latter trembled back to life. Extending one wrapped hand, he hoisted the blond back to his feet. After shaking on their fight, the hunter left the cage, yanked on his black hoodie, and headed straight for our corner of the barn under a landslide of cheers and whistles.

"I'm done for tonight." He wiped his brow, then took off his fingerless sparring gloves and stuck them underneath his armpit.

"I'm not going anywhere with you," I said.

Sweat made his forehead glisten. "You need to speak with Gwen and she needs to speak with you."

"I can't leave Cass—"

"I promised her father I wouldn't let her out of my sight," Cass lied, threading her arm through mine to lock me in place.

Kajika's eyes took on a feline glow. "You'll tell her father you never let her out of your sight, and then you'll tell him she slept over at your place."

"Influencing people already?" Ace said while Cass, whose eyes were vacant blue orbs, nodded robotically at Kajika.

"Let's go." Kajika started walking toward the barn door.

"You must be crazy if you think I'm going anywhere with you," I said.

He stopped midstride and spun around. "I thought you wanted her to stop interfering in your life." When I made no move to follow, he added, "Don't expect things to change then." He elbowed his way through the rowdy crowd, which was pressing toward the ring to observe the next fight.

Ace smirked. "Good choice, Kitty Cat."

I skewered him with a lethal look. "Cass, keep your phone on. I'll call you in an hour. And, Ace, if anything happens to her—"

"You're not seriously going?"

"I need to end this…this obsession she has with me," I told him, unlacing my arm from Cass's. "I trust you to get my friend home safely."

"I thought you didn't trust me."

"I'm begging you," I said, pulling on my coat, "and beggars can't be choosers."

Cass rolled her eyes. "Sheesh, I'm not a kid."

"I know." I hugged her, then ran to the door.

When I pushed through, oppressive, bone-chilling darkness slammed me. I pulled my black coat tighter around me, forgoing the buttons that would let air slip between the lining and the fabric of my dress. I squinted into the darkness for a man's shape, but the steel-colored clouds had obscured the moon and smattering of stars. The only light came from the high, slit-like barn windows. It did little to illuminate the parking lot.

Had he left already? I waited another minute. Still no one. I was about to return inside, when a rusty gray pickup truck swerved around the corner of the barn, wheels sending slushy snow flying all around. I hopped back to avoid getting soaked.

Kajika leaned over and rolled down the passenger window. "Changed your mind?"

I gave a sharp nod. As I opened the door, I said, "You have ten minutes of my time. *Not* the entire night."

I rolled the window back up, then strapped on my seatbelt.

Kajika veered down the narrow dirt road, away from the barn, eyes intent on the road. I prayed I'd made the right decision in accepting a meeting with Gwenelda. I prayed she would heed my demand for them to leave me out of their fight.

The car was as quiet as it was dark.

Too quiet.

Too dark.

Frigid obscurity bathed the fields around us.

Why the heck had I accepted a ride from a complete stranger?

Again.

I decided I had a serious problem with self-preservation. When had I become the sort of girl who hopped into cars with men I barely knew? What had happened to the Catori who prided herself on being street smart? Even as a kid, I never accepted candy from strangers—not even on Halloween. I was the girl who went around dressed up as a spooky ballerina or a dead Pocahontas, knocking on cobwebbed doors to see what horrific creature lurked behind.

The scarier the person's costume, the more I shrieked with delight. Maybe that was my problem: I didn't seek gratification; I sought thrills.

And apparently putting my life in strange men's hands thrilled me. I was seriously deranged.

I glanced at Kajika's face, which glowed from the dashboard's light. His nose was strong and sharp, as was his chin, his cropped black hair, his jaw, and his Adam's apple. Everything about him seemed honed and whittled with great precision.

"Where'd you get the car? Did you steal it?"

His gaze flicked toward me, before settling back on the road. I waited for him to answer, but he didn't.

I tried again. "Glad to be back?"

Again, he looked at me. Again, he didn't speak.

After a couple of really long and quiet minutes, I asked, "Giving me the silent treatment?"

Keeping his attention on the road this time, he said, "I'd rather not spend the ten minutes you're giving me discussing trivialities."

"It was a figure of speech. Like when people say, I'll be ready in a minute. It's rarely ever a minute." I sighed. "Look, I'll stay as long as it takes to convince you both to leave Rowan for good, and hopefully, it won't take all night."

"If that's your reason for coming with me, then I should drop you off back home."

"What? Why?"

"Gwenelda and I are not leaving."

"But you said—"

"I said I'd bring you to her so you could tell her to stop meddling in your life." His eyes locked on mine. "I didn't offer to host a farewell party."

Humiliation and anger warred within me. "I won't let you kill more people," I said through gritted teeth. "I don't think you understand how serious I am."

"Oh, we understand. We just don't have a choice. Our tribe must be reunited. It's time."

"Everyone has a choice!"

"Not when the Great Spirit chooses you."

"The Great Spirit chose *me*, yet you don't see me running around Rowan, sacrificing innocents to resurrect a clan of zombies!"

"We are not...zombies."

"You came out of a grave!"

"Where we were being preserved. We never died."

"And you think that's normal?"

"No. But the world isn't normal. You think faeries flying around are normal? Open your eyes, Catori. Open your eyes and look around. Your *normal* died with your mother."

My heart thumped like Ponytail's head back in the cage. "You're so insensitive."

"Being sensitive makes you weak."

"Well, being an asshole doesn't make you strong."

His eyes flicked back to the road. "No. I suppose it doesn't, but it makes you resilient. And after the hell I've lived through, I need every ounce of resilience I can get."

"Is that why you fought tonight? To test your *resilience?*"

"I was fighting because...because I was curious what my body and mind have become after two hundred years of magical inertness."

"You sure picked up driving quickly," I said.

"Blake"—he paused—"*taught* me."

The car became stiflingly quiet after that.

"Do you detest faeries as much as Gwenelda?" I asked after a long while.

"I detest them more."

"Why?"

"They killed my parents, my sisters, my tribe. They killed

everyone I cared for because our chief wouldn't agree to give them our land."

"I thought faeries lived in a *baseetogan*."

"They did, but they enjoyed roaming our lands and claiming them as their own. Fae are unsatisfied creatures who always desire more and more. They have a home in the *baseetogan*, yet they want another by the blue lakes, and another by the salty oceans, and another in the snowy mountains. They have mates, yet they're not faithful to them. Nothing is ever enough." His chest rose and fell and rose. "When my brother Menawa and I joined the Gottwas, we recounted the horrors that had befallen our people. We'd heard about their tribe wielding power over faeries, but these were tales woven around campfires. We did not know if there was truth to them, or if they were stories to help children sleep sounder at night. When Negongwa acknowledged their veracity, we offered our loyalty to the clan in exchange for their protection. I was eight, still a child, and Menawa fourteen, an adult already. Negongwa and his mate, Elika, took us in, fed us, clothed us, and tended to our wounds. Negongwa thanked the Great Spirit for bringing us safely to him. And then he asked Her to make the human world less attractive to the faeries, so they would stop persecuting humans. And She listened. She made the human world hostile to them."

"How?"

"Faeries aren't immortal, but they live very long lives. They used to be able to live out those years on our Earth, but She changed that. Now, they age at the same speed as humans when they venture outside the *baseetogan*. And She hindered their use of *gassen*. Before, they could replenish their stock of dust to create simultaneous illusions, but now, their supply is limited."

"If you and your brother weren't born into their tribe, how did you become faehunters? Did the Great Spirit bless you with powers?"

"A year after we'd pledged ourselves to the Gottwas, my brother mated with Gwenelda."

"You mean, married?"

Kajika's dark eyebrows knit on his forehead. "Yes," he finally said, as though he'd sieved through Blake's memories for the word. A chill shot through me when I realized that was probably exactly what he'd done. "They were each other's *aabitis*—halves. In Gottwa tradition, the couple paints opposite halves of their bodies with red earth, and slice their palms open with the tip of an arrow made of rowan wood and iron so that when they approach the shaman hand-in-hand, they are one."

I tried to imagine the ceremony. "Were they naked?"

"Yes. We did not hide our bodies underneath cloth like you do today. We cloaked ourselves with hides when frost descended on the land, laced leather around our feet, and wrapped strips of fabric around our sensitive parts to avoid scratches, but that was the extent of our attire."

My lips quirked up like a child's at the mention of sensitive parts. Thankfully, Kajika's eyes were on the road, and not on my face. I inhaled deeply to make my immaturity recede. "So they mixed their blood?"

"The truest bond is a bond made of *meekwa*."

I deduced *meekwa* was Gottwa for blood. "That's a great way to spread disease," the future doctor in me couldn't help but point out.

Kajika disregarded my remark. "A few weeks later, while we were out hunting for deer, a bear found us. Menawa rained arrows on the beast but he kept galloping, teeth bared. My brother grabbed my wrist and pulled me so fast through the woods, that the soles of my feet barely touched the ground. When we told our story to Negongwa, he turned very serious. He brought Menawa to the edge of the forest and asked him to concentrate on a pinecone perched in one of the tallest trees surrounding our camp. He asked him to make it fall.

"The tribe gathered around my brother and watched. The branch did not budge for so long that people returned to their wigwams, but Negongwa stayed put, and so did Gwenelda and

Elika. When my brother tried to abandon the effort, they urged him to keep his eyes on the branch. To concentrate. They stayed by Menawa's side until twilight filled the sky. Noticing how heavy my lids had become, Elika sat cross-legged on the cold earth and took me in her arms, letting me curl into her lap to sleep.

"At dawn, I woke to her chanting. Not only had the pinecone fallen, but so had every pinecone on the tree. There were mounds of them resting at my brother's feet."

"So Gwen's blood gave your brother powers?"

Kajika nodded.

"How did you get yours? Did they marry you off to someone else in the tribe?"

"I was only twelve. Too young for a mate. The Gottwas mate during their fifteenth summer."

"Then how—"

"Negongwa pressed his palm to mine. A few weeks later, I changed, like Menawa."

Enraptured by his story, I realized I had pivoted my entire body toward him. "Wait, you're not fifteen, right?"

"No. I'm twenty-one."

"Then you did eventually marry."

"I did."

"Is your wife buried in one of the rose petal graves?"

"My mate is buried, but not underneath any rose petals." His lips pressed tight and his nostrils flared. "It took many springs for the news of the transference to reach the fae who hadn't left the *baseetogan* since the Great Spirit cursed them. Realizing that Negongwa could potentially create more hunters—something he would never have done—fae poured into Rowan to annihilate the Gottwas. We lost so many that day, so ill-prepared were we for the attack."

"They killed your mate?"

Kajika was so very still, he seemed carved in stone rather than flesh. Finally, he nodded. "They only lost one of theirs," he continued in a voice that rumbled like the truck's ancient engine.

"Negongwa's son killed Maximus Wood, their ruthless, lawless leader."

"Maximus?"

"The faerie you brought tonight...Ace. He's Maximus's grandson. He resembles his grandfather so much that when I saw him, I thought it was Maximus risen from the dead. But I watched when Chesskan pierced Maximus's heart with an arrow. Maximus turned gray like a burnt log, before flaking apart, and drifting in the wind."

"That's how you kill them? An arrow through the heart?"

"Our arrows only immobilize them."

"Then how did Maximus die?"

"Chesskan had been bleeding, and some of his *meekwa* had stained the arrow tip. When a hunter's blood comes in contact with a faerie's heart, it kills them. Our blood puts out their fire. The Great Spirit had told Negongwa how to kill faeries, but he'd never shared the knowledge with us for fear of turning his people into bloodthirsty murderers.

"The attack made us vengeful, and the knowledge that we could now kill the creatures made us arrogant. Many in our tribe began to disrespect our chief. Like Maximus's body, people began to flake away from the tribe. Chesskan tried to gather them again, telling them there was strength in numbers, but they would not listen. Too many loved ones had been ripped from their arms during the attack.

"Several fights broke out over the years. We heard about them from neighboring tribes or from settlers' accounts. We did not know how many of our people had survived, but we imagined few."

"So you might not be the only hunters."

Kajika stayed silent. "We haven't found others yet."

After some time, I asked him, "What's different with your blood?"

"*Our* blood"—he watched for a reaction; I didn't give him one—"is pure iron."

"That's medically impossible. Then again, so is emerging from a two-century long slumber," I mused. "How do you like the modern world?"

"It's different, Catori. Faster. Easier in some ways, and harder in others. We had to hunt for food before. We had to trade with settlers. We had to skin animals and tan their hides. We didn't live to accumulate wealth like you do today. We didn't travel away from our families…unless we lost them," he added in a dismal voice.

I didn't want to feel empathy, but I did. "How did you end up in rose petal graves?"

"One day, their *gajeekwe*"—he looked at me—"you know who that is?"

I shook my head.

"He is the king's advisor. Like a minister. I believe they call him *wariff*."

"Yes. I've heard that word."

Kajika observed me. "You've spent a lot of time with faeries?"

"What did the *gajeekwe* want?" I asked.

He turned his gaze back to the winding asphalt road. The woods around us were thick and unfamiliar. I believed we were driving by Manistee Forest, but I couldn't tell what side of it we were on.

"His name was Jacobiah Vega."

I stopped contemplating the dark trees. "*Vega?* Was he related to Cruz?"

"He was Cruz's father." I bit my bottom lip as Kajika continued with his story, "He came to speak to Negongwa. He supposedly wanted to make peace with the hunters. We believed he wanted to trick our people but our chief trusted him. They spoke at length of a truce. On the day Negongwa agreed to meet Jacobiah to sign the treaty, the *golwinim* ambushed us. They descended upon our people, slashing through our bodies, filling us with their poisonous fire, asphyxiating us with their *gassen*."

"I know *gassen*."

"Good."

"I also know what the *golwinim* are."

"I know. You taught Blake what they were."

The reminder made my stomach roll. "How long will you keep his memories?"

"I don't know. Maybe I'll always have them. Or maybe they'll fade away in time."

"Is it strange?"

"Sharing a person's mind?"

I nodded.

"It's unpleasant. And hard, since I have to differentiate between his and mine. When I saw Cass earlier, I thought of her as my friend...I trusted her. But I can't tell if it's my instinct that dictates me to like her or Blake's memories."

"Probably Blake's memories. He adored Cass."

"He adored you more." His voice felt as dark as the night pouring over the frostbitten landscape.

"It must be very confusing to be around me, then," I said softly, coiling a long strand of hair around my fingers.

The ensuing silence was painful and awkward...painfully awkward. So I asked him about the *golwinim's* attack.

"Only thirteen people survived this time. After the tribe scattered, we were still over a hundred. They massacred us. And then they took pleasure spearing dead hunters with poles which they planted around the rowan circle Negongwa and twelve of us had managed to reach."

The images he painted were so vivid that if I closed my eyes, I was able to hear the screams, smell the blood, picture the carnage.

"We called it *Makudewa Geezhi*. The Dark Day." His Adam's apple dipped and rose in his throat. "When twilight came and concealed the misery around us, when the *golwinim* flew away, Negongwa implored the Great Spirit for help. She came to him in his sleep and instructed him to locate the *bazash* who grew perennial roses."

"*Bazash*," I whispered, rolling the word on my tongue. It didn't sound unfamiliar. Had I read about it in *The Wytchen Tree* or had Grandma Woni taught it to me?

"A *bazash* is a half fae and half human," he explained. "It took us days to find her. But eventually we came upon her hut. When we returned to camp with several bundles of roses, the eleven others had built coffins from rowan wood. Do you understand how low we had sunk to envisage such a solution? We accepted to bury ourselves alive under faerie-grown roses."

I did not want to offer him pity. Besides, I doubted Kajika was after my pity. "Did you have to go into the *baseetogan* to find the *bazash*?"

He snorted. "A hunter can't enter the *baseetogan*. Only faeries or humans willing to become faeries' slaves may enter. Fortunately for us, they repudiate most *bazash*. They call them the fallen even though they don't *fall out* of the faerie kingdom, they are tossed out, like rotting carcasses."

Kajika's loathing for the faeries was so strong it was something tangible, something sharp, and deadly, and bitter. His jaw juddered with it. The tendons in his hands moved with it. The vein in his neck throbbed with it.

"Why did the *bazash* help you?" I asked, to reroute his soundless rage before he unleashed it on the car—which he was driving too fast—or on me. I didn't think he'd kill me, but I sensed he didn't particularly appreciate me...in spite of Blake's memories.

"They helped us because faeries are unkind to them. *Bazash* are not considered equal to faeries; their magic is weaker. They are ostracized and bullied within the *baseetogan*, relegated to menial positions. The *bazash* who refuse to kowtow to faeries are thrown out, left to fend for themselves." He tipped his chin toward the windshield. "You asked earlier where I got this car—"

"It's Holly's car."

His lips parted in surprise.

"She's a good friend of my family's. She used to drive baskets of tomatoes over in this car. But that was before she taught my mother how to grow them herself. After that, she stopped coming. I was really small but I remember. It was around the time my grandfather died." As I dug through my memories of Holly, I recalled the day she'd made an orchid bloom before my very eyes. "Is she a *bazash*?"

"No."

"Oh." There went my conspiracy theory. Then again, if she were a faerie, she wouldn't be helping hunters. "What happened to the rose-growing *bazash*?"

"She died a long time ago. Outside the *baseetogan*, their lifespan is equal to a human's."

I toyed with the seatbelt. The fabric was darker in spots, timeworn like Holly herself. "Is that where you're hiding? At Holly's?"

"We are not hiding."

"Right..." I drummed my fingers against the armrest and was about to ask why Holly lent him her car, when a shape materialized on the road ahead. The high beams hadn't reached it, yet it glowed. "Kajika! Watch out!"

He jammed his foot on the brake pedal. The car skidded, swerved, and spun, but miraculously, didn't topple over. It must have unfastened Kajika's seatbelt as his body airlifted before dropping over mine like a heavy blanket, knocking the breath from my lungs. The car stopped spinning, but my heart didn't.

My fingers crawled to the seat belt buckle. Trembling, I pressed it open, pumped the door handle, and then pushed against Kajika's hard body, managing to shift him just enough to squeeze out of the car. I dropped to my knees against the freezing ground and vomited until only bile came up. And then, only then, did I trail my eyes up the glowing bare feet and legs hovering before me.

25

THE SISTER

"*A*re you crazy?" I yelled at Lily.

Lily brandished her phone in front of me. **Ace asked me to check on you.**

"Well, next time, text me." I spat, trying to remove the sour taste in my mouth.

"What are you doing here, *pahan?*" Kajika stood next to me, legs solidly planted in the ground, unfazed by our near collision. Unlike him, I was a quivering mess. Pressing myself back up was a feat. Staying up was an even greater feat as my limbs shook.

"She came to check you hadn't offed me," I said in Lily's place.

"*Offed* you?"

"Killed me off," I explained.

"I would never kill one of my own."

"Good to know." I rubbed my palms against my dress. My stockings were ruined, with holes extending down my calves and up my thighs.

Lily brandished her phone. Ace's name flashed on the screen.

"I really don't feel like speaking to him, Lily," I said.

She shook her head and pointed to Kajika.

He swiped the phone out of her fingers and pressed it against his ear. "Ace Wood," he growled. I expected him to rip him a new one, but those were the only words that came out of his mouth. Instead, he listened. And as he listened, he shifted away from Lily and me, muscles coiling in his bare calves. How was he not freezing, standing barefoot in a pair of shorts?

Lily poked my arm. The heat from her skin penetrated right through my jacket sleeve. I turned toward her. She connected her thumb and index finger in the okay signal.

I nodded. Then arms crossed, I kept watch on Kajika. Finally, the hunter ended the call and stalked back to us. He handed the phone to Lily.

"Practical things, phones," he said.

"What was that about?"

"I'm going to drop you off at home."

"What about meeting with Gwen?"

"You'll see her tomorrow, or after tomorrow. We're not going anywhere."

"But—"

Kajika tipped his head down so that he was facing me. "Not tonight," he said, his voice between a growl and a whisper. He whipped his head toward Lily who still hovered close to me, gaping at Kajika. If she were standing, the top of her head would reach his pecs, but hovering, she was the same height. I suddenly felt short, which had never, ever happened. "Lily, your brother said you should go home. Apparently, your mate needs to speak with you."

After getting over the shock that he'd used the word *mate*—which sounded downright bestial—to describe Cruz, I gaped at Lily. She didn't meet my gaze. I supposed, or maybe I hoped, things had gotten back to normal for her. From the tight expression that marred her alabaster face, I supposed they hadn't.

For the longest time she didn't budge, but then her gaze flicked to mine. Her eyes glistened like polished silver. This time, I was the one who connected my fingers in a circle to ask if she was okay.

She gave me the weakest shake of her head. I frowned, and she dropped her gaze to the ground below her hovering feet. "Kajika, can you wait in the car?"

He strode away from us, but made no move to get into the car, nor did he afford us much privacy as his eyes stayed trained on us.

"What's up?" I asked Lily, in a soft voice.

Her fingers flew across her phone's screen. **Cruz and I can't agree on what flowers to pick for our wedding ceremony.**

"Seriously?"

No. But if you think I'd confide in you, then you're delusional.

"I said I was sorry. I didn't know you were engaged."

The second time, you knew.

"Ace said faeries were polyamorous," I countered. Granted, he'd told me just tonight.

Well, I'm not. And Cruz promised me—she erased the last two words and replaced them with—**vowed to love only me.**

"He does love only you," I said.

Then why does he still ask about you? She looked at me, head tipped to the side, pale cheeks splotched with emotion.

"Because he marked me, Lily. Find a way to break the bond, and he'll stop asking."

Her head straightened. **The only way to break a bond is death.**

My stomach hardened. I regretted my suggestion, and backed away before she could fill me with her faerie dust, but then I remembered she'd used it on Blake, so she probably didn't have any left.

She shook her head and with trembling fingers typed, **I can't believe you'd think me capable of that. I may be hurt, but I'm not cruel.**

And with that, she shot up into the sky, piercing the thick layer of ashen clouds.

"A faerie marked you?" Kajika asked.

I exhaled slowly. "What did Ace want?"

Kajika marched toward me and picked up my hand. "Where?"

I yanked it away from him, heart galloping, and said, "Don't touch me." The top of my hand glowed faintly. I blinked in surprise.

"This is how they're tracking us!"

I stuffed my hands into my coat pockets. "One more reason not to hang around me."

Kajika shot me a feral look that made a breath snag in my throat. "Which faerie did this to you?" he asked, his voice low and *very* rough.

I didn't answer.

"Who is Lily's mate?"

I still didn't answer. He would find out sooner or later, but it wouldn't be from me.

"I'm surprised he hasn't killed you yet. You do understand the function of faerie branding?"

"I heard." Faeries marked to kill, yet I couldn't believe that's what Cruz had in mind when he'd linked me to him with his magic. He was a kind faerie; he'd saved Gwenelda. "I think he marked me to...as you said earlier...keep track of hunters."

"We must kill him."

"Absolutely not!"

"You are putting us at risk, Catori."

"At risk? This isn't the nineteenth century, Kajika. There are satellites and phones and something called the Internet. All faeries need to do today is click on a computer to locate a human. This mark is just a quicker access."

"You don't understand how our world works!"

"Well, you don't understand how *this* world works!" Annoyance blistered my tone, which, in turn, blistered the hunter's face.

"At least I'm trying to understand. I've been around for three days now, which I've spent trying to catch up on two hundred years while being haunted with memories that aren't mine." Jaw pulsing, he rounded the truck's hood and got in, slamming his door shut.

I balled my fingers into fists and started walking. Like Dad said at the funeral, I was stubborn. The truck rumbled to life, and then two beams of light carved the night, illuminating the way. I willed Kajika to drive away.

"You're going to freeze to death." His voice drifted through the open passenger window.

"That should break the bond, no?"

Kajika growled while I walked on. And on. Minutes went by and still the truck rattled next to me.

"Just leave me alone already," I said.

"When your father found your mother, he wanted to die. He cut his wrist open with a scalpel."

I whipped my face toward Kajika. "What are you talking about?"

"He phoned Blake. Told him what he'd done. Asked him to take care of you. Blake ran out of the restaurant and drove over to your house. He found your father lying next to your mother, soaked in his own blood. He managed to stop the bleeding. Apparently, you taught him how to make a tourniquet right before he left for the army. You made him do it over and over. You were afraid he'd get hurt if he didn't master the technique."

I stopped walking and faced the car, which stopped in turn. "How do you—" I paused midsentence. Goosebumps crawled over my skin. I shivered and drew the coat tighter around me, as though tugging on the fabric could release more heat.

"I don't know if he ever told you," Kajika continued, "but he managed to save two lives thanks to you. A boy from his platoon whose leg was blasted off by a landmine, and your father's."

"Why are you telling me this?"

"Because you mean the world to your father, Catori. Without you, he will end his life, and this time, Blake won't be around to save him. If you don't want to become a murderer—like us—get in the car."

Although I didn't like taking an order from Kajika, I pulled the door open and climbed in. "Don't ever use Blake again to get me to do something." I rolled the window back up.

His face darkened, and as soon as I attached my seatbelt, he took off, tires screeching so loudly the trill penetrated right through the windshield.

I crossed my arms and my legs, partly in annoyance and partly because knotting my limbs up like a pretzel helped conserve some heat.

We drove in silence for several minutes. Kajika's forehead was ridged in concentration. He didn't seem like he'd forgotten the way so I imagined he was thinking of Ace's phone call. I didn't ask him about it, certain I would see the faerie soon enough.

Silver sand dunes rose in the distance, and then the gnarled trunks of Holly's cherry trees appeared resembling a colossal, natural fence.

"The youngest of my sisters...she froze to death one winter night."

Kajika's voice startled me out of my topographical contemplation.

"We were moving to find shelter from a violent snowstorm. The air was white with snow. It accumulated so fast that after barely an hour of walking, I couldn't see my legs from the knees down. I remember it being painful to move. My calves felt like they were covered in bruises and insect bites. They burned and prickled yet I pushed on because there was no other option. By the time we'd reached the rock wall in which my father had spotted a cave during a hunt, my mother called out all our names to gather us around her. And that's when we saw that one child was missing. My father and Menawa rushed out of the cave and retraced their footsteps. They were gone so long." He paused.

I knew the ending. He'd started with it, yet I didn't want him to pause. I parted my lips and sucked in some air, and then I uncrossed my arms. "Did they find her?" I asked so that he would finish the story.

He nodded. "When they returned, she hung over my father's shoulder, wrapped in many furs, limp like the fabric doll she'd sewn for me that summer. At first, even though her thin legs were purple,

I thought there was still life inside her, but then my mother wailed, and that's when it hit me that my sister had passed on to the spirit world. I was only six, Catori. And she was only nine. It was the first time I realized that age didn't matter when it came to dying."

I took slow breaths, trying to rid my mind of the images Kajika had conjured up. "Life can be unfair," I whispered.

"That is why, when you have a fair chance at making it, you don't throw it away."

"Would you have driven away?"

"No."

"Because I'm a hunter?"

"Because I will not cause another person's death."

"Yet you spoke about killing the faerie I'm bonded to."

"Faeries are not people to me. They are evil molded in the form of a person."

I ground my lips together. I didn't have the strength or the desire to argue with Kajika, who was apparently as stubborn as I was. I never thought I would meet my match, but I had.

A few minutes later, we reached the cemetery and my dark house. Dad was not waiting up for me. Had Cass phoned to tell him I was sleeping at her place? Kajika slid the truck in front of the porch. He didn't stop the engine, nor did he look at me as I got out, his eyes on the ten remaining graves.

26

TREE OF LIFE

My head still full of Kajika's stories, I went to bed, but didn't sleep until the sky lightened. I dreamt I was plowing through a snowstorm with my mother. I couldn't see her, but I could hear her whispering that I shouldn't be scared. That once I stepped through the yellow door, I would be safe.

I never stepped through the yellow door. I woke up before reaching it, drenched in sweat, heart beating like the tail of a frightened fish. My hand prickled. I twisted it in front of my face. It didn't glow like it had last night, but there were two white marks on it, like an old scar.

I lay in bed a long time, trying to make sense of my jumbled emotions. I watched my yellow dream catcher, which made me think of the yellow door. Strange how my subconscious had turned it into a conduit to safety when I'd always considered it a gateway to something so dreadful I'd painted it white.

With my heel, I felt the lump under my mattress. I got up, the hardwood floors cold against the soles of my sleep-warmed feet, dug the book out, and settled back under my comforter to read. I landed on the page with the drawings of the hunters' faces and studied Kajika's. Its accuracy made me flip back to the front of the book in search of the author's name, but none had magically appeared. Had another hunter written this book? That would mean the twelve graves outside my window hadn't been the resting place of the last hunters…that others had survived.

Of course. Kajika had mentioned they were thirteen, which stirred an old memory. The thirteenth hunter, the one who'd buried his kin, was my great-great-great-grandfather. What was his name again? I massaged my temple until it came back to me: Taeewa. Had *he* written the book? But then, if he'd written it, why was it *sent* to us? Shouldn't we have owned it?

I rocketed out of bed, tumbling to my knees, and yanked the book's packaging from underneath my bed. Styrofoam peanuts scattered all around, clinging to my sleep shorts and to my comforter. I dusted them off, then pulled the tabs closed and read the label affixed to it. Our address was handwritten on the front. There was no return address and no postage, yet I remembered the mailman offering to send it back.

I rushed around my room, pulling on black jeans and a white shirt, then brushed my teeth and hair at record speed. Before leaving, I hid the book under my mattress, next to the opal necklace, and rearranged my comforter so that my bed looked somewhat made.

My father wasn't home, but he'd left a note next to the coffee machine telling me he'd gone to see Bee. I pushed aside the white curtains my grandmother had crocheted and peered through the kitchen window. The sky was silver and slate, but it wasn't snowing. Stuffing the box in one of Mom's fabric totes, I headed out.

The walk was quiet. No faerie buzzed about, no hunter lurked. Ice-laden branches tinkled as I passed beneath them. Snow crunched under my shearling boots. I walked past the sand dunes, past the crooked cherry trees. Smoke drifted from Holly's house. Temptation to pay her a visit was so great that I almost gave in, but then I remembered the hunters were staying there. I wouldn't willingly approach the place where they dwelled. After all, I'd asked them to stay away from me. Therefore, I had to stay away from them. Logic at its best. So I kept walking, past the pontoon that stretched like a pointed finger inside the dark blue lake.

In the quiet marina, tarpaulin-wrapped boats and goldeneye ducks bobbed like bath toys while gulls circled above, scavenging for food. Out in the distance, a handful of fishing boats braved the white crests and the freezing spray shimmying across the surface of the lake to bring in northern pike. Blake's grandfather had been a fisherman. He took us trawling one winter. Even though he'd bundled me up with polar fleece blankets, my teeth chattered throughout the entire trip, and my fingers turned white and stiff. It took a steaming bath and two mugs of hot chocolate to thaw me out.

I smiled sadly at the memory. After contemplating the boats a while longer, the sound of waves filling me like a familiar pulse, I started walking again. As I passed Astra's Bakery, I doubled back and went inside to buy something to eat.

In the warm months, the place brimmed with people in shorts and visor caps, and children in candy-colored swimsuits and inflatable armbands. Today, the long wooden tables and benches were populated with a handful of people. Tourists, I assumed, since I didn't recognize any of them. Some openly stared at me as I made my way to the counter. Although they kept talking, their conversations became hushed, as though someone had turned the volume down on their voices.

I concentrated on the appetizing display of baked goods, all homemade by Astra Sakar. At least, that's how it used to be when I was a kid. She was an old lady today, with terrible arthritis, who'd left the running of her shop to her daughter, Stella.

Since no one was behind the counter, I called out, "Hello?" and peered through the round window of the swing door.

"Coming." A couple seconds later, Faith pushed through the swing door. "Well, if it isn't Catori Price," she said, drying her hands on a red-and-white checkered kitchen towel. She tossed it underneath the counter and splayed her fingers against the white marble countertop. Her long, layered auburn hair shone red underneath the glass pendant light, and her blue eyes gleamed with the same malicious sheen they'd always possessed. She tipped her neck back to look at me. "Haven't stopped growing, have you?"

Come on, you're nineteen, not five. "Haven't sprouted a heart yet, have you?"

Her lips curled with a smile.

"Weren't you enrolled in the actor's studio?" I asked.

"Weren't you studying to be a doctor?"

I hadn't meant it as criticism. "Really, Faith? Even though you didn't show up at the funeral, I know you heard what happened to my mother."

"Yeah. I heard."

No *I'm sorry for your loss.* Whatever. I didn't need Faith Sakar's condolences.

"Did you come to tell me what a bitch I was, or did you want something to eat?" she asked.

"I'm not hungry anymore."

As I headed back toward the door, she called out, "At least I attended Blake's wake without running off for a three-way with Cass and Ace Wood."

The muted conversations around me stopped altogether. My cheeks flamed, as did my hand. To think that during our junior year of high school, I'd saved Faith from choking on a piece of meat. Maybe I shouldn't have meddled with Mother Nature's plan for her. I spun around, about to set her straight, when I noticed Lily sitting at one end of the long table. Twisted around on the bench, she stared at me. As did the two girls beside her, who I assumed were faeries, since I couldn't imagine Lily hanging out with mere mortals.

The four men sitting at the opposite end of the communal table were also observing me with eyes that gleamed gold. I had this niggling feeling that they were faeries too. And my niggling feeling grew so strong, it intensified the throbbing of my scarred hand.

"What are you doing here, Lily?" I asked.

Her eyebrows slanted with a frown.

"We're having breakfast," one of her friends said. The tips of her hair were dyed pink, the same pink that was smeared over her lips and fingernails. "Is it true?"

"Is what true?"

"You and Ace Wood?"

I glowered at Faith who'd folded her arms in front of her chest smugly.

"Cruz, Ace... Who's next?" asked Pink Hair.

I felt like I was in high school all over again, but this wasn't high school. Didn't faeries have better things to do than gossip? I shook my head, exasperated and angry, with them and with myself. If I hadn't succumbed to Cruz's charm, there wouldn't be rumors about me circulating through Neverra and Rowan.

"I heard your boyfriend was bored, Nadia, so maybe *he'll* be next?" a familiar voice said from behind me. I whirled around. Never had I been so thankful to see Ace in my life. And never in my life would I have expected the faerie—any faerie for that matter—to stand up for me.

Pink Hair, aka Nadia, sat up straighter, as though some invisible force pinched her shoulders, and the four men rose in unison, the metal feet of the bench scraping against the hardwood floors. Rigidly, they bowed their heads to Ace.

Ace paid them no attention, his gaze wholly focused on his sister. She made a few brisk hand movements. Instead of speaking, he signed something back. I wasn't sure if it was a quicker method of communication or a more secretive way of passing information. Lily glanced at me, then at her brother, then finally twisted back around on the bench.

"Your friends were just leaving, weren't they?" he asked Lily.

She gave the slightest nod, and the golden bun of hair pinned at the nape of her neck bobbed and glinted in the yellow glow of the glass ceiling light that dangled over her end of the table.

Lily's friends stood up, and, flanked by two of the golden-eyed men, walked out of the bakery. I watched them through the large windows, wondering if they would shoot up into the sky, but then remembered Faith was watching them. Instead of flying, they walked toward the little boathouse.

Faith cleared her throat loudly. "I hope you're planning on paying for the people who left, Mr. Wood. We're not a soup kitchen."

Ace clicked his fingers, and one of the men who'd stayed behind shot toward the counter. He took a wad of bills from his jacket pocket, and peeled two hundreds from the roll.

"Keep the change." Ace walked toward the seat Nadia had vacated. "So where did they get the heinous idea that we hooked up?"

Heinous indeed. I nodded toward my nemesis.

Faith, whose repertoire of emotion varied between disdain and malice, became agitated. "Are you denying you went out with Cass and Catori last night, Mr. Wood?"

"Faith, right?" he said.

She didn't bother acquiescing.

"Although I rarely deny being involved with a pretty woman— be it true or not—Catori turned me down last night. So it would be highly unjust, for her sake, to perpetuate such a rumor."

I whipped my head toward him. He winked at me. *Twice*. This was the second time in a matter of minutes that Ace stood up for me. Why was he being nice? Did he need something from me?

"So you just did my cousin, then?" Faith asked.

Ace shot her a censuring glare. "I'd like a coffee. Black. Cat, come sit with us."

"I should get going. I need to stop by the post office before it closes."

"Two minutes. Come here for two minutes." He patted the seat next to him.

"Why?" I frowned.

"Don't you want to know what Kajika and I discussed?"

I did, but I really didn't want to sit with Lily, who despised me, and rightfully so.

"Two minutes, Cat. It's the least you can do after I defended your honor."

I snorted, but then I made my way toward him. I did microscopically owe him for calling out Faith. "So what was so urgent you almost had me killed?"

Ace frowned. "Had you killed?"

"Lily appeared on the road, right in front of the car. We almost crashed."

He glanced at his sister who lowered her gaze to her empty teacup.

After a too-quiet minute, I said, "So what did you tell Kajika?"

He slid his blue eyes back toward me. "I told him not to invite any more relatives to visit. The same goes for you."

Faith brought his coffee over. Even though she didn't look at us, I could tell she was listening from the indolent way she deposited the complimentary jug of milk and pot of sugar. Faith never did anything slowly.

"Have you forgotten what I think of my extended family?" I asked.

Ace linked his long fingers together and placed both hands on the table in a business-like manner. "I feared what you thought of them might've changed after speaking with Kajika."

"It didn't."

"Good." He tipped his chin toward the tote I'd placed between us on the bench. "What's in the bag?"

"Something I need to mail out today."

"What is it?"

"A book."

"What sort of book?"

"An encyclopedia on venereal diseases. Perhaps you'd like to read it?"

He smirked. "Sounds lovely, but I'll pass."

"Catori?" I looked up at the perky voice that belonged to none other than Stella Sakar, Faith's mother. Plucking off a pair of tan leather gloves, she moved swiftly toward me, but paused when she noticed Ace and Lily Wood. Did I imagine the slight dip of her head as she stared at them? The Woods *were* celebrities in the human world, I reminded myself, which would explain Stella's odd reaction to them.

"Hi, Stella," I said, standing up.

She set a paper bag by her brown suede boots and hugged me. "How are you, sweetie?" Her skin looked golden and tight, as though she'd gotten plastic surgery on some tropical island, and her auburn hair gleamed with amber highlights.

"I'm okay."

"Back so soon from your trip, Ma?" Faith said, an accusatory edge to her voice. Her tone brought back the loud fight they'd had during prom. Stella had come as a chaperone, which had incensed Faith. She'd yelled at her mother about trust and boundaries. *If you don't stop meddling with my life, you'll drive me away just like you drove Dad away,* Faith had said.

Stella Sakar stroked my cheek, flicking the memory from my mind. "As soon as I heard what happened to Nova, I boarded a plane to come back. And then I received the news about Blake. It's so awful. You're such a brave girl." I was about to tell her I wasn't, when she continued, "I was just at Bee's, and your father was telling me how wonderful you've been at taking care of him, how lucky he is to have a daughter like you."

How had such a tender woman spawned a girl like Faith? My former schoolmate must have gotten her forked tongue from her father, who, like her cousin's father, had run off on them. Rumor had it he hadn't left for another woman, though... I didn't know if he was gay—and didn't care, unlike some more close-minded folks in our small town—but if he was anything like Faith, I was relieved he hadn't stuck around Rowan. The town wasn't large enough for two vipers with oversized egos.

"Objectivity isn't in my father's DNA," I told her.

"You forget I've known you forever too, Catori. I *know* you're an extraordinary girl."

I wrinkled my nose, about to repeat that I really wasn't, when Ace spoke up, "I think you forgot to put your book in the package."

I turned around, about to yell at him for going through my things, when I noticed that my bag had fallen and that the ripped cardboard box had slipped out. I kneeled and stuffed it back inside the bag.

"Why are you lugging around an empty box?" Ace asked.

I was about to tell him it was none of his business, but decided that would just spark his interest. "Because I'm trying to track down who sent it to me."

"Did you peel the postage off?" Stella asked as I stood back up.

"No. There wasn't any."

One of her eyebrows hiked up. "But it came in the mail?"

"Yes. Matt dropped it off."

"Maybe he's the one who sent it to you, then," she said.

"Matt wouldn't send me a book about—" I stopped myself short. I was in the presence of faeries. Even if I trusted Stella, I did not trust the others. "About gardening."

"Gardening?" Stella said. "That's Holly's expertise."

A strange stillness draped over the bakery.

Faith snickered. "Maybe Holly's looking for someone to help her till soil. After all, isn't she turning a hundred this year? You'd look so cute in a pair of her overalls, Cat."

I frowned, not because of Faith's tactless jab—I was used to those—but because a part of me wondered if Holly could've sent me the book.

"I know her handwriting," Stella said. "If you show me the package, I can tell you if it came from her."

So I showed her the package. After scrutinizing it, she confirmed it was Holly who'd written out my address. Apparently she was the only person in Rowan who drew loopy Os.

She handed me the box, then bent at the waist to retrieve her paper bag. "I just made these divine purple-velvet cupcakes, Mr. Wood. They have candied beetroots in them. Would you care to sample one?"

"You had time to bake cupcakes, Ma?" Faith asked. "Didn't you just arrive?"

Stella opened a plastic container filled with her purple-frosted creations and presented them to Ace. After he picked one out, she tendered the box to Lily who stared at her brother. When he nodded, she delicately extricated one and took a bite. She chewed slowly, swallowed, then gave Faith's mother an approving tilt of her head.

I used the distraction to leave the bakery. "It was nice seeing you all." I really only meant Stella.

"Wait. You have to try one," she said.

"Um, I'm...not really a beet person."

"But these are special beets." She winked at me.

Lily ate another bite, and I swear her eyes took on a hazy sparkle, as though she were slipping into some altered state of being. Could the cupcakes really be *that* good?

"I hope they'll be to your liking, Mr. Wood," Stella said when Ace still hadn't touched his. "And to yours too, Cat."

Biting my lip, I felt obliged to reach for one.

"Aren't you allergic to beets, Cat?" Ace asked.

I was about to say no, but realized he was giving me a way out. "Oh, gosh, I am."

Stella glanced from me to Ace. "What a shame. I'll be sure to make vanilla next time."

Lily licked her fingers, sighing blissfully. Her cheeks were tinted the softest shade of pink. Either sugar had a strange effect on faeries, or it was the beets—

My phone rang, startling me. I pulled it out of my pocket. My college roommate's name flashed on my screen. "I need to take this." I was so eager to leave, I all but jogged out of the bakery, barely waving goodbye.

"Hey, Cora," I said as I walked toward Morgan Street.

"Hi. How was—I mean, did it go okay?"

"Yeah."

"Good." After a long pause, she added, "I wanted to know if you were coming back anytime soon."

Since I didn't think she was particularly concerned, I suspected she had other motives, like making Duke a permanent resident of our dorm room in Danielsen Hall. "No. I'm going to stay out here for the semester. I sent the dean an email before leaving."

There was a short pause, then, "I think it's good that you're spending time with your dad. That's what I did when my little brother passed away."

A chill crawled up my spine. I'd forgotten she'd lost her little brother. I'd heard her boyfriend, Duke, speak about him, but I'd never wanted to pry and ask her for specifics. Besides, she didn't strike me as the sort of person who'd want to have a heart-to-heart with another human being. Well, besides Duke. They had a special bond, one only shared history could explain.

"Well, let me know when you're coming. We could have lunch or dinner," she said.

"Sure. That sounds nice. I'll check flights later and message you. Thanks for calling," I said before hanging up.

As I turned the corner onto our town's main street, the lunchtime bell rang in Rowan High, the great brick building in which I'd spent my entire childhood. Students poured out into the courtyard toward the greenhouse my grandfather had helped convert into a cafeteria when I was still in preschool. I watched them, listened to their conversations about the upcoming Valentine's Day dance. When had January faded into February?

I left them to discuss dresses and dates, wishing those could be my greatest concerns too. When I reached the post office on the next block, the door was locked and the place was dark.

Damn.

Even though Stella could have been right, I wanted to ask Matt if he remembered. Sighing, I crossed the street toward Bee's. A car honked at me, making me jump. I lifted a shaky palm to thank the driver for stopping, then leaped onto the sidewalk. The closed sign was hanging on the door, but the restaurant was lit, and a dozen or so patrons were sitting inside. I went in and scanned the room for Cass, but she wasn't there, and the kitchen was dark, yet people had food in front of them, along with beers and various other drinks.

"Hey, Catori," Mr. Hamilton said, blotting his thin lips with a napkin. "Derek's upstairs."

"Oh. Thanks." I started walking but doubled back toward Mr. Hamilton's table. "Is Cass here?"

"Nope."

"Then how do you all have food and drinks?"

"It was your dad's idea. After Bee went to sleep last night, he asked us to come and hang around the inn so that Bee didn't feel alone. I made this here sandwich at home. As for the drinks, we're serving ourselves and leaving money in the big jar behind the bar."

"That's...that's really nice of all of you."

"This is a good town, Catori. It takes care of you." He readjusted his tweed cap. "Your dad said it well during your mother's burial; Rowan is unique. I would even say it's magical."

I coughed, then cleared my throat. "Magical?"

"Yeah. You know, delightful, remarkable?" He squinted. "You okay? You're as white as my underpants."

Eww... "I should go see Bee and Dad."

"Can you grab me another Red Stripe?" Mr. Hamilton brandished a five-dollar bill. "It's $4.95. Don't bother bringing the nickel back. I'll take it on my way out."

I smiled. Mr. Hamilton was a renowned penny-pincher, but at least he was here, showing support. I grabbed his beer, uncapped it, and brought it over before going upstairs to the tiny suite Bee had moved into since her husband's passing a couple years ago. Every surface was either covered in doilies or framed pictures.

I knuckled the door and waited.

Dad greeted me, draping his arm across my shoulders and pulling me inside. "Did you walk all the way here?"

"Yeah. It was nice actually. Hi, Bee," I said, going over to where she was sitting on the rocking chair by the window, nursing a steaming cup of tea.

I bent over to kiss her cheek.

She looked at me and a gossamer smile materialized on her lips. It vanished quickly though. She turned back toward the window, shoulders hunched, face drawn, a sunken version of the woman who breathed life and joy into everything she touched. I hoped it was temporary. I sat down next to her and told her about running into Stella, and then I shared my recollection of the freezing fishing trip, hoping that speaking of her loved ones would alleviate the ache in her chest.

After a while, her lids closed and her face relaxed in sleep. I took the mug from her knobby fingers and set it down. It read: When nothing goes right, go left. Blake used to say that to me all the time, adding his own twist at the end: "...and straight up into the tree house."

Sighing, I approached Dad, whose watery eyes were fixed on a picture of Mom and Bee standing in front of the inn, both grinning, arms slung around each other's shoulders. I traced Mom's features, from her shiny, crinkly eyes to her silky black hair. I remembered curling my fingers through it as a child. What I didn't remember, but was told so often it had transformed into a memory, was that I would brush the ends of her locks underneath my nose to fall asleep as a baby.

"I was thinking of going to Boston," I said, still looking at Mom.

Dad sucked in a breath. "I suppose you can't take the semester off—"

"I'm not returning to study, Dad. I'm returning to pack and get my car."

"Oh." His expression faltered. "Oh!" A smile flickered on his lips, and then it flickered off like a faulty light bulb. "You're sure that's what *you* want?"

"That's what I want."

Dad smiled widely. "When are you going?"

"I'll check airline prices later, but I hope to get everything done this week."

"That's a good idea."

"How long are you planning on hanging out here with Bee?"

"Another hour or two." He lifted his sweater sleeves. His left wrist was bandaged. When he saw me looking, he dragged his sleeves back down. "I cut myself on a broken wine bottle last night."

I blinked, surprised he was lying to me, surprised Kajika had been telling the truth. Dad stared down at his boots, shuffling them awkwardly on the navy carpet. I decided to let it go. "You think I can borrow the car? I wanted to go see Holly."

A breath whooshed out of his mouth, the sound of relief. "You heard she wasn't doing well?"

"What? No!"

"Isn't that why you're going to see her?"

"What do you mean she's not doing well?"

"She called the day after your mom died to tell me she couldn't make the funeral, that she'd be there in spirit." Dad sighed. "She *is* ninety-nine. It's sad but not unexpected at her age."

A horrible thought pinged inside my mind. Was Gwenelda holding her hostage? "I should—I'll go check on her."

"I didn't mean to worry you, Cat. I should've kept quiet."

"No! I'm glad you told me."

"Speaking of Holly, want to know something weird?" Before I could respond, he said, "Around New Year's, right after you left, your mother decided she wanted to research her genealogical tree. You know how she was…once she set her mind to something, she just had to see it through right away. Anyway, I don't know if she ever told you, but she always wondered why her great-grand-mother, Chatwa, was buried next to Holly's mother."

"Weren't they sworn enemies? A fight over some boy or something like that?"

Dad shook his head. "This is where it gets weird. Not only do they share the same birth year, but apparently they share the same birthday."

"Birthdays aren't exclusive—"

"But her name was Ley. Not L-E-I-G-H but L-E-Y."

"So?"

"It's Gottwa, honey. It means light. And Chatwa means darkness."

I shivered.

"Nova believed they were twins."

I shivered again, which made the weightless tote bag slide off my shoulder. "So that would make Holly…that would make her—"

"Family."

My jaw slackened.

Dad laughed. "Yeah. That was my exact reaction, too."

And here I'd asked Kajika if she was a *bazash*. "Did Mom ask her about it?"

"Did your mother ever leave anything alone?"

"What did Holly say?"

"Holly said it was your great-grandmother Iya's decision to keep it a secret."

"Why?"

"I'm not sure, but your mom said Holly was going to send her a book that would explain everything." His jovial expression turned subdued. "Unfortunately, Nova never got it. Why don't you ask her about it, Cat? Maybe she'll give it to you."

She already gave it to me...

Even though the window was closed and I held no seashell against my ear, the waves of Lake Michigan crested and crashed against my eardrums. It was the sound of everything reasonable and rational disintegrating.

Stella had been right; Holly sent me the book. And she sent it to me because my ancestors were hers too.

27

GOTTWA AND FAELI

*T*he drive over to Holly's was a blur. I parked alongside her truck and walked up to the house. Hoping Holly hadn't started locking her door, I turned the knob but met resistance. *Damn it.* I placed my hands on the metal knocker but then thought better of announcing my presence.

Body flush against the clapboard exterior, I crept over to her living room window. I peered inside but the room was dark. Still, I studied each section, from the open kitchen to the mustard-yellow living room, to the Spanish-tiled floor. Thankfully, Holly's body wasn't lying there. I slinked around the corner and was about to steal a glance into the next window when two hands wound around my biceps like vices.

I yelped.

My captor twisted me around.

Helpless, I blinked up at Kajika, breathing too hard to speak.

"What are you doing here, Catori?" he asked. "I thought we were supposed to keep our distance."

I ripped my arms out of his grasp and stepped back. "I came to see Holly. Not you. Not Gwen."

He nodded. "You should use the door, then."

"It was locked."

"Were you going to climb through a window?" His voice buzzed in my ears.

"No. I...I wanted to make sure she wasn't sleeping. I didn't want to disturb her."

He tipped his head to the side. A lock of silky black hair fell into his eyes. He brushed it away, but it fell again. "She wants to see you. Gwenelda was going to ask your father to bring y—"

"Gwen better stay away from him," I snapped.

He straightened his neck, nostrils flaring.

A window scraped open next to me. I spun around.

"Catori," Gwen said, head darting through the opening. "How wonderful that you have come. Holly is waiting for you."

"I heard." I hadn't seen Gwenelda since the night she'd awakened Kajika, yet her face was almost as familiar to me as an old friend's. She wasn't an old friend, though.

Gwen stared beyond me, at the hunter. "Kajika, *gwayekgin?*"

I bet he was going to tell her I didn't trust her around my father.

"I'm fine," he said gruffly before striding away toward the enormous tree stump Holly used as a picnic table for all those who helped her pick cherries during the harvest months. Kajika lifted an axe along with a large piece of wood. He placed it on the stump, and with one fluid stroke, sliced it in half. And then he felled it again, and again. He bent at the waist and grabbed another log. I left him with his axe and pent-up anger, and made my way back around the house. This time when I tried the doorknob, it yielded.

My heart tripped as I stepped inside and almost collided with Gwen, who stood in the gloomy entrance.

"You know, there's such a thing as electricity nowadays." I was about to take my coat off, but the air was so frigid inside the house, my breath puffed out of me. "It's like a freezer in here. Have you turned the heating off?"

"Kajika took the money he made last night to the person who controls the electricity, so it should be restored soon."

Kajika had fought for money? That wasn't what he'd told me.

The air smelled of fire and ashes and frozen snow. I glimpsed dying embers in the living room's chimney. "Holly ran out of money to pay her bills?"

"Yes. Your mother gave her a little a month ago, but that was not enough."

"Why didn't she call us? My dad would've helped. Everyone in this town would've pitched in."

"She did not think she would live long enough to need more money." Gwenelda gave me a somber smile that looked out of place on her usually impassive face.

"Where is she?"

"In her bedroom. She does not leave it anymore."

I walked down the narrow hallway until I reached the door at the end. I nudged it open. "Holly, it's Catori. Can I come in?"

A feeble 'yes' answered me, so I inched into the dusky room.

When I saw the ancient gardener nestled underneath a heap of blankets, my breath snagged in my throat. I came closer. Her face was framed by sparse wisps of silver hair and bones pushed against her paper-thin skin. If I hadn't heard her speak, I would've thought she was a cadaver.

A weak smile broke over her face as I approached, shifting the sharp bones. "I was hoping...you would come," she said, her voice as insubstantial as the pale cloud that formed when her breath hit her bedroom air.

"Dad just told me that you are"—I paused—"that you are family. Is that true?"

Her eyes sparkled with the residue of life that had deserted the rest of her body. They were the same eyes that had looked down at me when I'd marveled at the blooming flower. "It's true."

"I received the book."

"I hoped—" She wheezed. Gwenelda, who was lighting candles on the dresser, rushed to Holly's side and cradled her head until her lungs quieted. "I hoped it had reached you." Gwen replaced Holly's head and tucked the covers back around her shoulders.

"Where did you get it?" I asked.

"I wrote it when I was very...young. It's our story. Your history." Whistling breaths partitioned her sentences. "Would you like me to...tell you about us?"

Us. One tiny word that held such enormous meaning. "If it's not too hard on you, Holly, I would love for you to tell me about *us.*" I raised my gaze to Gwen when I spoke the word. *Us* meant Holly, my mother, Aylen, and me; it didn't include her or Kajika. I hoped she knew the distinction was crystal clear in my mind.

"Sit, child. It's a long story."

I dragged the armchair in the corner toward the bed. The handstitched lily print on it reminded me of the bedspread on my grandparents' old bed. Mom had put it in storage when Grandma Woni passed. Had it been cut from the same fabric?

"It started in 1817, with a man named Taeewa...and a woman named Adette. He was"—her eyes moved toward Gwen—"Gwenelda's youngest brother."

"The favorite," Gwen said, a winsome smile filtering across her taut features. "He was a most charming boy."

"He's the one...who drew the hunters," Holly whispered.

Gwen's smile absconded from her lips. "He is also the one who buried us."

"The thirteenth hunter," I mused.

Gwenelda nodded. "A few months before he met Adette, days before he buried us, a faerie named Jacobiah Vega"—she eyed me for a reaction—"you know who he is, Catori?"

"Kajika told me. Apparently, Cruz's father tricked Negongwa into thinking the faeries wanted to make peace with the hunters. The tribe named it the Dark Day."

"*Makudewa Geezhi,*" Holly whispered.

"That was what we thought when our bodies were lowered into the earth." Her gaze flicked to my great-great aunt. "I have learned recently that Jacobiah truly wanted to make peace. It was not a ploy to disarm us. He returned to Rowan after the *Makudewa Geezhi*. He was ordered to end the remaining hunter's life to prove he was no traitor to the Woods." Gwen pinched her lips, as though this part of the story was particularly difficult for her to voice. "He found Taeewa while he was on his way to the woman who supplied my mate with the rose petals. Did Kajika tell you about her?"

"Yes."

Gwenelda's gaze grazed Holly's. "When Jacobiah found my little brother, he gassed him. Filled him with his dust. The powers my brother had confiscated were returned to two eager, unruly faeries."

"If Jacobiah killed him, then how am I here?"

"You are here because Jacobiah brought him back."

I leaned forward in my seat.

"Before he gassed my brother, Jacobiah struck a deal with Taeewa: Jacobiah would let him live if he promised to inform him of the hunters' awakening. You see, faeries always demand something in return, a favor. A *tokwa*. That is how we call it."

"Cruz didn't ask me for anything."

Holly's lids closed and opened, like the shutter on a reflex camera, and Gwen sighed.

"Unfortunately, Catori, when a fae undertakes the wish of a human or a hunter, and no bargain is struck beforehand, he may ask for *anything* in return, at *any time*, and you will have to oblige him."

"Maybe he won't ask for anything," I said, which won me an eyebrow raise from Gwen. "What?"

"She's young, Gwenelda. This is all…new for her," Holly said in her wispy voice.

Yes, this was new to me. And *yes*, I was still wrapping my head around it all, but was I truly as naïve as they were both making me out to be? "Taeewa's dead, right?"

Gwenelda blinked, then frowned. "Of course."

"Then how did the faeries find out you were back?" I asked.

"Holly had to uphold her ancestor's *tokwa*. She had to inform Jacobiah."

"But Jacobiah's dead also, isn't he?"

"He is, Catori. But a favor owed does not perish when a faerie dies. It passes on to the next of kin. Just like it was passed down to Holly. When I stirred, she was obliged to inform Cruz Vega."

"How did she do it?"

"She spoke his name into a faerie portal," Gwen explained.

This time, I was the one who frowned. "She went all the way to Traverse City and talked to the lighthouse?"

"You're reading...the book." Holly smiled, and then her white lips shifted. "There is a closer one now...right here, in Rowan."

"Where?"

"In the boathouse," she said. "Locker number four."

"A locker?"

"If you open the metal box," Gwen explained, "it transforms into an entrance, but only if you are fae, or if you have the sight. You cannot enter it, though, even if you have the sight, but you will see inside."

Is that where the faeries had gone after leaving Astra's? To the boathouse? Had they crawled into a locker?

"Do you recall the summer day you went to the shore with your mother, aunt, and cousins? The insufferably warm one that ended with a lightning storm." Gwen spoke softly, yet her words prodded me like metal spokes.

She had my mother's mind, and I hated her for it. But then, my anger turned to shock as I remembered the day in question. Shiloh and Satyana were four and I was fourteen. I had a million other places I'd wanted to be, but Mom and Aylen insisted we make it a girls' afternoon, so I'd had to tag along. We were all wading in the cool water when Shiloh remembered she'd brought an inflatable pink swim ring and ran back into the boathouse to grab it. Seconds later, she'd trundled out shrieking—

"Shiloh saw a man climb out of the metal box," Gwenelda said.

"Shiloh has the sight?" Holly asked. "How wonderful."

I didn't agree, but I kept this to myself. "If you speak into *the locker*"—I felt foolish asking if the lockers were walkie-talkies—"does your voice carry to the *baseetogan?*"

"Yes. Gwenelda, *meeggwe manazi...ta* Catori."

I spun my head toward her. "You speak Gottwa, Holly?"

Holly did that faint head gesture again as Gwen opened the dresser's top drawer and extricated a small, leather-bound book.

"It's a dictionary," Holly murmured. "I know Woni wrote one... but this one, it's different." She smiled up at me. It strained the fragile net of skin shielding her bones.

I took the book and unwrapped the leather tie that laced around it several times. "Mom tried to teach me Gottwa when I was younger. But I wasn't very patient."

"Perhaps now...you will have patience."

I opened it to the first page. There were three columns. The first was in English. The other two were in foreign tongues. I recognized a Gottwa word in the second column, but in the third, I recognized nothing. I looked up at Holly. "In what language is the third column?"

"It's *Faeli*...the fae's tongue," she said, a hint of pride playing on the corners of her lips that were the color of freshly laundered linens.

"You learned the faerie's language?" I asked. It was a stupid question considering I had proof right there, on the paper.

"I am *gingawi*," Holly murmured. "Like you. Like Nova. Like Shiloh."

"*Gingawi?*" I repeated.

"Mixed," Holly said.

Gwen turned toward the window and looked out onto the graying day, hands clasped behind her back.

"Part hunter...part fae."

The book slipped through my fingers and fell onto the carpet. Too startled, I didn't move to pick it up. "How?"

"Adette was the *bazash*'s daughter." Holly's eyes sparked again in the thickening darkness. "Faeries sense we're different, but they believe...it's because our hunter magic has been...diluted from mixing with humans."

"I thought faeries had kept tabs on the hunters. Wouldn't they know that Taeewa had children with a *bazash*?"

"Only Jacobiah knew...that Taeewa was still alive. Before parting with him...the faerie instructed him...to always carry an opal..."

"Because opals make hunters invisible to faeries," I said, which earned me an approbating nod from Holly. I chewed on my lip. The mist, which had settled over my mind the day I discovered magic really existed, was slowly starting to clear. "Then how come faeries knew I had hunter blood?"

"They assumed you were a descendant of the tribe," Gwen explained. "They do not know you come down directly from Taeewa."

"But back at the cabin, you told me we were the last ones. That there were no other hunters. How—"

"There are no other hunters, Catori. Over the years, faeries have killed every human they encountered who possessed even an ounce of hunter blood."

"They didn't kill me..."

"But they were tracking you."

"They didn't kill Holly."

"Because I am fae," Holly wheezed.

"But you're also a hunter," I countered.

The mound of covers atop Holly lifted and dipped to the rhythm of her inhalations and exhalations. "Not anymore." She wheezed again, then coughed.

Gwen turned away from the window and moved to Holly's side.

She boosted Holly's head up. "*Danimogwe*," she murmured. "*Danimogwe*. Breathe."

"What does she mean, *not anymore?*" I asked Gwen.

"She chose to annihilate her hunter side to become a full-fledged faerie."

Goosebumps rose over my arms. "Will I have to choose?"

"If you do not choose, you will remain human." Gwenelda rested Holly's head back, ran her fingers through the old woman's feathery gray hair, then smoothed down the covers around her. "You will keep the sight and whatever faerie magic you possess."

I was taken aback. "*I* have a faerie magic?"

"Remember the robin...that flew into my glasshouse?" Holly whispered.

The little red-breasted bird hadn't seen the clear glass and had hit it with a teeth-grinding thump. I'd raced outside and collected its limp, dazed body.

"It broke its neck," she continued.

I frowned. "No it didn't. It took flight."

"Because you healed it, Catori..." Holly murmured. "Healing is faerie magic. The greatest doctors...possess a little faerie blood."

I brought my hands up in front of my face and twisted them. They didn't feel like my hands. They felt like a stranger's hands. I balled my fingers into fists, which I laid on my thighs. "Could I heal you?"

She smiled. "I am too old to be healed. Besides, I am tired of living."

I supposed that ninety-nine years was a long time to live. "Is it reversible? Once you choose?"

"No," Holly said.

"And if I were to choose, how and when do I do it?"

"During a blue moon," she whispered. "As to how...read *The Wytchen Tree*, child."

The mist thinned some more. "Holly, why did Chatwa and Ley fight?"

"Because Ley chose...to become fae, and Chatwa, hunter. Like religion...it tears people apart."

"Did you get along with Chatwa?"

Holly's gaze went unfocused. "Chatwa despised faeries...so she despised me." There was so much sadness in her voice that I regretted having asked.

I stood up, collected the fallen dictionary, and tucked it against me so it wouldn't escape again. "I think I'll stick to human, then." I wouldn't have to undergo gene therapy after all. "Aylen doesn't have the sight. Why is that? Isn't she mixed?"

"Her faerie side...must be stronger," Holly answered in a voice that exposed how deeply scarred her lungs were. "If she chose...she could be a hunter." She wheezed, the tendons in her neck contracting. "Come closer."

I approached, my skin prickling as I lowered my head toward Holly.

"There are many secrets...within *The Wytchen Tree*'s pages." The shell of my ear tingled with her words. "Within..." she whispered again.

I stood back up, my spine as taut as a tightrope.

"It was so nice to see you...Catori." Holly's lips bent into a weak smile. "Thank you for coming."

"Of course," I said. "And I'll come back soon. Very soon, I promise."

Holly spoke softly to Gwenelda with words that weren't English. I imagined she was speaking in Gottwa.

"Can I speak to you before I go?" I asked Gwenelda as the old gardener's lids finally closed in exhaustion.

Gwen nodded. I followed her out of the bedroom and into the small kitchen, which looked as though it hadn't been updated since the turn of the twentieth century.

"What did she just tell you?" I asked her.

"She told me to erase the mind of your father, Catori. She said it would be better if no one knew you were related to her."

"Don't you dare mess with my father's head!"

Gwen pressed her lips into a thin line. "I would never have done so without your permission."

"Well I don't give you permission."

"As you wish, Catori."

"*I'll* tell him to keep it secret."

Doubt gleamed in her eyes, yet she nodded.

My father wouldn't tell anyone. He wasn't the sort of man to gossip. "Tell me something, Gwen. Holly's a faerie, but you don't seem to hate her. Why is that?"

"The memories I share with your mother make me trust her. Her memories of your mother make her trust *me*."

Heat pulsed underneath my skin as an image of my mother imprisoned in Gwen's mind arose. I had to reason with myself that it wasn't completely Gwenelda's fault; my mother's insatiable curiosity led her to forage for a mystical grave.

"Why did you wake Kajika? Why didn't you bring Menawa back?" I asked her.

Gwen frowned before saying, "The graves are unmarked, Catori. I do not know where Menawa lies." Her voice was as heavy as the obscurity cloaking Holly's house. "I wish I had awakened my beloved instead."

Had Ace lied to me? Were their names not on the headstones?

"Why do you ask me that, Catori?"

I shrugged. "It was just...just a question."

She waited for me to say something else, but I didn't deliver what lurked in the back of my mind.

"Thank you for going to the fight last night," she said.

"Aha! I was right. It was no coincidence."

"No, it was not. I influenced your friend to bring you along because I was worried something would happen to Kajika. I could not leave Holly's side, not in her state."

"And you assumed I would help him?"

"You would have taken care of him. Like you took care of me. I would no longer be here if you had not saved me, Catori. I owe you my life."

"Well, Kajika took Blake's life, so I wouldn't have helped him."

She tapped two fingers against her forehead. "You cannot watch someone get hurt without helping. Your mother *showed* me this. She showed me when you performed the maneuver of Heimlich on a girl named Faith in your school cafeteria. You did not like her, yet you did not let her choke."

I stared at her wide-eyed again.

Her long hair frolicked around the baggy blouse. It was the one Kajika had worn in The Earth Market. Gwenelda had added a belt to it, so it looked more like a dress than a misadjusted garment. On her feet, she wore the glossy red boots she'd had on the day the *golwinim* attacked...the day she'd died.

"It is incredible how much you resemble Ishtu," she said in a soft voice.

I jerked my gaze away from her boots. "Who's Ishtu?"

"She was Kajika's *aabiti*."

"His mate?"

Gwenelda nodded. "When I first laid eyes on you, I believed I was seeing Ishtu, but then I heard your name being spoken, and I knew it was just a genetic coincidence."

"Who was she to you?"

"My cousin, on my father's side."

A great clattering sound startled us both. I spun around to find Kajika standing in the doorjamb, logs arrayed helter-skelter around his bare feet. "*A ma kwenim*, Gwenelda! *Mawa*!" He turned and rushed out the door like a wounded animal.

"*Gatizogin*," she yelled after him, but he was already too far away to hear her. "I am sorry," she whispered. "*Gatizogin*, Kajika."

"Why is he so angry?" I asked Gwen, trying to make out his shape against the chalk-white land.

"He did not want me to tell you about her."

I picked up an armful of logs and tossed them into the crackling hearth, then fished my wallet out of my coat pocket and handed her the few crumpled twenties inside.

She shook her head. "We have enough. For now, we have enough, thank *Gejaiwe*."

"Who's *Gejaiwe*?"

Gwen smiled. "The Great Spirit."

I stuffed the money back into my wallet.

"Catori?"

"Yes?"

"I am sorry about Blake."

I looked at her a long time without speaking. Regret was etched all over her face. Regret would never be apology enough, though. Not for me.

"My father's worried about Holly, so he'll probably stop by. Don't hang around when he visits. He thinks you murdered the medical examiner."

Gwenelda's forehead furrowed, but she didn't voice her confusion. "I will not let him see me then."

I nodded, then headed back to the hearse. I sank into the driver's seat and shut the door. As I drove away, I scanned the land for Kajika, but didn't find any broody, hooded figure. I stopped the car and opened the dictionary that I'd placed on the passenger seat. I thumbed through it until I found the word he'd spoken: **kwenim**. *Memory*. And then I found his other word: **mawa**. *Mine*. I didn't remember the rest of his sentence, but those two words were enough for me to understand he was telling Gwen that Ishtu's memory belonged to him.

THE TREE HOUSE

*T*wo days later, we lowered Blake into the earth in a simple oak casket. Like at my mother's funeral, everyone in Rowan converged on our estate to bid him farewell with swollen lids and aching throats.

Bee tried to speak over the deep hole, but her words kept tripping over each other and meshing with her relentless tears until she heaved so deeply, my father and Stella had to lead her into the house, away from the distraught mourners.

Even though my eyes burned, I didn't cry. My heart had begun to thicken, padding itself with protective layers to weather the chaotic storm raging across my life. I sensed this wasn't the last death on my horizon. Cass, who held on to my arm, kept blowing her nose and tossing the used tissues into her pink purse until it could no longer close.

When it was over, when we'd all thrown our reverent handfuls of dirt over Blake's remains, I wandered toward the copse of Rowan trees. Someone had removed Kajika's empty coffin. I supposed it was my father, or perhaps it was being held for evidence by the police. I studied the remaining headstone. Three curved lines ran parallel to each other like the symbol for water. I racked my brain for their meaning. Had Mom ever told me? She must have…

I moved to the next grave and again found only the same pictogram. I spun around slowly, taking in all the headstones. All twelve were identical. For the first time, I hated Gwen a little less and disliked Ace a ton more. He'd tricked me into thinking the hunters' names were etched in the stone.

Why was I so surprised? Faeries were masters of chicanery after all. Even Cruz had confessed to this.

"You think you're going to have to dig out the remaining graves?" Cass stood next to me, nose as red and cheeks as white as candy canes.

"Why would we?" I asked, horrified.

"I just thought that since the ground started caving in, you'd need to dig them all up, that's all."

"I hope it won't come to that," I said quietly.

"Why do you think they were filled with rose petals?"

"How do you know about that?"

"Jimmy told me."

"Gottwas believed roses would preserve their bodies. Like mummification."

"Well that didn't work out too well for them did it?"

"You never told me how last night went?" I asked, to change the subject.

"Once you left with the hottie, the party was over. We didn't even stay for another fight. And then, during the entire drive back, Ace was on the phone. So, not much fun."

"Who was he on the phone with?"

"I heard Lily's name at some point. He spoke to her in some weird language. But then he spoke English. He said something along the lines of, *if they raised one more, Gregor and the gold-something would come to Rowan to clean up the mess.* I think that's what he said. It sounds weird, huh? You think he was talking about building a mall or something? I'd like a mall. It sure would liven up this place."

They were most definitely not talking about building malls. I wondered who this Gregor was. A faerie, I imagined. One I probably didn't want to meet. As Cass looped her arm in mine and dragged me back to the house, muttering how cold her feet were, I looked over at Blake's grave, and at the large picture Bee had printed of him. It was before he'd left for the war, before his face had been irreparably altered. I'd forgotten how baby-faced he'd looked before going off to Afghanistan, with a soft jaw, fuzzy chin, and smiley eyes. After the blast, when he'd returned to Rowan, his jaw had become uneven and angular from a prosthesis that made his chin stick out in a way it never had before. But his eyes had changed the most. Or rather his remaining eye; it had lost its sparkle. Blake-before and Blake-after had been two very different boys, but they'd shared the same virtuous heart and the same noble mind.

A tear rolled down my cheek. Okay, perhaps I was wrong about having built a fort around myself. A fence maybe. And everything gets through fences. Unless they're made of iron or rowan wood.

My silly musing made me think of what Cass had said, which called back Kajika's reaction to the phone call. It had put him on edge. I established Gregor must be someone to fear. I left Cass downstairs and headed to my room. After locking the door, I flipped through Holly's book, hoping to find something about Gregor. I wasn't sure how I would detect a name from thousands of lines of text. Futile hope spurred me on, though.

Twenty minutes went by before I closed the book with a sigh. I'd ask Holly, or I'd ask Ace. Before someone came looking for me, I put the book away and headed back downstairs. I found Cass by a platter of sky-blue vanilla cupcakes Stella had made. Although her gesture was kind, they looked better suited for a baby shower. In a way we were celebrating a boy's life, but it was a departed life, not an impending one.

"Burying your grief underneath frosting?" I asked Cass.

She crinkled her nose as she chewed. "That's a pretty tasteless joke."

"I live over a morgue; I'm allowed an odd sense of humor."

Cass swallowed, and then she smiled. "Wait, wait. Rewind. *You* have a sense of humor?"

"Haha."

She grinned wider, which made her puffy eyes squint. "Did you see who came?"

"Who?" I scanned the room, expecting to see Ace or Kajika. Instead, I caught sight of Faith. She wore a tent-like black dress, which was odd considering her wardrobe consisted only of spandex and lycra. If it wasn't tight, she didn't wear it. "Am I the only one who finds it weird she's wearing a muumuu?"

"Nope. New York must have changed her."

"New York did not change her." In a hushed voice, I told Cass about our run-in at Astra's.

She sighed. "Once a viper, always a viper."

We studied Faith until she caught us in the act.

"Cass, was Blake suicidal?" I asked, grabbing a Styrofoam cup and pumping coffee from a thermos into it.

Cass combed her hand through her bangs as she averted her gaze. Eyes scaling back up to mine, she said, "Yes." She bit down on her lower lip, then released it. "Yes, he was."

"How bad was it?"

"He didn't come to work one morning, and he wasn't answering his phone, so Bee sent me to get him. I searched the house. He wasn't there, but since his Jeep was, I thought he'd gone out for a run. I got back in my car and drove around. And around. I kept phoning him, but there was no answer. Finally I drove back to his house and phoned him one last time.

"I heard his ringtone coming from the garage. I found him sitting in his grandfather's old Buick, head lolled back, eyes closed. The car was running, so I assumed he'd fallen asleep. But then I saw this hose snaking from the exhaust pipe right into the passenger window. And that's when I panicked. Like, I *really* panicked. I called 9-1-1. They told me get him out of the car. He'd locked all the doors. It was awful, Cat. I had to smash the car window with a baseball bat to get the doors open, and then getting him out...He weighed a ton. I dragged him out. I don't know how I managed but I did."

Something hot and wet dripped through my fingers, down the sleeve of my black turtleneck. And then my coffee cup came crashing down at my feet. Styrofoam didn't shatter yet it felt like it had. Perhaps it was just the sound of something breaking inside of me. I would've said my heart, but my heart hadn't mended enough to break.

Cass grabbed a fistful of paper napkins. "Are you okay? Did you get burned?"

"You should've called me," I whispered as she patted my wet, stinging hand. "I would've come home."

"He made me swear not to tell you. He made me swear not to tell anyone, but especially you. Besides, when someone's determined to hurt themselves, there's not much anyone can do to stop them. I'm just sorry he had to end it underneath your window. It must've been awful for you." She chucked the balled napkin onto a paper plate. "Your hand's really red. We should run some cold water over it. Or put ice on there. I'll go grab some."

I made a sound, something between a sob and a gasp. Blake's death was ruled a suicide, and forever more, he would be remembered as the depressed boy who'd given up on life. "Aw, Cat. I shouldn't have said anything..."

I don't know when and from where she came, but Faith was suddenly standing next to us. "Are you really pitying *her*, Coz? *She* turned him down; *she* made him drive into a tree. His death...it's all on her."

"Stop it, Faith," Cass mumbled.

"You're the one who told me Catori must've said no. That this was why he'd slit his wrist and driven like a madman through the cemetery."

Horrified, I backed away from them. Until then, I'd known his death had indirectly been my fault. If Gwen hadn't been at his house that night, Blake wouldn't have died. I hadn't realized my friends were convinced unrequited love had been his downfall.

I lowered my gaze to the puddle of spilled coffee pooling around their black boots. It was so much easier to look at than the reproachful faces around me.

"Catori, wait," Cass blurted out, but I was out the door before anyone could stop me. I ran and ran, my shoes sinking into the mushy snow. Slush and mud splattered against my black jeans, making the material stick to my legs. Blood pumped through me, funneling heat through my muscles. I'd forgotten my coat, but was warm enough. When I arrived in front of the house in which Blake had been raised, I stopped running.

After his parents died, the bank had repossessed it because Bee couldn't afford the mortgage. It had remained vacant ever since. I crossed the backyard toward the large oak and looked up. The tree house was still there, its roof shielded by a thin coat of snow. I gripped the rope ladder and climbed it. Inside, the floorboards were humid and dusty, but still I sat, with my back to a wall and my knees tucked against me. And then I let the overwhelming grief and guilt wash over me. When the tears finally subsided, the sky had gone dark. I rested the back of my head against the clapboard wall and closed my sore eyes, finally blissfully numb to everything inside and outside.

"Your father's looking for you."

My eyes snapped open and zeroed in on Kajika. "What are you doing here?"

He tipped his head to the side.

"Did you follow me?"

His head straightened. "No."

"Then how—"

"It's your safe place."

I sucked in a breath. The reminder that he possessed Blake's mind was bittersweet. "How do you know my dad's looking for me?" I asked after a long moment.

"He stopped by Holly's house."

Worry supplanted all other feelings. "Did he see you? Did he see Gwen?"

"No. We stayed out of sight, but we heard him ask if you were there. He seemed frantic. Did you get into a fight?"

Breathing a little easier, I stared back down at my knees that seemed particularly knobby. "Everyone thinks Blake killed himself because I couldn't love him back."

In a low voice, Kajika said, "He did."

I jerked my gaze back to him. "No, *you* killed him; Gwenelda killed him."

The hunter was still crouched in the entrance. "He cut his wrist. Gwenelda found him bleeding out in his armchair. She tried to save him, Catori, she really tried, but she didn't know how to stop the hemorrhaging. So she drove him out to the graveyard and unearthed me." Kajika padded in toward me in a crouch, barefoot as always. "Gwenelda thought that if she used his life to wake one of us, in a way, she'd be saving him."

My heart missed a beat. A very long beat. "So I"—my voice cracked—"so I really"—I swallowed—"*I* killed Blake?"

"*He* killed *himself*. It wasn't your fault, Catori. He gave up on life. When he saw you with the...with the faerie"—Kajika's eyes gleamed like burning coals—"he decided he didn't stand a chance."

I took a long breath. "We're even now."

He frowned.

"You have...*mawa kwenim* too," I whispered.

Kajika blinked, and then a faint smile softened the set of his jaw. "*Ma kwenim*. My memory, not mine memory."

"You're really giving me a grammar lesson right now?"

He smiled a bit wider, then sat down beside me and stretched out his legs in front of him. When I was a kid, we could be four up here and still have wiggle room. Now, between Kajika and me, there remained very little space.

I kept my gaze on the wall in front of us, on the white tic-tac-toe board Blake and I had painted a long-ago summer. We'd used paintbrushes soaked in water to draw the circles and exes. Once the heat evaporated our old game, we'd start a new one. In the meantime, we'd write ephemeral messages or things that bothered us on the walls, and watch those fade away. Blake had a theory that if we externalized our feelings, we'd feel better.

"Not only do you share my Ishtu's face, but you have her character," Kajika said, making Blake and our juvenile games fade away. "She was mighty strong-willed, yet her name meant sweetness. I teased her often about changing her name to Mashka."

"What does *mashka* mean?"

"Tough."

"She must've loved that."

He smiled, and then he didn't, and his face turned forlorn. "You know what I miss most about her?"

"No."

"Her laugh. She had such a beautiful laugh. A laugh that could turn rainclouds into sunshine."

I looked at Kajika, really looked at him. I would never have pegged him for a romantic or a poet.

"You know what Blake liked most about you?" he asked.

"My surly attitude?"

Kajika's eyebrows pulled in. "*Gejaiwe* knows how, he grew immune to that."

I poked the hunter with my elbow, shook my head, and then I laughed until tears bloomed at the edge of my vision. After the shit day...the shit week, my laughter felt liberating, like a sailor spotting land after months at sea. It rumbled up from my toes that didn't even feel like my toes anymore; it thrummed inside my chest, vibrated in my throat, prickled my palate, and tickled my lips. I rested my head back until the very last blissful spasms escaped through my icy lips. "I don't know when the last time I laughed was," I said. "Thank you for that."

Kajika had stiffened. He probably thought I was becoming crazy, and maybe he was right. Maybe I was experiencing a nervous breakdown. Honestly, I didn't care much, because if this was a nervous breakdown, then it was sublime.

"So what did Blake like most about me?"

Kajika didn't answer right away. His eyes had closed as though he were trying to retrieve the memory from an armored drawer. After a long moment, his lips and eyes parted with my answer, "What he liked most were your eyes. The way they slanted upward like a cat's. The way everything you felt was reflected in them. The way they held no condemnation even though he was a monster."

"A monster?" I murmured.

Kajika nodded.

I dragged my palms over my face, resting my fingertips against my tingling lips. "He was no monster."

"I agree. Most monsters wear beautiful faces." Kajika studied me when he said this.

Saddened by his prejudice against faeries, all remnants of bliss shriveled up inside me. "Did you hear I was part faerie? Do you think *I'm* a monster?"

His Adam's apple bobbed up sharply in his throat. "You're not a faerie until you choose to be one."

"What if I do choose to be one? Will you think me an abomination then?"

"Yes."

Feeling as though he'd slapped me, I crawled toward the opening. My legs burned and ached, but I made it out to the platform.

"You think you know them, Catori. But you don't. Why do you think we were created? If there was goodness in them, they wouldn't need hunters to keep them in line."

I didn't want to argue with someone whose mind was airtight, and yet I couldn't help but say, "Jacobiah wanted peace."

"Just because Holly says this, it doesn't make it true."

"Catori!" came a distant, anguished voice. "Catori!" Dad yelled again.

"You should learn to trust people. You'd be a hell of a lot happier," I told Kajika as I slid my feet onto the rope rungs of the ladder.

"I don't seek happiness, Catori," Kajika said, staring at me through the small opening. "I was happy once, and the faeries killed my family, and then I was happy again with my new family, with Ishtu, and again the faeries killed my happiness. What's the point in pursuing something that places you at another's mercy?"

"What's the point of living without happiness?" I countered.

"Perhaps it isn't my destiny to be happy."

I rolled my eyes. "You make your own happiness, Kajika. Just like you create your own destiny."

The hunter traced the patchy pools of light on the grimy wooden floor. "When I awoke and saw you"—he raised his eyes to mine—"I thought my wish had been granted."

My spine tingled. "What wish?"

"To reach the other side and be reunited with those I loved. But I didn't wake up on the other side, and you weren't Ishtu."

"Catori?" Dad shouted. I crawled to the entrance. He was standing several yards away from the tree house, cheeks flushed even though the rest of his face was deathly pale. "Oh, sweetheart! I looked everywhere for you. I thought..." His voice crackled like an old record player.

I climbed down the ladder. When my feet touched the ground, I almost keeled over, but caught myself on the broad trunk. Dad strode over to me, then looped his long arms around me.

"I thought you'd left for Boston. I thought you weren't coming back," he said.

"I would never leave without telling you. I just needed space after I heard"—I sighed, and it hurt my chest—"after I heard that it wasn't an accident."

Dad nodded against my shoulder, and then he released me, and his eyes poured his emotions straight into mine. I could feel the anxiety, and the terror, and the guilt. It was like taking a shower with my head tipped up and my eyes wide open. "I should've told you the truth. I was just so afraid of what it would do to you."

"Thank you, Daddy."

"For what?"

"For protecting me."

He hugged me again. "Let's get you home."

I nodded. Before leaving, though, I looked up. I wasn't sure what I wanted to tell Kajika, but I couldn't just pretend he wasn't up there.

Kajika crouched on the platform, as though he were about to spring off. His eyes glowed as he watched my father and me.

"Dad, I'd like you to meet a friend of mine. He's visiting from Boston."

Dad looked up. Kajika's body immobilized in alarm, mirroring my father's, although I doubted my father's reaction to him was out of fear. More like surprise, and wariness.

It took my father a moment to snap out of his trance-like stupor and acknowledge the hunter who was hurtling down the ladder.

"Hi, I'm Derek."

Hesitantly, he shook my father's outstretched hand. "Kajika."

Dad looked him over, from his earth-stained feet to his baggy sweatpants and black hoodie. "Kajika," Dad repeated. "Is that Gottwa?"

The hunter's eyes grew wide.

"Funny story," I said. "He's Holly's great-nephew."

"I thought he was your friend from Boston."

"Well, he is, but when we met, and I asked him where his name came from, he told me he had a great-aunt in Rowan."

"But you didn't know Holly was Gottwa," Dad said, releasing Kajika's hand. *Damn.*

"No...I didn't know Holly was *related* to us," I said. "I knew she had native blood."

Dad studied Kajika again. After a long while, he said, "Then that sort of makes you family," Dad told Kajika.

"Yep," I said.

One of Dad's eyebrows curved up. "Your face looks awfully familiar. Have we met before?"

"No, sir," he said.

My palms slickened. Even though they were cold, I had to rub the sweat off against my pants. Had Dad found my book? Had he seen the pictures of the faehunters buried in our backyard?

"I've been in town a few days now. Maybe you saw me from afar?" Kajika suggested.

"Maybe." He looked him over again. "Can I ask why you're not wearing shoes, son?"

"I..." Kajika stumbled to find a plausible excuse. "I forgot them in Boston."

I almost laughed—almost because the reality was pitiful.

Thankfully, Dad didn't ask how he hadn't noticed he was shoeless when he was boarding a bus or a plane from Boston to Rowan. "Well, you look to be about my size. I'm sure I have a few pairs gathering dust in the back of my closet," Dad said. "My wife was always hounding me to get rid of stuff, so you'd really be doing me a favor if you accepted a pair."

In that moment, my father became more than just the man I loved above all others. He became the man I admired above all others. Mom had *never* asked him to go through his closet and discard unworn items of clothing. If anyone was a packrat, it had been her.

"Well, let's get ourselves home. Catori looks like an icicle, and you don't look much warmer yourself."

"No, I should get back—" Kajika started.

"Not without shoes. Did you bring a coat or did you forget it in Boston too?" The way Dad asked him told me he hadn't been fooled by the lie.

Kajika lowered his eyes to the ground. "In my haste to get here, I left it back home."

"Well, you're in luck. I have this great coat that I just can't zip over my belly." Dad shook his head. "Internet shopping gone wrong."

Kajika looked at Dad again, eyebrows pulled in. Even though he had Blake's memories, he didn't seem to understand what Internet shopping was. Or maybe he didn't get why a complete stranger was being kind to him. No. Negongwa had showed him kindness. It was probably the Internet shopping that stumped him. "O-okay," he finally said.

And so we trudged out toward the hearse. Dad raised the backseat for Kajika who got in with great reticence.

"How did you know where to find me?" I asked Dad as I settled in the front next to him.

"Bee suggested it when I told her I couldn't find you anywhere."

Dad placed his hand on top of mine as he drove back, as though he were afraid I'd dash away again. Several times, I glanced back at Kajika, who was staring out his window, hands clasped firmly in his lap. After we parked, the hunter insisted on waiting by the car, but Dad made him go inside. Kajika stared wide-eyed around him. I did too, but for an entirely different reason. Our living room and kitchen were spotless, with no hint of the reception we'd hosted only hours earlier.

"You have a very nice house, sir," he told Dad, who glanced around appreciatively too.

"That was all Nova. She had a real talent for decorating."

As he said this, my gaze struck the door I'd repainted. I didn't regret changing the color, but erasing Mom's cheery yellow had hurt my father, so I regretted that. I decided that before leaving for Boston, I would rebuild the iron wind chime as a gift to him.

"I'll be right back," Dad said, heading upstairs. "Cat, why don't you whip up some hot chocolate?"

"Gladly...that is, if I can get the blood to return into my hands," I said, making my way to the kitchen. I rubbed my palms together to generate heat. Once I could bend my fingers again, I grabbed a deep saucepan and filled it with milk. I held my hands over the simmering liquid. Soon, I was pushing the sleeves of my turtleneck up.

When I turned away from the stove, Kajika was still standing in the foyer, rigid as a totem pole.

I broke up a bittersweet chocolate bar and tossed the pieces into the milk, then turned off the heat and stirred. "You can come closer. I won't bite."

He inched toward the kitchen on bruise-colored feet. When he saw me looking down at them, he stopped moving.

"Sit," I told him, tipping my head toward one of the kitchen chairs.

Slowly, he did.

I filled the water heater and put it to boil, then I pumped some of Aylen's fresh rosemary soap into the plastic basin we kept underneath the sink. Before the electric kettle clicked, I added the warm water to the soap. It foamed and diffused a crisp green scent over the aroma of molten chocolate. I placed the basin by his chair and a clean kitchen towel on our dining table. He stared at the water as though it were the strangest offering he'd ever received...*he*, the hunter who'd been buried underneath spelled rose petals. "It's a footbath," I said.

He pushed an unruly lock of hair off his forehead. It fell right back into his eyes.

"To clean and warm your feet," I added, in case he wasn't familiar with the term. Maybe Blake had never had one.

He shifted in his seat, dipped one foot in, then the other, and hissed.

"Too hot?" I asked. "I'm a sucker for soaking in super hot water, but maybe you aren't."

"It burns," he said, his voice husky.

I drew the freezer door open and grabbed a fistful of ice cubes. I was about to toss them in when he caught my wrist.

"Don't. It's lovely."

I didn't shrug his hand off, too stunned he'd deigned to touch me—me, the abomination. The ice began to melt. Cool water dripped down my wrist to my elbow, and still he didn't let go. And still I didn't push him away. When I shivered, he grabbed the towel with his free hand and wiped my arm slowly, eyes never leaving mine.

"So this is what I—" Dad stopped short.

I yanked my arm out of Kajika's grasp, cheeks hot. I tossed the shrunken ice cubes into the sink and returned to the stove to stir the hot chocolate. Thankfully, the silence didn't last long. Dad explained to Kajika how he'd bought all these pants and shirts and sweaters and socks in the wrong sizes. If my pulse weren't still beating erratically, I would probably have grinned at my father's bevy of lies.

Hands shaking, I poured out three mugs of hot chocolate and gave the men their mugs, or rather I tendered Dad his mug and placed Kajika's on the table.

"I'm going to go sleep now, Dad," I said, grabbing my mug and starting up the stairs.

"But it's only five-thirty," Dad called after me.

"I'm really tired."

I hurried up the stairs before Dad could guilt-trip me into staying. I heard them talk a while longer. And then I heard the front door close. I walked over to the window and watched a bundled-up Kajika make his way across the cemetery in a pair of Timberland boots and a thick army green parka. At least he'd be warm from now on. I was about to turn away when he looked up and caught me staring. He didn't wave, nor did I. He tipped his head in goodbye or in thanks, and then he whirled around and ran until he was just a speck in the darkness.

That night I checked airline tickets. I found one for the end of the week. It would put me in Boston around lunchtime, which would give me ample time to pack. I'd sleep one last night in my dorm room, and then I would drive back to Rowan. Maybe I could find an internship at Mercy Hospital in Mullegon, so as not to go completely crazy during the coming months. I had many flaws, but idleness wasn't one of them.

29

FAERIE CAKES

*T*he next morning, awake too early, I took the book from underneath my mattress and flipped through it. I looked for the secrets Holly mentioned, but all I found within the pages of *The Wytchen Tree* were accounts of hunter rituals and faerie traditions, as well as more myths like the one about the *mishipeshu*.

There was a lot of information, which Holly had related in the third person and woven with such copious details it felt more like historical fiction than an actual account. Although I searched carefully, I found no mention of how to pick between my faerie side and my hunter side. Everything I learned was interesting, but it did not clear the mist from my mind. Toward the last chapter, my eyesight began to go unfocused. I was about to close the book when I noticed a diagram—narrow rectangles arranged in a circle. I blinked and sat up straighter.

The diagram was gone.

Yet I was sure I'd seen it.

I brought the book closer to the lamp on my nightstand, but it didn't magically reappear.

I brought it closer to my face, but I didn't see it.

Had I hallucinated?

I stared at the lines of text, but no rectangles materialized. Annoyed, I rubbed my eyes, closed the book, and then replaced it next to my necklace underneath my mattress.

After taking a warm shower, I headed to the attic to sort through Mom's things. The light that trickled in through the fan-shaped window was golden gray, as though the sun was finally challenging the thick clouds. As I unpacked, made piles, then repacked, the light grew warmer and brighter. I found myself holding out old shirts, contemplating them, remembering days when she'd worn them, smelling them, filling myself with her. Orange rind and cut grass. That had always been my mother's scent.

It had been the first body oil Aylen had mixed in her home laboratory. She'd named it after Mom, her very first customer. She'd paid Aylen a hundred dollars for a lifetime's supply of that oil. Instead of investing it, Aylen had framed the bill. She showed it to us when we'd visited a couple years back. It had moved Mom that she'd preserved the memento instead of investing it.

I thought of Aylen and wondered if she'd want to keep anything. I started making a pile of things she might like. Once I filled a box, I wrote her name with a thick felt-tip pen. I scanned the remaining heap of clothes. I grabbed a new box and laid them inside. I contemplated giving them away to the Salvation Army, but decided to swing by Holly's and see if Gwenelda needed anything.

Footsteps sounded on the staircase. "So that's where you're hiding," Dad said, peering over the balustrade at me. "I brought you sustenance." He handed me a plate with one of yesterday's blue cupcakes.

"Thanks." Stomach hollow, I bit into the cupcake. When the sugar hit my tongue, my brain hummed, almost as though I was being hot-wired. I hadn't realized how low on fuel I was running. "These are really good."

"Sweetie, I wanted to talk to you about something."

Dad's face was so strained I set the cupcake down. "What?"

"I wanted to know... Is something going on between you and Holly's great-nephew?"

Relief flooded me. Here I thought he was going to tell me he didn't believe Kajika was related to Holly, or something along those lines. "God, no." Suddenly ravenous for more food, I broke off a chunk of cupcake and tossed it into my mouth.

He let out a deep breath. "Good. Because, even though he isn't your first cousin, he's still family and"—he wrinkled his nose—"it's probably not very wise, genetically speaking, to grow too attached to a family member."

This felt like the-birds-and-the-bees discussion all over again, except instead of being twelve, I was nineteen, and instead of my mother explaining how it worked, I was speaking with my father about boys. Pretty icky. "You really don't have to worry about that."

Dad smiled, and it was like watching a bud burst open. His lips were cotton candy pink and his teeth, incredibly white.

"What toothpaste do you use?" I asked him.

Dad stared at me as though I'd cracked my head open. I felt my forehead in case I had. Smooth skin met my fingertips. Wow... My skin was awfully soft, like velvet or silk. Hmm... What was softer?

"Cat, honey, you okay?" Dad asked, crouching down in front of me.

"Huh?"

"You've been rubbing the same spot on your forehead for about five minutes. Does it hurt?"

I tore my fingers off and it felt like peeling a strip of Velcro. I could almost hear the scratchy ripping noise. "What? No."

He looked at me with his blue eyes, the same shade as Aylen's swimming pool back in Arizona. Such a pretty blue. Why couldn't mine be blue too? Instead of black, or were they technically dark, dark brown? *No.* Black. That's what was written on my driver's license. I'd need it soon for Boston. *Woo-hoo!* Boston. I was suddenly very excited for the trip. Or maybe I was just excited to get out of this teeny, tiny, puny, godforsaken, faerie-infested town.

"Sweetie?" Dad's voice resonated in my ears. He brought a glass of water to my lips and made me drink it.

It tasted like waterfall water, fresh and wild. Then again, I'd never tasted waterfall water. Maybe it didn't taste good at all. The liquid coated my throat and fell with a rumble into my stomach. Or maybe that noise was hunger pangs. I eyed the cupcake and was about to take another bite when Dad said, "Thank you so much for going through your mother's stuff."

A shiver shook me. I tore my eyes off the cake, looked at Dad, then stared at the piles of sorted clothing.

Mom.

"I put some stuff aside for Aylen," I said.

Dad was still studying me. "That's great. I'll call her. See if she's planning a trip out here or if I should ship them." He tipped his face to the side. "Cat, did you sleep okay last night?"

I blinked. "Better than I've slept in a long time."

"That's good." He rose from his crouch. "I slept well myself." He started toward the stairs but turned back. "By the way, I remembered where I've seen Kajika."

My neck stiffened. "Really?"

"In that odd dream I had a couple nights ago. You know, the one with the swing?"

"Weird," I said.

"Yeah. Weird. Your mom would've said the Great Spirit was offering me a vision."

I busied myself with a new box.

"But I doubt it since he's family." Halfway down the stairs, he called out, "Does he have tattoos?"

"Yes," I said, but immediately regretted it. Now Dad was going to wonder how I knew. "He's an ultimate fighter, so I've seen him with his shirt off. Like all fighters. I don't think they're allowed to fight fully clothed."

What I could see of Dad's face turned incredibly pale. "Ultimate fighting?"

Man oh man. I should've said we'd gone swimming or something. "Don't tell anyone, Dad, okay? He needs the money and he likes fighting, so it's fitting."

"I don't care what he does. I care what my daughter does. You've been to a lot of these ultimate fighting matches?"

"Just one."

"Please be careful, Cat. It's not really a place for girls."

"I'm careful. Plus, I only go with friends."

"I can come with you next time. If you want."

His suggestion was so ludicrous I grimaced. I quickly wiped the expression off my face. I didn't want to upset him. "There probably won't be a next time."

"Okay. Good."

"Dad, there was something I wanted to ask *you*. Did you tell anyone about Holly being related to us?"

"I told Stella yesterday. Why?"

"Holly doesn't want anyone to know."

"Oh." He scratched his head. "Shoot. Well, I'm having lunch with Stella today, to thank her for cleaning up our house. I'll tell her not to share the information."

"Okay."

He went down a step. "Although if you have time, I'd rather have lunch with you."

"I'm planning on getting all of this"—I gestured toward the still unopened boxes—"sorted out today, so I probably won't be done for a few more hours. Mom had *a lot* of stuff."

"I know. Such a hoarder."

"Such a hoarder," I mused with a smile. "Thanks for giving Kajika all those clothes yesterday."

"The poor kid looked like he needed help. Does he do drugs?"

"Drugs?" I shook my head no. "Why?"

"The last person I saw walking around without shoes in the middle of winter was Stella after her husband left. I don't know what she was on, but she was definitely in an altered state. Anyway, I'll let you get back to your…sorting."

"See you later, Dad."

"Bye, sweetheart," he said, before disappearing down the stairs. Moments later I heard the front door open and close, and then the hearse's tires crunching against the mix of gravel and granular snow.

Propped on my knees, I opened the flaps of yet another box when I heard a knock. I rocked backward and landed on my butt. My gaze sailed to the window where a fist knocked again. How could a fist reach a window that was three stories high? And then a face pushed against the glass, and I understood how.

"Mind opening this thing?" Ace's voice was muffled by the glass.

I hesitated, but then I pushed myself up and walked over. "Now, why would I do that?"

"Because you're in danger, and I'm the only one who can save you."

My breath snagged. I unlocked one side of the window and pushed it out. Ace floated through the narrow space like an astronaut gliding through airlocks on a spaceship. "Does this have to do with Gregor?" I asked, heart stampeding, hand prickling.

"Gregor?"

A message pinged on his phone. He typed back.

"What the hell's going on, Ace?"

He tucked the phone back into his jeans. "Loverboy was concerned about your escalating heart rate."

I put my hands on my waist. "I'm not asking about your text message. I'm asking about the danger. What danger?"

"It was just a ploy to get you to let me in."

"Ugh," I groaned. "You are so annoying!"

"How did you hear about Gregor? Did Kajika tell you about him?"

"No. Cass mentioned his name. Is he a faerie?"

"Yep. The loveliest kind."

I knew sarcasm, and that was sarcasm. "Is he coming to Rowan?"

He sniffed the air. Without asking for permission, he picked up the half-eaten cupcake, held it underneath his nose, and then tossed it back down on the plate. "One of Stella's?"

"Yeah."

"What do you think of them?"

I frowned. "They're tasty."

"Just tasty?"

What was he getting at? "Yes."

He eyed me for a long while, and then he eyed the cupcake.

"What do you think of them?" I asked him.

"I don't like them, then again, I don't like losing control."

My pulse quickened. "Why would a cupcake make you lose control?"

"There's mallow inside."

"Mallow?"

"It's like faerie weed. It affects humans by making them overeat. Especially Neverra-grown mallow, which is what's inside these. And it turns faerie brains into mush. It doesn't affect hunters though."

The lightheadedness I'd felt after sampling the cupcake returned with a vengeance. This time though, it was due to my rapid intakes of breath. "Stella's a…she's a…"

"Stella and Cometta are *calidum*. Half faeries. I believe you hunters call them *bazash*."

I'd never heard anyone utter Etta's full name out loud. "And their kids? Cass, Faith, Jimmy?"

Ace sat down on the daffodil-colored rocking chair my grandfather had built for my mother when she was pregnant with me. It was the only place I slept during the first six months of my life, nestled against my mother's breast. The second she would lay me in my crib, I would wake and screech.

"Cass and her brother have a microscopic amount of faerie

blood, because their dad was one hundred percent human, but Faith's father is one hundred percent faerie. Which makes Faith more of a faerie than her mother. It's all math and blood. Holly's a faerie too, but I think you know that already."

I nodded, deciding there was no point in lying.

"Speaking of Holly, what book did she send you?" Ace asked.

My guard came back up, cinching around me like armor. I didn't despise Ace as much as before, but I wasn't sure I could trust him either. "A history book."

"About?"

"Rowan's history."

"Does it contain any mention of faeries and hunters?"

I let out a frustrated sigh. "Why are you so interested in it?"

"Humans love to write tales about us, but they're all speculative. If Holly sent you a book, then the information inside must be accurate. And call me crazy, but I'd like to see what she wrote about us."

"Do I owe you something now?"

He frowned. "Huh?"

"You defended my *honor* back at the bakery. Do I owe you a *tokwa*?"

"A *tokwa*?"

"A favor." I pushed the box aside and pulled another one toward me. "Apparently faeries only do kind things for gain."

"Hooking up with a hunter is majorly frowned upon, so technically, I was defending *my* honor. Plus, I'm the prince of Neverra, Cat; I get first pick. I don't take another man's spoils."

I rolled my eyes. "How does all that arrogance fit into such a small body?"

"Small?" He chuckled. "I'm bigger than you. And you're anything but small."

Irritation pulsed through me. Why did he have to remind me how freakishly tall I was? I tipped over the box and dumped everything out. Hands shaking with anger, I started sorting through the mess of hair accessories, socks, and belts.

"What?" he asked.

"Nothing."

"Did I say something?"

Shouldn't fretting about faeries and hunters take precedence over worrying about my height? I shoved my insecurity away. Hopefully, one day, it would stop surfacing altogether. "Faith can't fly, can she? And she doesn't glow."

"Because she hasn't come to Neverra yet. If she never visits the Isle, her blood won't turn into fire."

I exhaled sharply. "Does she know what she is?"

"Nope. Stella doesn't want to tell her daughter yet, so don't you dare fess up, or I'll drag you to Neverra and never let you out."

I met those brilliant blue eyes of his straight on. I bet a lot of girls had succumbed to him because of those eyes. Thank the Great Spirit I was immune to them. "First off, I'm not a gossip. And secondly, I'm a hunter, so you can't take me to Neverra."

A shadow crossed over Ace's face, tingeing his bright blue irises violet. "Right."

Silence settled over the attic. It was neither pleasant, nor unpleasant. It was just really quiet. I tugged another box toward me as Ace rocked in Mom's chair. I tossed the scuffed shoes onto the pile of things to discard, paired the newer-looking ones, and then placed them back inside the box. Mom's feet had been tiny. I didn't have huge feet, but none of these would ever fit me. I knew they wouldn't fit Aylen since her feet were a size larger than Mom's. She'd always complained about never being able to borrow her older sister's cool shoes.

Did Gwen have small feet? Now, that was a thought I never imagined would cross my mind. I wrote a large G on the box and shoved it aside.

"I don't think they'll fit Gregor," Ace said.

I smiled in spite of myself. "Since you're *still* here, tell me more about this Gregor."

"He's the current wariff. A soulless narcissist with no values and too much influence."

"There are two of you in Neverra?"

He winced. "Ouch."

"Is Gregor in Rowan?"

"Nah. He's too scared to come, what with the regulations on our dust Negongwa implemented. But he's sending more *lucionaga* to patrol the town."

"*Lucio*-whattas?"

"*Golwinims*. Faerie guards. You know those lovely large men with the golden eyes? The ones you met at Astra's?"

"I knew it!" I stared at my hand, feeling the phantom burn one of them had inflicted on me the night Kajika rose. Had it been one of the men at the bakery? Or had it been Cruz's mark?

"Apparently Cruz and I did a subpar job at keeping the hunters in line. At least, that's what Gregor told my dad, and my dad eats up everything he says. I have to agree Cruz didn't behave suitably, what with canoodling with you, but *I've* been exemplary."

I tried to dismiss what had happened between Cruz and me under a thick coat of humor. "And you say you're not a narcissist?"

Ace grinned.

I started on a new box. "Cass can penetrate the circle of rowan trees, yet she has faerie blood."

"She has too little for it to make her sensitive to rowan wood or to iron."

"What about Faith? Can she penetrate it?" I asked, looking up.

"Until she visits Neverra, yes, but she'll get a really bad rash if she touches that dirt or those trees."

I pulled another box toward me and peered into it. Gardening tools. What were they doing up here? I had to take those down to the shed. "Why didn't you ever use normal humans to dig up the hunters?"

"Have you ever tried plowing through metal with a shovel?"

I stopped folding the cardboard flaps of the box in front of me.

"Between the iron sediments and the tree roots, the earth is rock solid to anyone without hunter blood," Ace explained, rocking back and forth.

I carved my hand through my hair, forgetting I'd tied it up. I tugged the elastic off, shook out my head, then smoothed it back and secured it while Ace watched on as though ponytails were some thrilling hunter ritual.

"I've been ordered to *punish* Holly for sending you the book."

"Punish her? Why?"

"For sharing information with hunters." Tendons shifted underneath his bare forearms. Or maybe it was fire.

"It's just a bunch of stories. There's nothing dangerous to faeries in it."

"Give it to me and I'll spare Holly."

"Spare her?"

He looked out the window, at the winter sun, which had finally managed to assert itself in the sky, bathing Manistee Forest in pale light. "Gregor has ordered me to kill her."

Pain bloomed in my jaw; I was clenching it too tightly. "Kill her?" I shook my head in disbelief. "It's a book, Ace. Just a book. Trust me, there's nothing inside that warrants murder."

"Trust you? You're a hunter, Cat. I can't trust you, just like you can't trust me."

My pulse pinged against my eardrums. "I won't give it to you, so please leave. I have a lot of things to do before my trip."

"Your trip? Where are you going?"

"Nowhere."

"You forget we have this amazing tracking device in you," he said, rising from the rocking chair.

I balled the fingers of my branded hand into a fist. *Damn mark.* "Boston."

"I love Boston," he said.

"Don't you dare show up there."

He started toward the window and pushed it open. Levitating, he turned around. "You should go to a restaurant called The Passage. It's a great scene."

"Please go away."

"The Passage. Write it down. *Valo.* That means goodbye in Faeli."

"How do you say *go away* in Faeli?"

"*Vade.*"

"Then *vade.*"

He smiled, but it didn't quite reach his eyes, then glided out the window and soared upward. Seeing a person take to the skies without an engine and wings was still a thing of wonder for me. I used to dream of flying when I was a kid. If I chose to become fae, I would be able to fly.

I shivered from the temptation. No. I would remain human.

That's what I wanted.

That's what I needed.

Besides, I didn't even know how to become anything else.

I wrote the word *human* in thick black letters on the back of my hand, right over Cruz's mark.

30

TATTOO

*A*fter two more taxing hours of sorting through my mother's boxes, I decided to immortalize the word I'd written on my hand.

So determined was I that this was a brilliant idea, I didn't let the small factor of being carless stop me. I recovered my bike from the shed behind the house. The metal body was as cold as snow, and the leather seat as stiff as dried plaster, but it beat taking the bus, which made so many stops along the way it took a whole hour to reach Ruddington.

My muscles were rigid, but by mile three, pedaling became easier. And then I flew down the cleared roads, swallowing lungfuls of crisp air and admiring the silver-gilded landscape.

Ruddington was another harbor town with under ten thousand inhabitants. Like Rowan, its heart beat on a single street where mom-and-pop shops competed with corner bookstores and quaint restaurants. Unlike in Rowan, one of the streets that branched off the main street housed a biker bar, a strip club, and a tattoo parlor.

The tattoo artist looked at me funny when I told him I wanted the word *human* inked on my hand. I was surprised my choice received an eyebrow raise. It wasn't as though I'd asked him to embed a working compass into my flesh.

"Want the equivalent in Chinese?" he asked.

"No."

"And you really want it on the top of your hand?"

"Yes."

"Most women get inked on the inside of their wrists."

I smiled sweetly at him. "I'd like it right where the pen marks are."

"You sure?"

"Couldn't be surer."

Finally, he set to work, dabbing a damp cotton disk over my hand to erase the traces of marker.

When I saw him studying the V-shaped white lines of Cruz's mark, I said, "Birthmark." He probably thought I'd carved my own skin.

About half an hour later, I had the pretty cursive word etched into my skin for all of eternity.

As I paid, he asked, "Why *human?*"

"As a reminder."

He tipped his head to the side as he handed me my change. "Because you forget?"

"Not yet."

He rubbed his pierced eyebrow, confused.

I left before he could ask me anything else. When I stepped outside, my bike was gone. The chain I'd wrapped through the front spokes was still there, clipped neatly in half. I grunted in frustration, went back inside the tattoo parlor, and asked if he had security cameras. The man looked at me funny again.

I returned outside, clutching my cell phone angrily and pressed on the first number I had on my speed-dial list. It rang and then an automated message informed me the number had been disconnected. I looked at the screen and, in horror, read Mom's name.

I dropped the phone, my heart squeezed so tight it felt as

though it were being vacuum-packed into this tiny flat thing that could not possibly contain a pulse.

For a long time I didn't move, but then I bent over and picked my phone back up. Fingers shaking, I did one of the hardest things: I deleted Mom's contact and then I did the same for Blake's. Their names vanished into thin air, yet their phone numbers spooled through my mind on a loop.

My favorites list now consisted of three numbers: Dad, Aylen, and Cass.

I phoned Cass, not wanting to worry my father.

"Hey, Cat," she said. I could hear voices in the background. She was probably at work.

"Any chance you could swing by Ruddington to pick me up?" I asked, on the off chance she wasn't busy. "Someone stole my bike."

She sucked air through her teeth, or maybe that was the sound of the milk steamer. "Can't. There's a party of eight who just walked in. What are you doing in Ruddington?"

"I got a tattoo."

"You what?" she exclaimed. "You're so badass."

I grimaced. "I bet you'll change your mind when you see it. Is Dad around by any chance?"

"He's upstairs with Bee. But your friend is here. Let me ask if he can come."

"What friend?"

"The hot one."

"Which hot one?"

"True. You got a bunch of hot friends." She lowered her voice. "The fighter."

I would rather have taken the bus than requested Kajika's help. "Don't ask him. I'll call Dad."

I almost hung up, but then I heard her on the other end of the line speaking to someone.

"Cass, no," I said loudly.

"He's on his way."

"He doesn't even know where I am," I grumbled.

"I told him you were next to the strip club. He didn't ask where it was," she said, with a lilt in her voice. "I suppose he's a regular like most of the men in this town. Really gotta go now. Come keep me company later?"

"Sure," I mumbled.

After hanging up, I squeezed the phone in my hand. What was I supposed to do? Just stand there until Holly's old truck rumbled through town? I checked my watch. It would take him at least twenty minutes to get here. I was most definitely not waiting on a street corner with a hand covered in Vaseline and saran wrap in sub-zero temperatures.

I went inside the biker bar and scooted onto one of the bar stools. I was expecting it to stick to my gray jeans, but it didn't. The bartender came over, a big man with tattoo sleeves and thick ropey muscles. He placed his palms on the bar in front of me, then inspected my face.

"Could I get a beer, please?"

"I'm going to have to see some ID first."

Shoot. I rummaged through my bag. I'd left my fake ID in Boston. I didn't like traveling with it. Finally, I sucked in a breath, took out my real driver's license and handed it over.

Leveling my gaze on his, going almost squinty-eyed, I tried something crazy...I tried to influence him. "I was born on June 7th, 1995."

He didn't blink. His eyes stayed wide, and then he nodded. He slid my driver's license across the bar. It skidded noiselessly toward me.

"What sort of beer would you like?"

I gaped up at him, stunned my influence had worked, then slotted the card back into my wallet. "Um, what do you have on tap?"

"Stella, Nooner, Amstel."

"I'll take a Nooner," I said at random.

"Comin' right up." He filled a tall, frosty glass and set it in front of me. "Whad'ya get tattooed?"

I rubbed my fingers over the piece of plastic wrap. "My new mantra."

"I started with one of those. Lyrics from a Metallica song." He pointed at them. "Then I got more. And more. My girl told me I looked like the bulletin board in our apartment building, but whatev, right? I like them, and that's all that counts."

"Agreed."

"Enjoy the beer. It's a good one."

I dipped my lips in the creamy foam and tipped the glass back. It tasted like chestnuts and quince and a spring meadow. I took another sip and checked my emails. I had a hundred unread ones. Most were newsletters I'd subscribed to or college announcements. I started going through them, but then decided I'd done enough sorting for one day. Instead, I opened an Internet page, and typed "iron wind chimes" in the search bar.

I got a few hits, one of which was titled, "Keep pests out." Halfway through my glass of beer, I had to read the headline twice to make sure it said pests and not pets. Finally, I clicked on it. I was sent to a page with a picture of a wind chime that looked exactly like the one Mom had built. I added it to my cart, then browsed to see what else was sold. Their other products were horseshoes, mezuzahs, evil-eyes, and crosses made of Rowan wood and red thread. I smiled as I imagined how enthralled Mom would have been by this website.

Draining my glass, I took out my credit card and filled out the information to have it shipped to the house. I received an order confirmation email just as someone slipped onto the barstool next to me.

"You found me."

"You didn't make it easy," Kajika said.

"I want another beer. You want one?" I stuck my hand in the air to catch the bartender's attention. "My treat."

"I don't drink alcohol."

I whirled toward the hunter. "Seriously? Why not?"

"It alters the senses." He grabbed my hand, the one with the tattoo. "What is this?"

I pulled my hand out of Kajika's just as the bartender walked toward me. "I'll take another one."

"What did you do to your hand, Catori?"

"I got a tattoo," I said defensively.

Kajika went statue-still. Only his eyes moved, from my hand up to my face. "You seized a power?"

"Huh?" It took my beer-addled brain a second to connect the dots. "No. Someone made it."

"What do you mean?"

"Some guy used this magic pen and drew it on me," I said, just as the bartender brought my beer. "You see *his* arms? Same thing."

Kajika looked at the bartender. He frowned, then laid his gaze back on me. "Why would you do that?"

"It's her body. Her choice, man," the bartender said.

Kajika glared at him, and his eyes shone like those brown-gold stones Aylen loved...tiger-eyes. Pretty appropriate considering Kajika's gaze was as savage as a tiger's. "Leave us alone," he told Tattoo.

Transfixed, the bartender nodded, then he blinked and walked away.

"I did that too," I told Kajika, feeling mighty proud.

Kajika turned his attention back to me. All of his attention. If it weren't for the first drink pleasantly buzzing through me, I would most probably have looked away. "Did what?" he asked in that raucous voice of his.

I leaned in toward him. "Made him believe I was twenty-one." I smiled, delighted with myself.

"You're supposed to use your influence for good."

"Like you just did?" I snorted, then drank a large gulp of beer. Foam stuck to my upper lip. I licked it off. Kajika stared at me as though I were an alien descended from another planet. He was the alien. Not me. "You are such a killjoy, you know that?"

Shadows pooled over his face.

"What are you even doing here?" I asked him, placing the glass back down on the coaster. I twirled it, watching the coaster rotate as though it were the kaleidoscope I'd made with Mom for school five years ago. Our acrylic tube, triangular mirrors, glue, and glitter had won first prize.

"Cass told me your bicycle was stolen," Kajika said, thrusting me off memory lane.

"Could've just said you were busy."

"I wasn't."

"What? No faeries to discipline?"

"Not today," he replied, way too seriously.

I drank in silence. Without asking permission, he peeled off the piece of plastic wrap and read the word.

"I was reminding myself of the choice I'll need to make soon," I explained, "in case I'm tempted by something else."

His brow puckered. "You're tempted by something else?"

I took a long swallow of beer, looking at him over the rim of my glass. He was wearing Dad's shoes, a pair of jeans that actually fit him, and a black T-shirt that made him look narrow even though I knew he wasn't.

"Which side of you?" he asked.

I debated whether to tell him the truth. Since Kajika hated faeries, voicing it might get me killed, and I hadn't finished my beer yet. Okay, it wasn't because of the beer as much as I just didn't feel like dying. For Dad's sake, and for my sake. I squared my shoulders and said, "The abominable one."

He squeezed his eyes shut. It lasted so long I wondered how angry I'd made him on a scale of one to ten. When he opened his eyes, I decided he was hovering between a nine and a half and a ten. He planted his elbows on the bar, and then hung his head in his hands.

Goosebumps popped up on my arms. I felt wicked. Why was I feeling wicked about a choice that was mine to make? "That's why I'm staying human, Kajika." I drank more beer to drown the guilt I had no reason to feel. "Plus, I wouldn't want you as my enemy. I'm pretty sure you'd hunt me down and kill me in a second, and an arrow through the heart is not the way I want to leave this world."

He shook his head. Joggled his knee. I laid my palm on his thigh to calm him down.

He jerked off the barstool. "Don't!"

Short-fused and dangerous, that's what he was. He stared me down; I stared right back. I shrugged, then looked away. "You can leave. I'll get the bus." I signaled the bartender. He glanced my way before dropping his gaze back to the glass he was drying. I waited. "I'd like another," I said loudly, but he still didn't acknowledge me. Other patrons did, but I didn't want *their* attention.

In my peripheral vision, I saw Kajika push through the door. At least *he'd* gotten the message. I asked the bartender a third time for my beer. Even though the man lifted his eyes to mine, he still wouldn't approach. Huffing, I tossed ten dollars on the bar, and got up. When I stepped out, a wave of cold slammed into me. I blinked to make sure the bar hadn't been transported to the edge of the lake, and that I wasn't walking straight into a body of water. But the only thing I waded in was a typical Michigan winter night.

I walked to the bus stop, hands stuffed in my pockets to keep them from becoming ice cubes. Ahead of me strolled a couple who glowed brightly, as though lit from within. I looked at their feet, expecting them to hover off the pavement, but they weren't flying. They were no longer even moving. When I looked back up at their faces, I found them staring at me, sniffing the air, frowning.

Shoulders hunched, I crossed the street, praying they wouldn't follow me. I tried to calm myself down. I wasn't really at risk, was I? I peeked over my shoulder. They were gone. I was about to exhale a deep breath when I knocked right into something.

Regaining my balance, I looked up, straight into one of their unfamiliar faces.

"What do we have here?" the male asked. He was blond, almost silver-haired, and pale.

His companion was the exact opposite, ebony-skinned, glimmering like a black diamond in the darkness. She sniffed the air. *"Ventor."*

I guessed it meant hunter. Unless it meant, "Kill her." I really hoped not.

I backed away, heart thrusting against the walls of my ribcage. My hand prickled. *This would be a really good time to show up, Ace,* I thought. I half expected him to shoot down from the sky, but he didn't. My phone vibrated in my pocket. I drew it out. Cruz's number flashed. I slid my finger against the screen to answer.

"She's marked," the woman faerie said, grabbing my hand with her burning one. She yanked on my fingers so hard to show her partner that my phone fell. The smell of charred flesh stung my nostrils, but the only thing I worried about was whether I'd answered the phone.

A flash of darkness shot out behind the faeries. Was I about to pass out? I always saw black spots before passing out. The woman dropped my hand, and spun around. She held her palms out in front of her. Flames licked her dark skin. "Another one," she said, head turning, searching the darkness.

And then a wall of black appeared in front of me, so close my nose smashed against it. It smelled like my father. Instinct took over. I pushed him aside. Dad couldn't protect me against faeries, but maybe I could protect him.

An arm shot out and struck my stomach, knocking the breath out of me. "Stay behind me, Catori," a voice—not my father's —growled.

Gasping, I cowered behind Kajika.

"So the rumors are true. The hunters have returned." It was the male fae who said this.

"Leave before I repossess your sinful power," Kajika said, his voice low, menacing.

He snorted. "I'll turn your little friend into ashes if you even try."

"She's marked," the female said, placing a hand on the male's outstretched arm. Fire pulsed underneath his skin. "She's not ours to kill, Marcus."

Without lowering his hand, the male levitated, and then his companion did the same, and they shot upward. I trailed their ascent, heart still hammering. I kept my gaze on the sky long after they'd left, terrified they could still set me on fire. The wall moved. Not a wall, I reminded myself. Kajika.

He turned, tipped his head down. "Did they hurt you?"

"I...I..." My teeth chattered. "They scared me, that's all."

He inspected my hand. "She burned you."

My mouth and my throat felt bone-dry. I tried to swallow but ended up coughing. I looked down at my hand that Kajika still held. Three of my fingers were badly blistered. "It doesn't hurt."

"Because you're in shock." Kajika released my hand.

I nursed it with my other hand. The blisters started deflating and then the purple skin peeled off. I was healing. I suspected my faerie blood was to thank, but I didn't say it out loud. Kajika stared at my hand, then he stared away. Strips of dead skin flaked off, replaced by pale pink flesh that darkened to my normal color without leaving a single scar. I wasn't a doctor yet, but I knew this process took days, weeks, not seconds. Instead of enchanting me, the magic I possessed scared me.

I curled my fingers and pressed my nails into my palm until I could feel pain. Pain made me feel human. "You didn't kill them," I whispered.

Kajika's eyes gleamed. "I'm only authorized to kill if they threaten us with dust."

My breathing had almost returned to normal. "Do you even have...arrows?"

He patted his jacket in answer. I supposed all that wood he'd felled wasn't just to make fire. "Still want to join them?" he asked, his face dangerously close to mine, and dangerously complacent.

"I'm not joining anyone."

A vein throbbed in his neck. He didn't move, and neither did I. If he was trying to intimidate me into admitting I feared faeries, it wasn't working.

His face loomed closer to mine, and then he sank to his knees and picked up my cell phone. "Here," he said, handing it to me. He spun around and strode across the street. A car honked at him. He didn't react. Once on the other side, he stopped. "Are you coming this time, or do you want to make more friends?"

I leveled my gaze on his. I couldn't tell if he was being humorous or bitter.

He waited. I swallowed a sour-tasting lump of pride and crossed the street toward him. I stayed silent and lagged behind him during the short walk to the car. Once in the car, I kept my silence, watching for more glowing passersby, but the few who passed by didn't glow.

Kajika turned left and then left again, driving through streets that didn't lead back to Rowan. "Too proud to ask for directions?"

"I was looking for your bicycle."

"Oh." I blushed. And then I shrugged. "It's probably inside someone's garage by now."

"Back in my day, when a thief was caught, his or her nose was cut off as punishment. It served as a warning to the people he interacted with, to alert them of his misconduct."

"Nowadays, a thief is fined or jailed, depending on the value of what was stolen."

"Then how do you know if they are a criminal when you cross paths with them in the street?"

"You don't."

"That's foolish."

However gruesome the thought of amputating body parts,

Kajika made a good point. "You do realize that if your punishment were still applied, you'd have your nose cut off?"

He frowned.

"You stole clothes."

His shoulders strained his coat. "I went back to pay once I had money."

Mouth slightly ajar, I studied his profile. He was kind, too kind. And so very righteous. Just like Blake had been. The comparison clawed at my chest.

He took some more turns in the side streets. I didn't stop him, even though it was hopeless. At some point, he must have given up sleuthing, because he took the road that led back to Rowan.

"What do humans see when they look at faeries?" I asked. "Do they see the fire burning on their skin? The flying?"

"When they levitate, faeries use dust to create illusions. Humans see them running away, or disappearing into a house, or whatever other illusion a fae projects. As for the fire, only hunters or fae can perceive it."

"How come I never noticed that Stella or Holly glowed?"

"They were probably careful around you because of your...ancestry."

"Cruz said that as long as hunters didn't know about faeries, faeries didn't know about them."

Kajika slanted his eyes. "Catori, they can smell hunters. Ever since you were born, they knew what you were."

"Then why did he tell me this?"

"I reckon because he's dishonest, but what do I know?"

I twisted my lips in annoyance, and watched as thick woods replaced concrete sidewalks.

"How are you going to explain your tattoo to your father?" he asked.

I studied the little word. "I'll tell him it's a reminder that nothing lasts forever."

Kajika stared at the empty, flat strip of road ahead of us while the car's vents sputtered bursts of heat that sounded like long, droning sighs. "I put some stuff aside for Gwen. Can you take it to her after you drop me off?"

He nodded.

"Do faeries frighten you?" I asked him when the sign welcoming us to Rowan appeared on the side of the road.

"No."

"Does anything frighten you?"

"No."

"Really?" I pivoted toward him in my seat. "Nothing?"

"Fear comes from the unknown."

"And you consider you know everything?"

"Yes." There was no conceit in his voice or on his face. He was serious. "I've tasted death. I've been hurt and tortured. I've been torn away from the people I've loved. What's left to fear, Catori?"

"Faeries tortured you?"

He smiled a dark smile that wasn't a smile at all, even though it resembled one.

"What did they do to you?" I asked.

"They burned me...tried to suffocate me. May I give you some advice, or will you tell me I'm being inconsiderate toward your friends?"

"I'll take the advice."

"If they bring out their dust, squeeze your nose shut and hold your breath. As long as you don't inhale it, it won't affect you."

"I'll remember that."

"Dust can penetrate your eyes, but not quickly."

"How many powers have you confiscated?"

"Twenty-two. I gave most back."

"Is it a time thing? Like a sentencing? You keep them a certain number of months?"

"No. It's a choice; the hunter's choice. If the faerie apologizes and behaves for an acceptable period of time, you release their power."

"So you deemed certain people unforgivable?"

He nodded.

"Will you eventually release the remaining powers?"

"I might return five of them, but two I will always keep."

"Why?"

His fingers tightened around the wheel. "Because they belong to the faeries who murdered Ishtu."

A shiver slithered up my spine. "Who were they?"

His Adam's apple jostled in his throat. "Borgo Lief and Lyoh Vega."

"Vega? Who's Lyoh Vega?"

"Your faerie friend's mother."

"Cruz told me she was dead."

Concentrated anger pulsed in his neck. "If she were, her power wouldn't still be inside me."

Cruz had lied to me. Again. Had anything he'd told me been truthful? A heavy silence filled the car. "Why did they kill Ishtu?"

"They said she was at the wrong place, at the wrong time."

"Why did you confiscate their power? Why didn't you just kill them, Kajika?"

"Stripping a faerie of power is like cutting off its nose."

"You thought humiliation was punishment enough?"

"No," he said, his voice as deep as a roll of thunder. It sent shivers all the way down my spine. "Catori, I don't want to talk about this with you. We are not friends."

It hurt. To pretend it didn't would be a lie. He was right, though. We weren't friends. Friends helped each other. Granted, he'd saved me back in Ruddington, but how had *I* helped him? The clothes he wore were given to him by my father. The house he lived in belonged to Holly. He'd opened himself up to me, shared secrets and advice, while I'd shared only my desire to stay human and my temptation to become fae.

We drove the rest of the way in silence. When he slowed down in front of my house, I asked him to wait. I lugged down two boxes full of clothes and shoes for Gwenelda, and one box with canned food, packages of crackers, and a first-aid kit. Maybe they could afford this on their own now, but in case they couldn't, they wouldn't have to steal.

Kajika heaved them into the truck's bed. "Thank you." Without another word, he walked back to the driver's seat, climbed in, and closed his door.

Arms wrapped around myself, I backed up and watched him leave, and for a moment, it felt like Blake was leaving me all over again. And it hurt all over again.

31

THE PASSAGE

*T*he trip to Boston couldn't come soon enough. I woke up before the sun broke over the horizon and arrived at the airport three full hours before my flight. Dad waited until I'd passed through security and then he waited some more for Aylen's flight to land.

She'd told Dad not to waste his money on shipping even though that wasn't the real reason she was coming to Rowan. The real reason was I'd asked her to come. I told her what Dad had done to himself after he discovered Mom's body. I didn't want him to be alone. I supposed I could have tasked someone else to father-sit, but Dad would've found it strange if the person insisted on sleeping over. Plus Aylen was so chatty she would steer his mind away from any morose thoughts.

The flight wasn't bumpy like it had been on the way in. I hadn't needed to clutch my armrests or take calming breaths. It took two hours to make the journey that would take me ten the following day. And that was if the weather remained fair. Snow would slow me down. I'd checked the forecast, and no snowfall had been predicted, but weather in New England was mercurial.

I took a cab to my dorm. Cora wasn't there, which made

packing restful. If she'd been around, I would've felt the need to make conversation. I crammed three duffel bags full of clothes, books, and toiletries. I didn't have many personal items besides those, only one framed photograph of my family on my bedside shelf taken the day of orientation. Mom had worn dark sunglasses to mask her teary eyes.

I slotted the framed picture between two scarves, then changed into my favorite pair of pants—black leather leggings I'd gotten my first year of college—and a boxy violet sweater. I zipped up my last bag, then one by one, I took them to my car, which was parked outside, camouflaged by two inches of crusty snow. It took several attempts to drag the trunk up as it was frozen shut. I couldn't wait for spring.

After placing all my belongings inside, I strolled around campus, then sat on a bench to watch the sun dip below the brick buildings and tinge the Charles orange. It was something I never did—sit still with no book to read or paper to study or phone to scroll through. Mom used to say stillness allowed you to perceive the invisible. Until that moment, I'd never realized what she'd meant.

I saw fear overtake a child's face when he lost sight of his mother, and then relief wash over him when he found her. I saw pain rumple a runner's forehead. I saw desperation in a teenage boy's eyes as he walked, knobby-kneed, hands stuffed inside his pockets. I sensed excitement ripple off a woman speaking on a phone.

Gorged on others' emotions, I made my way back to the dorm. Cora was there, concern lancing behind her dark, kohl-lined gaze.

"You took the sheets off the bed," she said.

"Yeah. I packed everything."

"You should spend the night and leave in the morning."

"I like driving at night. It's peaceful."

She grimaced, which made the silver stud in her nose glint.

"You're one strange girl, Catori Price. But I'll have you know you were my favorite roommate."

"Because I left?"

She smiled. "Because you were respectful. Because you didn't think I was some practicing Wiccan. Apparently, some girls on the third floor think I cast spells in my downtime."

All the nice buzzing inside my brain died out like a TV being turned off. Even though Cora had meant it as a joke, it reminded me of Rowan, of faeries and hunters, things that shouldn't exist but did. I rubbed my tattoo. Even if I chose to stay human, what sort of life would I lead carrying all this knowledge around?

"I'm not," she said, taking my silence for alarm. "Relax."

"Of course you're not."

"Come on. I got us a table at a restaurant I've been dying to try."

Looking around one last time, I turned away and followed Cora downstairs. We walked a few blocks, chatting about her classes and about Duke. It seemed like every student was out; the restaurants and coffeehouses were bursting with giggling, rowdy groups.

Rowan was *really* quiet.

"I'll be back in September," I said, although Cora hadn't asked. I was telling the streets, and I was telling myself.

We went inside a dark and narrow restaurant with no awning that looked like an abandoned bordello. Black and white pictures of sensual clichés adorned red walls. The loud lounge music made me want to dance. Several people were, in fact, dancing in the back of the restaurant. An L-shaped copper bar ran the length of the place with not a free barstool in sight.

"Is wearing lingerie in public even allowed?" I asked Cora, as the bedazzled-bra-and-panty-clad hostess guided us to our table. Granted she had fishnet stockings *and* knee-high boots, but those hardly counted as real clothes.

"I think so," she said, dark eyes mesmerized by the thick, swanning crowd.

The hostess handed us menus. When I read the name embossed

on the leather cover, I jerked my gaze up to Cora's. "Who told you to come here?"

"I read about it. The Passage has been voted best bar and restaurant in the Boston area."

I stared around me, expecting to see glowing people, but I didn't. Then again, faeries shone only in moonlight. Which meant everyone here could possibly be fae. My stomach roiled as I kept staring around all throughout dinner, unable to concentrate on a thing Cora was saying. Not that I could really hear her over the noise.

I was afraid of eating the food, wary mallow had been ground over each dish. I nibbled on a salad leaf, but then stopped. What if it was a mallow leaf? I drank water, but even that, I did carefully, spacing out each sip, testing if I felt funny. After a buzz-free half hour, I decided the water was safe and filled my churning stomach with just that.

Cora mouthed something. Well, she spoke it, but I couldn't hear her, so I leaned over. "What did you write on your hand?"

I showed her.

"Cryptic," she said. "But so true." She took a sip of her wine. "You should try this wine! It's unbelievable."

"I don't want to drink and drive," I yelled back.

Suddenly her gaze climbed up, to some place above my head, and her lips parted. I twirled around, half expecting to see Ace standing there.

But it wasn't Ace.

My hand burned and glowed.

The palm of the person behind me also glowed.

"Hello, Catori," Cruz said.

I was unable to articulate a response.

"May I sit with you?" he asked pulling up a chair from God knew where.

I blinked.

"You two know each other?" Cora asked, looking from me to Cruz.

I nodded, my throat feeling as though it had contracted to the width of a straw.

"I need to go to the bathroom. I'll be right back," she said, giving me a knowing look.

I wanted to tell her to stay but was still unable to speak. She waggled her eyebrows at me when she stood behind Cruz.

Cruz was looking at my tattoo. His brow furrowed and his really green eyes narrowed. "Human?"

I swallowed.

Another song came on, and then it ended, and I still hadn't said anything, too shocked that Cruz Vega was sitting inches away from me.

"I heard about Blake. I'm really sorry, Catori."

Again I swallowed. I seemed unable to do anything but freaking swallow.

"I also heard the new hunter is *nice* with you."

I frowned. How the heck had he heard that?

I must have said this out loud because he said, "Ace told me Kajika protected you from Patila and Marcus."

"Who?"

"The faeries you ran into a few days ago."

"Ace wasn't there. How would he know?"

"He was there. But so was...Kajika. He didn't want to intervene. He said the hunter had everything under control."

Cruz collected my hand in his, but I dragged it away, nestling it in my lap. Hurt tinged his handsome face.

"You told me your mother was dead," I said.

"She is."

"She's not."

"She is, Catori. To me, she is." His eyes clouded. "She died the day she executed my father in front of everyone in Neverra."

"She killed your father?"

He nodded. "I'm pretty sure she'd like me dead too." He smiled. "Don't look so shocked. That's Neverra for you. Everyone wants to either pierce each other's hearts or make them beat wildly. It's the fae way. At least, that's what Ace and I call it. *The fae way*," he repeated, his smile turning grim. "We'd like to change things, but we seem to be the only ones up in Neverra with that aspiration. Down here though, many want change. That's why, when Holly woke the hunters, we saw it as an opportunity."

It took me a second to process what he was saying, but especially the last part. "Holly? *She* told my mother to wake the hunters?"

He nodded slowly. "Everyone assumed the earth would shift one day, and the hunters would awaken. And perhaps it would have, but Holly wanted them to wake sooner. So she asked your mother to dig one up."

I'd finally found the person to blame, yet it brought me no solace.

I stared at Cruz, and then I stared around him, but I wasn't seeing anything. My eyesight was as unfocused as my mind.

A human shape materialized next to our table. I had to blink several times to make out Cora. She said she needed to join Duke at some party. When she rifled through her purse to pay, Cruz touched her arm. From the way she gaped at him, I thought he'd electrocuted her.

"It's a buddy's place. Friends of Catori aren't allowed to pay."

She thanked him, then bent over and gave me a one-armed hug as I sat there stiffly, sullenly.

"Please say something," Cruz told me once she'd left. "I don't like your silence."

"Holly killed my mother," I repeated robotically. "She *killed* my mother."

"She didn't know."

"You're defending her? I suppose you would since you're thrilled the hunters are back."

"I understand your bitterness, but don't direct it at me. I didn't ask Holly to wake your ancestors. And again, she didn't know what it would do to your mother."

"I'm so sick of hearing that excuse. You don't take stupid risks. Not when it involves someone's life."

"The greatest rewards come at the greatest risks."

I discharged a shrill breath. "It wasn't *your* mother."

"I wish it had been." The darkness in his gaze bled into his throat.

"Aren't you afraid someone will hear you say that?"

"It's not a secret. Some days, I detest being a faerie. I detest that I had to witness my father's death. I detest being engaged to an innocent girl because my mother and Linus Wood struck a deal." His black curls gleamed in the dim golden glow of the restaurant. "But what I detest most is being locked up in Neverra."

"You're here, so I guess you're not *that* locked up."

"I'm here because I agreed to Gregor's terms."

"Gregor's terms?"

"He wants something of yours, and I told him I could get it for him."

"What does he want?"

"Holly's book."

I snorted. "Why does everyone want the freaking book?"

"Because it tells in what grave each hunter is buried."

"So?"

"We need to wake Negongwa. He is the key to making peace."

"Is that why Gregor wants to wake him? To make peace?"

"No. Gregor wants to force him to annul the regulation on our dust."

"And kill him."

Cruz looked away from my face. It lasted a heartbeat, but it was long enough for me to know I'd spoken the truth.

"Have you heard of *gajoï*, Catori?"

"No."

"Hunters call them *tokwa*."

I stiffened. "Yes."

"I need to collect mine."

Something beat in the pit of my stomach, like a pulse. Fear maybe?

"Catori," he said slowly, "tell me where you put Holly's book."

I stared at Cruz and blinked. The throbbing in my stomach intensified and cut off my breath. I hugged my arms around myself and bent as an even more excruciating pain filled me. It felt as though I'd stepped into the ring with Kajika, and he was pounding me with his fists. But I was in no ring. And unfortunately, Kajika wasn't there. I looked down at my belly, but nothing was touching it. The pain turned so sharp, my lips unbolted with a gasp.

"It's going to hurt until you tell me, Catori," Cruz said calmly.

I hated him then. I hated him for torturing me. I didn't know how he was doing it, but I was certain he was controlling everything. "Make it stop," I yelped.

"It won't stop until you uphold your end of the bargain." Cruz's voice sounded all at once far away and too close.

Sweat coated my upper lip. It dripped into my mouth. "I never agreed—" A stronger blow crushed my insides, as though a hand were gripping my organs. I squeezed my mouth shut again, but the pain didn't let up, and soon, I was panting and gasping. "Stop it," I whimpered, and then I yelped as Cruz's magic shredded my insides. Tears bloomed inside my eyes, clung to my eyelashes. I wanted to look around, call for help, but I just sat there, huddled over, racked with pain.

"Where is it?" He was so fucking calm.

All this for a book. They could have their stupid book! "Under my mattress," I hissed.

Just as it had started, the pain stopped. Completely stopped. Numbness and hollowness replaced the excruciating pounding. And then anger supplanted the numbness. "How dare you?" I shrieked. I didn't care if I attracted attention. I was so goddamn mad. "That wasn't fair!"

Cruz typed something on his phone, and then he looked up at me. "I'm sorry, Catori, but I had no choice."

His leather jacket crackled as he squared his shoulders. It was the jacket he'd lent me the day Gwenelda had been gassed by vitriolic *golwinim,* the day I'd kissed him. *Ugh...*

"You *had* a choice," I said.

"You don't know what it's like up there."

I shook my head and shot to my feet. I'd found him so handsome, so trustworthy, but Kajika was right...he was just a selfish monster out to use me. "Is that why you saved Gwenelda? So I would owe you?" I spat.

"I saved Gwenelda because I want peace. Like my father wanted peace. Like Negongwa." He held my stare. "That you owed me came in handy."

I glowered.

"You know who else wants peace?" he asked. "Kajika. He agreed to work with Ace."

I gave a dark laugh. "He hates you more than I do. Actually, that's not true; I might hate you more."

Cruz's brow crumpled. "The pain ensures a person goes through with a bargain. I truly am sorry."

"Oh, save your apologies for someone who cares."

His cell phone rang. As he answered it, I yanked on my coat and made to leave, but he caught my wrist. "Don't go."

I threw his hand off. "Don't you dare touch me."

I forded through the restaurant but collided into someone. I tried to step around them, but the person caught hold of me. I looked up into bright blue eyes. "What happened, Kitty Cat?"

"What happened? Why don't you ask your *brother*?" I told Ace, my gaze murderous.

He frowned.

Suddenly, someone shoved Ace aside. I craned my neck up, and gasped when my gaze met Kajika's. The hunter stared back at me, giving my body one long, careful sweep. "What did the faerie do to you?"

"Kajika?" I looked at Ace again, then at Kajika again.

Both were really here.

Cruz took a step toward me. I backed away, my arm hitting Kajika's chest. "I told Ace to bring Kajika. I didn't think you were in any state to drive back on your own."

"Why? Because you just tortured a secret out of me?" My voice dripped with anger.

"He tortured you?" Kajika hissed.

"You know how a *tokwa* works, don't you, *ventor*?" Cruz asked. "The magic in the bargain creates pain."

Kajika folded his arms so tightly they looked like they'd merged into one thick limb.

"If you'd asked nicely, Cruz," I hissed, "I would've given you the book."

"Ace asked nicely. You didn't give it to him."

"Because he and I didn't share what you and I did," I said. "But apparently, that too was just an illusion."

Repentance or guilt cracked the hard set of his features. I didn't care which emotion it was because I didn't care about him anymore. "That's not true," he said softly.

My heart pounded. Stupid heart. And then my even stupider hand smoldered. And so did Cruz's. Both Ace and Kajika stared at our shining connection. But soon it was only Ace, as Kajika's face filled with too much disgust. He turned and walked out of The Passage. He would probably leave.

When I turned back toward the faeries, they were speaking quietly. They stopped when they saw me staring. "How did you get here?" I asked Ace.

"I flew." I didn't think he meant by plane.

"How did Kajika get here?"

"I carried him."

"He let a faerie carry him?"

"It was the quickest way to get here," Ace said. "I told him you were in mortal danger."

"You lied to him?"

"I didn't think driving ten hours on your own, in the middle of the night, foaming at the mouth, was the safest thing for you."

"So you knew what Cruz wanted from me?"

He combed his hand through his dark blond hair.

"Ace was just helping me"—Cruz looked at his future brother-in-law—"like I helped him."

I snorted. "You owed Cruz a favor? Lucky you. Is it an actual profession up in Neverra? *Gajoï* collector."

Ace smirked. "No, but it would be a good one."

"Does Kajika owe you now?"

"Are you kidding? The hunter would never, ever accept to bargain with a faerie. He even held an arrow to my throat during the entire flight. It was mega fun."

I smiled as I looked over at the entrance of the restaurant, hoping I would see him, but he was gone. My smile disappeared.

"He's still there." Ace tapped his nose. "I can smell him, remember?"

Right. "Like you can smell me?"

"About that…" He glanced over at Cruz. "Why doesn't she smell like the others?"

A nerve ticked in Cruz's jaw.

"I thought I reeked," I said.

"People were listening to our conversation, Kitty Cat."

Suddenly, a luminescent symbol appeared on their wrists. A perfect circle slashed with five irregular-sized lines. It reminded me of the way I used to draw suns when I was in pre-school.

"We are needed up in Neverra," Cruz said, staring at the strange sun. "I apologize for this mess, Catori."

I jerked my gaze off his wrist. "*Mess*? This is *way* more than a mess."

Cruz's expression grew somber. "I'll see you soon."

"Don't you dare come to Rowan."

Shooting me a regretful look, he turned and carved a path through the thick crowd. People parted around him as though he were magnetic. Taking support on the bar, he hopped over it, then crouched down and didn't reappear.

"I'm really sorry, Cat. I didn't mean to trick you into coming here," Ace said as he started walking away.

"Yes you did," I called out.

He turned and raised a rueful grin. "Okay. Maybe a little. *Valo*, Kitty Cat." Instead of angering me, the nickname made me smile. Or maybe it was Ace who made me smile. He felt like a friend, but was he? Or was I—and the rest of the hunters—mere pawns in their tortuous game?

As he made his way toward the faerie portal behind the bar, I made my way outside...toward Kajika. Like Ace had said, the hunter was waiting, eyes fixed on the flow of headlights and the ebb of people.

"American cities didn't look like this two hundred years ago?" I asked, coming to stand next to him.

He looked down at me, jaw set in a hard line. *The next ten hours will be such a blast.* Maybe I should've sampled the wine and the food, especially if they were spiked with mallow. As we started walking, I glimpsed a plane in the sky and imagined Kajika strapped onto Ace's back, and I chuckled. Kajika stared at me like I was an alien again.

Slowly, my laughter petered out, but my smile stayed in place. "Heard you and Ace shared a moment up there."

Kajika scowled. "It was most unpleasant."

All residual glee drained out of me. "This...us...them...this is all so insane." I rubbed my temples. "This must be a nightmare for you. Being around a girl who looks like your mate, but who isn't because two hundred years have gone by, and no one lives two centuries, but somehow, you did. And now her best friend lives inside your brain, and faeries are still manipulating everyone."

He dipped his head in ascent. "It is, Catori. But it's not just a nightmare. You have no idea how long I've wished for the faeries to admit their system was flawed. How long I dreamed they would take it upon themselves to change."

"I heard you agreed to help them. Do you trust them now?"

"Trust and help are two very different things. I'd like to think Linus's son can make his people see a different way of life. So that faehunters can cease to be necessary. So that I can pass on to the next realm."

I shuddered and quickened my step. The wind chill was violent, yet my anger at his selfish talk of ending his life rendered me immune to it. When I reached my car, he gripped my arm and turned me around.

"Isn't that what *you* want, Catori? Not being a hunter, not having to choose, not having me around to remind you of Blake?"

I looked up at him, and he looked down at me. So many emotions teemed in his dark eyes, in his hard jaw, in his smooth forehead. It was like standing on a spinning carousel, watching everything move while you stayed perfectly immobile. Kajika's eyes searched mine for an answer.

"Why did you come all the way here?" I asked.

"Because Ace told me Cruz was trying to take you back to Neverra."

"Hunters can't penetrate Neverra."

"But you're not just a hunter, Catori. If you wanted to go there—"

"I'd be out of *your* life." The air between us trembled with my words. "Isn't that everything *you* want?"

He shuddered, probably because he hadn't expected me to turn his words against him. His hand was still on my arm. When he saw me glancing at it, he loosened his grip, but didn't let go.

"Do you want me to let you go?" he asked, his voice hoarse.

I didn't ask if he meant to Neverra, or at that moment. My answer would've been the same.

"No."

His face hardened, and so did his hand, while his other arm swooped around my waist, bringing me so close I could smell the wind and warmth on his skin. Slowly, he brought his lips toward mine, but left a hairline gap between them. His breaths came in warm bursts against my mouth. When he closed his eyes, I held my breath.

"You should know—" he started, the words pulsing against my quivering lips. He took a deep breath, as though stalling to finish his sentence.

My stomach clenched. "What should I know?"

His eyes flew open, so very dark and so very serious. Direct conduits into the hazardous depths of his soul. "It's all or nothing with me, Catori."

My pulse, which already beat fiercely, soared as though it had grown wings. I swallowed and leaned back to see his entire face. "Define *all*."

"When I decided to make Ishtu my mate, we were bound together before the next full moon."

My shock must have registered because his already hard face shuttered up.

"Now define nothing," I asked.

"Our paths might cross, but I cannot be your friend."

A deep breath rattled up my lungs and escaped through my parted, trembling lips. When I gasped, his arm snaked off my waist. I would have fallen if he were no longer holding my arm. But then his wrapped fingers slid off. I jerked my hand toward the car roof for balance.

"That's what I thought," he murmured. "You're not sure."

I frowned. How could anyone be sure? How could *he* be sure? Maybe Blake had colored his feelings for me? We'd known each other only a few days... I was sure I was attracted to him, sure I could trust him, but were attraction and trust enough to agree on an all-or-nothing relationship?

The barrier he'd brought up around himself was so dense and barbed that there was no approaching him, no touching him, but my voice would carry through the wiring. "How can *you* be sure, Kajika?"

A sad smile grazed his lips. He pumped his fist against his heart. "You have awakened me." He pumped his fist again. "All of me."

My own heart banged against its walls, as though trying to breach my chest to reach Kajika's. And then my hand sparked, and both our gazes dropped to the reminder that I was connected to a faerie.

My hand belonged to another, but it was only a hand. Not a heart.

He drew the door open for me. "Let me know when you want me to take over."

THE THIRD ONE

*M*y arms ached as I gripped the steering wheel. I'd been driving for five straight hours, hours during which both Kajika and I had stayed quiet. My lower back hurt from my rigid posture. Every time I began to relax, a glance from Kajika made me sit up straighter. We stopped for fuel and coffee in a 24-hour gas station. Kajika tried to pay, but I wouldn't allow him to waste his money on a trip he hadn't needed to undertake in the first place.

I conceded the wheel, though. While he drove, I turned on the satellite radio to replace the silence. The music filed down the ragged edges of my mind until it finally shut down.

My phone rang in my dream. I tried to reach it, but it kept slipping away, further and further out of reach, as though coated in petroleum jelly. The ringing stopped. And then it started again. This time I didn't even try to reach it as strong hands stroked my waist. I looked into Kajika's face, wondering if he'd changed his mind. Or was I the one who'd changed my mind? I reached up to stroke his jaw, and he allowed me. He even pressed his cheek against my palm.

I feared my hand would glow, and he would jolt away from me

again, but Cruz's brand didn't flare up. Yet my heart was beating urgently, like my ringing phone.

Why wasn't it lighting up?

Cruz had been killed! Now that he'd complied with Gregor, the wariff had killed him! I should've been glad, but I was horrified.

"Catori?" Kajika shook my shoulder. "Catori, wake up."

I blinked rapidly. Kajika held my phone in front of my face.

"Ace needs to talk to you," he said.

My heart zipped around inside me like a deflating balloon. Had my nightmare been a vision? Was I connected to Cruz on some psychic plane? I was about to ask Ace if Cruz had died when his brand lit up. It was the first time I was relieved to see it. "Hi," I whispered, my voice hoarse with sleep. "What is it?"

"How far are you from Rowan?"

I rubbed my eyes to clear the too-real dream, then focused on the GPS. "Forty miles."

Wow, I'd been asleep for four hours. I was about to apologize to Kajika, when Ace said, "Put me on speakerphone."

I was fully alert now, as though a bucket of ice water had been thrown over me. "Okay. We can both hear you. What's going on?"

"Did you know your aunt is in Rowan?" he asked.

"Yes. I asked her to come."

"Did you ask her to wake up another hunter?"

"What?" I shrieked, or maybe I whispered it, or maybe I just gasped. There was too much pounding against my eardrums. "Please tell me— Please—"

"She's digging up a grave, Catori."

"Well stop her," I yelled.

"I cannot penetrate the fucking circle!"

"Yell for her to stop. She'll stop!"

"Your father told your aunt not to listen to me. She said I was the enemy. Asked me to prove I wasn't by stepping through the circle, but obviously I can't do that."

"Put me on speakerphone, Ace."

"I'm at Holly's. I'm going to bring Gwenelda. She can—"

"You made Dad believe she was a psychopath. He won't listen to her!"

"Call your father then," he said.

I hung up on Ace. My fingers trembled so hard I couldn't get them to dial. My cell phone clattered to the floor next to my boots. I tried to fish it off the mat, but it slipped through my fingers. Keeping one hand on the wheel, Kajika leaned over, grabbed it, and dialed my father.

The highway flashed by around us, the speedometer indicating 140 miles per hour. And still we were too far away.

The phone rang and rang and then it clicked to voicemail. I phoned Aylen, but the same thing happened with her phone.

I must have started crying, because something wet dripped off my chin.

Both of Kajika's hands were back on the steering wheel. "We're not going fast enough," he said.

I called Ace back. "Come and get me. Fly me there."

Kajika yanked the phone away from me. "You don't need a faerie. You have me." He tossed the phone on my lap and swerved onto the shoulder of the highway, slamming his foot down on the brake. "We'll run."

"Run?" My voice shook. "Wouldn't flying be faster?"

He snapped his seat belt off, then snapped mine off. "Not this time. I know where we are. Ace doesn't."

He jumped out of the car. I got my door open, but I couldn't get my legs to move. Kajika flung it wide, spun around, and knelt down. "Get on my back. And hold on."

Even though the idea of hanging on to Kajika felt ludicrous, my aunt and my father's lives depended on it, so I wound my legs around his waist and my arms around his neck, and then he leaped off the railing and raced down a grassy slope that led straight into the easternmost boundary of Manistee Forest. He ran so fast, the dawn-fresh wind flogged my cheeks and nose, and whipped my loose hair into a frenzy. When the trees grew denser, I closed my eyes and nestled my face in the crook of his neck, breathing in his familiar scent, borrowing some of his strength.

Kajika ran and ran, his footholds never faltering. Was he anxious to get there in time to greet the new hunter or was he sprinting to help me save the people I loved?

Suddenly, the wind stopped whistling, and the rising sun pricked the nape of my neck. I dared look up. The cemetery sprawled before me. I sprang off Kajika's back, and ran the rest of the way.

"Dad! Aylen!" I shrieked. "Stop!"

They looked up at me. Both looked up at me. Both were still alive! Yet, the grave was open. It was open!

Aylen clutched a small book. I kept running. Her eyes dropped to the book again. When I realized she was holding Holly's dictionary, I screamed, "Don't read another word!"

I broke through the circle of rowan trees and yanked the book from her hands. A page ripped.

"Did you translate the spell?" I asked, breathing so hard the taste of metal flooded my mouth.

"You know about *them*, don't you?" Dad pointed at someone behind me.

I thought he was pointing at Kajika, but when I turned, the hunter wasn't alone. Gwenelda and Ace stood next to him. Gwenelda walked toward us, her long hair swinging like my mother's used to when I tripped over rocks on the beach and she hurried toward me.

"What is *she* doing here? She's a murderer." Dad's voice roiled with anger and disappointment. "And him." He pointed at Kajika. "He's not Holly's great-nephew! Get behind me, Cat."

"We've all come to help," I said.

Aylen's eyes widened. "You're one of the twelve, too," she told Gwen. "I recognize you from Catori's book. You're one of them!" Her eyes darted to the open grave. "It's all true. You really rise!"

I let my gaze drop to the figure stretched out inside the rowan casket. It was a woman who resembled Gwenelda, but with hair in all different shades of gray.

Aylen's lips moved. I tried to make out her words, but she was talking gibberish. But then I understood the word *maahin* and realized it was Gottwa, not gibberish. She was speaking the spell.

"Stop reading!" I yelled, throwing myself at Aylen. "Stop it! It will kill you!"

Arms grabbed me around the waist and hauled me off my aunt. I tried to get away, but Kajika wouldn't let me go. He just wouldn't let me go.

"Will it really bring this one back too, Cat?" Dad asked, interrupting Aylen.

"Yes," I yelled, battling back sobs. "Yes."

Kajika squeezed me harder.

"Let me go, Kajika," I moaned.

Aylen started reading again.

"You have to stop, Aylen!"

There was white around my aunt's irises, as though she were possessed.

When her mouth moved again, I yelled, "Gwen, stop her!" But Gwenelda was somewhere else.

Pinpricks of light hovered around the tree grove. Fireflies. In my blurred eyesight, the *golwinim* resembled the burning stars of a detonated firework.

"Dad, if she reads that spell, then I lose you too," I wailed. "I lose you too." I tried to pry Kajika's arms off me, but he just wouldn't let go.

"*Naagangwe*, Gwenelda," Kajika said. "*Naagangwe.*"

Gwenelda raised her eyes to Kajika. So filled were they with melancholy that my heart pounded louder, and my hand...my hand felt like I was holding it over an open flame, like the skin was melting off. Cruz wasn't dead.

In a flash of movement, Gwenelda shot to her feet and slapped her palm over Aylen's mouth. My aunt tried to shake her off, but Gwen held on.

"Are you crazy, woman?" Dad roared.

Gwen backed up fast, too fast for Dad to catch her. And then she stopped and fixed Dad with her gleaming eyes. Her lips moved. "You will forget about what you and Aylen have just done. You will forget all that you have learned and all that you think you know about faeries and hunters and Nova's family. And you will never, *ever* venture into this sacred part of the cemetery. Now return to the house and remain there until Catori comes to you."

Dad stumbled back, then blinked, and then he turned and walked into the house without looking at me, without looking back. I stared until he'd shut the door. With the back of my hand, I stifled a relieved sob.

When I turned back, Gwen had stalked around Aylen to capture her attention. Before she could wipe my aunt's mind, I asked in a shrill voice, "Who told you to dig up this grave?"

Aylen stared at my retreating father, then at Gwen, and finally at me. "Stella and I found a book in your room, Cat. A crazy book that said our ancestors were still alive underneath the earth, preserved by some magical rose petals."

"Did *she* tell you to dig one up?"

"No one told me to do it. I wanted to know if it was true. I was curious. Gosh, Cat, weren't you curious when you read the book?"

"No." I shook my head vigorously. "No, I wasn't because I knew what bringing one back entailed."

Aylen frowned.

"A life for a life. It costs a life," I croaked.

Aylen paled. Even underneath her thick foundation and streaky blush, she paled. "Nova didn't die of a heart attack?"

"No."

Fat tears formed in her eyes, rolled down her cheeks. "So I almost...almost—"

"Died or killed Dad? Yeah. You almost did."

She clapped her hand in front of her mouth. "I didn't know. I didn't know, Cat." Her voice was choppy and her breathing labored.

I swallowed, then turned toward Gwenelda and whispered, "Please make her forget. Make her fear approaching the circle of rowan trees."

Aylen widened her shiny eyes. "What are you talking a—"

"You will cease to remember tonight," Gwen said, her hoarse voice echoing through the cemetery. "You will cease to remember that faeries and hunters exist. You will forget everything you have read and heard, and if anyone tries to make you remember, you will not listen to them. You will not believe them. And you will never penetrate the sacred circle of rowan trees, because for the rest of your life, you will believe it is cursed."

I held my breath until Aylen's lids lowered and rose, until her expression turned blank, until she mindlessly walked off, until Kajika's arm fell away from my waist. The fireflies hung motionless in the air. I couldn't see their eyes, but I could feel them. Were they waiting to see what we would do with the exhumed huntress?

Gwen dropped to her knees in front of the grave. Eyes closed, she started chanting something. Was it the spell?

"Is she going to use *my* life?" I murmured.

"We'd never use your life, Catori. She's saying goodbye to her mother." Kajika's voice, although firm, caught when he added, "To our mother."

"Why?"

"Once the body is exposed, life must be given immediately... before the petals dry."

I whirled around to face him. "Then we have a couple of hours to find someone." I couldn't believe what I was suggesting. "The petals don't desiccate right away. They were still pink in Gwenelda's grave for a day after—"

"Because it was opened inside your house, protected from the wild air."

"But—"

"I was still next to my grave when mine grayed."

I wiped my cheeks as Gwenelda's lament grew louder and faster.

Dread rippled over my skin. "We can't just let her die."

"We don't have a choice."

"She's your mother, Kajika. We have to save her."

"Elika is with the Great Spirit now. Soon she'll be reunited with her loved ones," he said, and I swear he sounded wistful.

His longing made everything in that moment worse. Tears spilled over my cheeks. They were tears for him, for his adoptive mother, for Gwenelda, for my father and my aunt whose lives had dangled dangerously close to the point of no return. They were tears of terror, tears of relief, and tears of sorrow.

My aunt was in the kitchen. She had her back to me, so I didn't know what to expect when she turned around. Reproach, guilt, anger…

"Aylen," I called out gently, closing the front door.

She whipped around and her face broke into a huge smile. "Cat, you're home!" She tossed the mixing bowl and the whisk on the kitchen table, and approached me, arms held wide.

I froze as she hugged me.

"I was making a chocolate cake. Stella gave me the recipe last night," she said.

"Stella?" Had Gwen's influence not worked? "Stella came over?"

"Yes. She stayed for dinner. It was such fun." She stretched her arms. "Boy do my arms feel sore from all this mixing. I try not to bake too much at home. For the sake of Tony's waistline." She leaned back, then kissed both my cheeks. "Your father's been good. No talk of dying." She arched an eyebrow and inspected my face. "Is someone having boy trouble?"

"What?"

"Your eyes are as red as poppies. You want to tell me about it? I'm an expert at boy trouble."

I smiled sadly. If only *boy trouble* were to blame. "Let me go see Dad first, and then I'll tell you all about it."

I climbed the stairs and knocked on his door. A minute later, he swept it open, clothed in a fluffy gray bathrobe, blond hair still wet and soapy. He scooped me up in a giant hug. "Glad you're back, sweetheart." He squeezed me once more before setting me down. "Let me dry up, and I'll come down to help you with your bags."

My bags. My car. *Shoot.*

"You still have shampoo in your hair," I told him.

He ran his hand through it, saw the foam, and then returned to the bathroom.

I didn't move until he came back, this time, shampoo-free. "My car broke down forty miles back," I lied.

"Why didn't you call me?" Dad asked, as he went into the adjoining walk-in closet. There was this big mirror against one of the walls in which I used to model my mother's heels when my feet barely filled the toe part.

"I tried, but your phone was off."

Dad came back out in a pair of jeans and a flannel shirt. He checked his phone on his nightstand. Sure enough, he found my missed calls. "Did you contact the towing company?"

"Yes."

"Did they tell you what was wrong with it?"

"I ran out of gas."

Dad frowned. "Really?"

I nodded.

"You're sure you didn't get into an accident? You look like you've been crying, Cat."

"No accident, Dad. I promise. It's just been a long night."

"I told you that you should've slept in Boston and driven during the day, but you are *so* stubborn."

If I hadn't been stubborn, I would've lost him. "I heard Stella came over last night."

"When she heard Aylen was in town, she just had to see her.

Those two were so close in high school. You should've seen them last night. They binged on the leftover cupcakes, which turned them into these raving cleaning ladies. Sugar does strange things to women. They wiped and dusted and mopped and changed all the sheets in the house. I tried to stop them from going into your room, but they just had to clean that too."

So that was the cover Stella had used to steal my book. She posed as Aylen's accomplice when in fact she was Gregor's.

Dad picked up his wallet. "I'm ready. Let's go get your car."

"Kajika offered to drive me."

"Oh." His blue eyes clouded with disappointment. "Well, then"—Dad pulled a credit card out of his wallet and handed it to me—"put whatever it costs on this, okay?"

"It's *my* mistake, Dad."

"And you're *my* little girl. I'm taking care of you, whether you let me or not."

"Okay, Daddy," I whispered. "Okay." I took the card from him, then locked my arms around his neck. "I love you. I hope you know that."

"What you feel for me pales in comparison to what I feel for you." He kissed the top of my head. "I hope *you* know *that*. Now go get your car so you don't leave me too long with that nutty aunt of yours."

I smiled. "Whom you love to pieces, right?"

"Yeah. But one doesn't cancel out the other." He winked at me. "I think I'm going to lie down for a bit. I'm feeling battered."

I nodded. After shutting Dad's door, I went to my bedroom. The comforter lay bare and bunched at the foot of my bed, and the mattress had been stripped of its protective sheet. I never thought I would identify with bedding, but at that moment, I felt exposed and jumbled too.

I tossed the dictionary into my sock drawer, then clambered down the stairs. "I need to go get my car," I told Aylen, heading for the front door.

"Your car? Didn't you just drive it back?"

"I ran out of gas."

"That happened to me once. In Death Valley of all places—"

"I got to run. Save me the story for later?"

"Sure, sure."

When I stepped out of the house, I found Kajika standing in the rowan circle, shoveling soil over the rose petal grave. My car could wait. Wordlessly, I waited near him. Even though I hadn't unburied her, I felt responsible for her death. Like I felt responsible for Kajika and Gwen's intractable heartaches.

It didn't take him long to blanket his adoptive mother with the soft soil as the grave wasn't deep. Gently, I pried the shovel from his hands and put it away in the shed before anyone else could use it. When I returned, he'd dropped to his knees with his forehead pressed against the ground. I stood by one of the tree trunks, watching him bid the huntress farewell. When I heard him speak Ishtu's name, my muscles pinched, as though I were an instrument made of strings that someone plucked. Each pull pulsed inside of me, vibrated in my sinews, resonated in my tender skull.

I turned around and walked away. He was probably asking Elika to inform Ishtu of his imminent arrival. For a long time, I ambled aimlessly, trying to untangle my feelings and thoughts. I ended up at the tree house.

I always ended up at the tree house.

I climbed up the rope ladder, crawled inside, and sat exactly where I'd sat the afternoon of Blake's burial. I gathered my knees against me and rested my cheek on my knees.

Not long after I arrived, the floor creaked. I looked up to find Kajika crouched in the small entrance, his forehead smeared with dirt. He moved toward me and sat exactly where he'd sat before. And even though everything looked the same as the afternoon of Blake's burial, nothing was the same.

"I'm sorry for your loss," I said, angling my head toward him.

Although tainted with grief, his face wasn't full of its usual hard lines. "I thought I would be saying those words to you."

I sealed my mouth to prevent a rising sob from escaping.

"Hey," he said, his voice low and raspy. "Come here." He extended his arm behind me and tucked me against him. I let my head fall against his shoulder.

The last twenty-four hours played in a loop. An endless, horrible loop. If only I could shut off my brain. "Thank you," I murmured after a long, silent while. "For your kindness. For your sacrifice. For everything."

He stroked my cheek with his fingers. They smelled like earth and wood and metal.

"I don't want you to—" My voice was weak. "To leave too."

His fingers stilled. "What makes you think I'm going anywhere?"

I lowered my eyes to his dirt-stained boots. "Isn't that what you want? What you were telling Elika?"

His hand fell away from my cheek. "I was telling her I would see her on the other side...but I won't be going to the other side for a long time still. There are many things I need to take care of here."

I breathed in and out slowly. "Am I one of those things?"

"Would you like to be?"

I looked up at him. He went very still. Even his breathing seemed to have halted.

"You spoke about all or nothing, Kajika. I can't accept those are my only two options. I want *something*. But can that something be friendship for now?" His arm stiffened behind my back. "I'm not in a good place, and however resilient *you* are, I don't think you're in a good place either." I wrung my fingers in my lap. "Let's get to a good place. Together." I tried to smile, to let him know it was okay if he didn't want that, even though, deep down, it would hurt like hell if he turned down my offer.

In such a short amount of time, he'd filled a hole in my heart I didn't think anyone would be able to fill, let alone reach. Maybe it was because he carried Blake inside him. Whatever the reason, I knew I didn't want us to become strangers.

His chest rose and fell as he rested the back of his head against the clapboard wall and shut his eyes.

He would say no.

Disappointment surged behind my breastbone, yet I schooled my features into a brave smile.

"I don't know if I can," he said, his voice hoarse. "I'm not Blake, Catori."

A breath snagged in my throat. "I know you're not." I sat up straighter so that my body no longer touched his. "Just like I'm not Ishtu. Haven't you wondered if you were attracted to me because I resemble her? Maybe once you get to know me, friendship will be the only thing you want."

Even though his eyes remained closed, his mouth curved.

"What?" I asked.

"I've seen you at your meanest. At your angriest. At your weakest. And at your kindest. You've screamed at me. You've cried in my arms. And yet you think I don't know you?"

"We met just a few days ago."

His eyes opened and fixed me. "Time is of no importance, Catori. Sometimes you spend a lifetime with a person and never truly know them. And sometimes, you spend an hour with someone and you know everything about them. But if you need more time to realize this, then take more time. I've waited two hundred years to meet you. I should be able to withstand a few more days…or weeks."

My heart skyrocketed into my throat, filling my mouth with a frenzied pulse and my cheeks with warmth.

He caressed my cheek again.

I shuddered.

"Friends can touch each other, can't they?" he asked.

It was my cheek, yet it felt as intimate as if he were running his fingers over my bare thigh. "No friend of mine has ever touched me like that."

"I would hope not." Kajika smiled. I was too shaken by his confidence to smile. "Lean into me again, Catori. I need comfort, and feeling you against me gives me comfort."

I was too perplexed to move, so his arm wrapped around my shoulders and pulled me back. Everything zinged and tightened in me. I wasn't sure how my proximity could help him unwind; it did the exact opposite to me.

He tucked a strand of hair behind my ear, letting his fingers glide down my neck. Goosebumps rose in their wake. His hand traveled down my arm and came to rest on top of mine, on top of Cruz's mark. It burned as he slotted his fingers through mine. All of me burned. "I'm sad you never got to meet Elika. She loved so deeply and so fiercely."

His fingers were cold. They didn't tremble, but they were so cold. I covered them with my free hand, hoping I could bring him the warmth he deserved and the comfort he craved.

"Sounds like my mom."

"Tell me about her."

So that's what I did, and as I spoke, I burrowed in closer to Kajika. His thumb stroked mine, and his breaths warmed my forehead. Each memory made my heart coil and twist, as though it were wringing out the lingering pain her absence had left behind. And then I asked him about Elika.

When we finally grew silent, the entire day had passed and the sky had darkened with stars. My father would be worried. Aylen too. And yet, I didn't want to leave the tree house because leaving meant parting with the hunter, and I wasn't ready to let him go.

Not yet.

Not after I'd just found him.

WANT TO KNOW WHAT HAPPENS NEXT IN CATORI'S LIFE?
Dive into **Rowan Wood Legends** today.

WANT ANOTHER PARANORMAL ADVENTURE?

If you're in a witchy, slow-burn romance mood, then travel to the coldest and mistiest town in France with a ragtag crew tasked with bringing magic back into the world in
OF WICKED BLOOD.

Prefer enemies-to-lovers stories with alpha males and heroines who know their own mind? Then you'll love my wolves. Start *The Boulder Wolves* series with **A PACK OF BLOOD AND LIES.**

You could also head over to the City of Lights with my angels in **FEATHER** for a modern and darkly romantic retelling of *Romeo & Juliet.*

ACKNOWLEDGMENTS

I have been fortunate to meet some truly extraordinary writers and readers in recent years. And I'm even more fortunate to be able to call them my friends. When I need to vent about story and characters, they listen and hand over miraculous advice that help shape my books into genuine novels. A photographer can't take portraits without a model, and I can't write novels without my beta readers.

Theresea, you are the absolute bestest! I am so lucky to have you as my friend and confidant. Thank you for taking the time to read and correct each one of my books. You are a fabulous reader and a fabulous writer. I cannot wait to see your own manuscripts in print.

Vee, sister, editor, problem solver, sounding board, fellow mother, shoulder to cry on, person to laugh with, woman to vent to. Although we spend hours talking each day, they are never enough.

To Katie Hayoz, one of the authors whose writing I adore. You deserve fame and fortune. Your books are incredibly crafted, with characters and storylines that leap off the page and take root in your heart. Read her books!

Astrid, my favorite cousin and an exceptional writer. You have found a way to seal wit and humor into each one of your sentences. Pick up *A Cunning Plan*, people! It's ridiculously funny and entertaining. We may live thousands of miles apart, but yet, we've never been closer. I love that we share the same passions: for our children —even when they drive us mad—and for our craft—even when we want to toss our computers on the floor and stomp on them.

Melanie Karsak, the amazing NYTimes bestselling author of *The Airship Racing Chronicles*. Thank you for reading *Rose Petal Graves* when I started doubting everything about it. You have renewed my confidence in Catori and in Rowan.

To Alessia Casali, you are so darn talented and you have soooo much patience with me. To designing many more covers together!

Becky Stephens, you were the first editor to read *Rose Petal Graves* when it was still just a novella. From the beginning, you were enthusiastic and kind in your much-needed critiques.

Jessica Nelson, my other fabulous editor. You have a way of catching my tragic writing flaws and forcing my darlings to walk the plank. I'm so very thankful for that.

Josiah Davis, proofreader *extraordinaire*. Enough said.

To you, reader, thank you for the time and investment you've put into this book.

ALSO BY OLIVIA WILDENSTEIN

YA PARANORMAL ROMANCE

The Lost Clan **series**

ROSE PETAL GRAVES

ROWAN WOOD LEGENDS

RISING SILVER MIST

RAGING RIVAL HEARTS

RECKLESS CRUEL HEIRS

The Boulder Wolves **series**

A PACK OF BLOOD AND LIES

A PACK OF VOWS AND TEARS

A PACK OF LOVE AND HATE

A PACK OF STORMS AND STARS

Angels of Elysium **series**

FEATHER

CELESTIAL

STARLIGHT

The Quatrefoil Chronicles **series**

OF WICKED BLOOD

OF TAINTED HEART

YA CONTEMPORARY ROMANCE

GHOSTBOY, CHAMELEON & THE DUKE OF GRAFFITI
NOT ANOTHER LOVE SONG

YA ROMANTIC SUSPENSE

Cold Little Games series
COLD LITTLE LIES
COLD LITTLE GAMES
COLD LITTLE HEARTS

ABOUT THE AUTHOR

Olivia Wildenstein grew up in New York City, the daughter of a French father with a great sense of humor, and a Swedish mother whom she speaks to at least three times a day. She chose Brown University to complete her undergraduate studies and earned a bachelor's in comparative literature. After designing jewelry for a few years, Wildenstein traded in her tools for a laptop computer and a very comfortable chair. This line of work made more sense, considering her college degree.

When she's not writing, she's psychoanalyzing everyone she meets (Yes. Everyone), eavesdropping on conversations to gather material for her next book, baking up a storm (that she actually eats), going to the gym (because she eats), and attempting not to be late at her children's school (like she is 4 out of 5 mornings, on good weeks).

Wildenstein lives with her husband and three children in Geneva, Switzerland, where she's an active member of the writing community.

Her first book, *Ghostboy, Chameleon & the Duke of Graffiti,* about a little boy who dreams of great adventures, received rave reviews and has been nominated for a 2015 **Indiefab Book of the Year award**.

Her second book, the first part of the MASTERFUL series, *The Masterpiecers*, a darker tale of twin sisters locked up in two very different worlds, has been compared to GONE GIRL meets ORANGE IS THE NEW BLACK. It won gold at the 2016 **Chil-**

dren's Moonbeam Awards. The follow-up, *The Masterminds*, which has been called thrilling and pulse-pounding is also available, and has been nominated for several awards.

oliviawildenstein.com
press@oliviawildenstein.com